»»» ««

# The Sins of ...

## and Other ...

»»»»»»»»»»»»»«««««««««««««

# Bolesław Prus

# The Sins of Childhood & Other Stories

TRANSLATED BY BILL JOHNSTON

NORTHWESTERN UNIVERSITY PRESS

EVANSTON, ILLINOIS

Northwestern University Press
Evanston, Illinois 60208-4210

English translation and compilation copyright © 1996 by
Northwestern University Press. Published 1996.
All rights reserved.

Printed in the United States of America

ISBN 0-8101-1274-4 (cloth)
ISBN 0-8101-1462-3 (paper)

Library of Congress Cataloging-in-Publication Data

Prus, Bolesław, 1847–1912.
    [Short stories. English. Selections]
    The sins of childhood & other stories / Bolesław Prus ; translated by
Bill Johnston.
        p.   cm. — (European classics)
    ISBN 0-8101-1274-4 (alk. paper). — ISBN 0-8101-1462-3 (pbk. : alk.
paper)
    1. Prus, Bolesław, 1847–1912—Translations into English. I. Title. II.
Series: European classics (Evanston, Ill.)
PG7158.C6A25   1997
891.8'536—dc20                                              96-42276
                                                                CIP

# »»» CONTENTS «««

## »»» ««««
# Staś's Little Adventure

The hero of this story is an individual who is just over a foot and a half tall, weighs around thirty pounds, and has been in existence for barely eighteen months. This class of citizens is known to grown-ups as children, and they are not treated at all seriously.

For this reason, it is with a certain trepidation that I present little Staś to my readers, and above all ask them to be forbearing. Staś is a handsome, clean child who is fit to be kissed by any fine lady in four-buttoned gloves. He has flaxen hair, sapphire-blue eyes, a coarse wool shirt, and as many teeth as are needed to deal with one's own bread. In addition, he possesses a yellow cradle painted with black and green flowers, and a cart whose only defect is that each wheel seems to run in a different direction.

I would be most disappointed if the aforementioned recommendations did not make you like Staś, who otherwise has no unusual qualities. He is a legitimate child, not a foundling; he has not shown the slightest talent for thievery or playing a musical instrument; and, what's worse, he doesn't even have the touch of silliness that would entitle him to be considered well-born.

And yet he is an exceptional child; at least that's the opinion of his father, Józef Szarak, a blacksmith by profession, his mother, Małgorzata, née Stawińska, and his Granddad Stawiński, the miller, not to mention the relatives, friends, and all those upstanding people who had the opportunity to lose their cool at the baptismal ceremony.

Staś's very birth was the product of an unlikely combination of circumstances. First of all, God had to create two families: the Szarak family of blacksmiths and the Stawiński family of millers; then He had to arrange for one family to have a son and the other a daughter; and third, He had to break a particular iron part in the mill and bring young Szarak to repair it at the very time when Małgosia's heart had bloomed like the flowers of the water lilies on her father's millpond. "A true miracle!" – as old Grzybina rightly used to say as she divided her time between begging and casting charms against sicknesses, occupations that give old village women the right to know a miracle when they see one.

Since, in the unanimous opinion of women of experience, Staś took after his mother, we shall be so bold as to devote a few words to her. This is all the more necessary because the blacksmith's wife will take on the role of heroine in the story, which, we are sorry to confess, will concern neither a criminal act nor an outrageous romance.

By a dike that could only be crossed once in a blue moon, and next to a large pond with a luxuriant covering of verdure bordered by an alder grove, stood the mill. It was an old black building with grated windows, and on its right flank it possessed two enormous wheels, thanks to which it had shaken and rattled for thirty years, bringing quite a fortune to its owner, Stawiński.

The miller had a son and a daughter, that same Małgosia. He had sent his son out into the world to search for ways of producing the finest flour, but he kept his daughter by his side. She lacked for nothing, since her father never scrimped either on clothes for her or on the household. The only thing she did not have was affection.

The old miller was not a bad man, but he dealt coldly with people, spoke rarely and sharply, and lost himself in his business affairs. He had to watch the apprentices to make sure they didn't steal anyone's grain; he had to see to it that the pigs snorting under the floor of the mill were regularly given their portion of bran; he had to count the interest from money he had loaned, setting aside certain sums and investing others.

In such circumstances, Małgosia lived alone with nature, and she loved her mill. In the daytime, when she was working in the orchard or feeding the chickens or the big fat ducks, or stroking the cows, who came running like dogs at the sound of her voice, the mill would rumble and clatter out solemn, unheard music. In its rattling could be heard all the different instruments: fiddles, drums, organ. But they played something that no band, no organist, would have been able to perform.

Nature seemed to Małgosia to be an immense lake whose reflection reached up to the sky and whose droplets were the villages scattered across the countryside, the alder grove, the meadow, the mill, the pear trees along the hedgerows, the birds, and Małgosia herself. Sometimes, as she stared at the clouds that came out from behind the black wall of the woods, took a look at themselves in the pond, and hurried on behind the jagged hills, and as she listened to the sound of the wind ruffling the water and the corn in the fields, or the moaning of the reeds swaying over the marsh, she would ask whether her own existence was just a reflection of everything she saw and heard around her, like the images of the trees and the sky that can be seen in the waters of the pond. At such times, for no reason, tears would spring to her eyes. She would stretch as if wings were about to grow from her arms and whisk her away over the clouds, and she would sing in an unknown melody things that were never heard in any folk song. In the end, her father would come out of the mill and say morosely, "What's that you're singing, girl? You'd be better off not doing that. People'll laugh at you."

Małgosia, embarrassed, fell silent, but her friend the mill repeated every word and every note of hers, even more gracefully and beautifully. And was it possible not to love that mill, even though it looked like the fearful head of a bizarre creature with many legs, and even though it breathed heat and dust from its maw, and howled and shook as if it wanted to crush those riding across the dike with its immense fangs?

On holidays the mill fell silent. Only the rusty weather vanes on the roof creaked mournfully, while the thin streams of water murmured through the sluice gates and fell weeping onto the slippery mill wheel. On these days, when the summer evenings were warm, Małgosia would sit in a boat and row far out onto the pond, where only the top of the mill could be seen.

Here, sitting pensively over the deep water in which the round-eyed fish flitted past, she would listen to the whispering of the clumps of sweet flag and the cries of the waterfowl calling to each other, or, hanging her head over the side of the boat, she would watch the stars appear one by one from the bottom of the pond, while a swathe of moonlight shimmered on the surface of the waves. Sometimes she could see garments, finer than spiders' webs, which the water maidens hung on droplets of dew . . . There was a veil . . . there a cloak . . . and there a flowing gown. She rowed toward them, but the wind blew them onto the meadow, over which a lake of silvery white mist appeared at once, filled with dancing flashes and shadows. Who was at play there, and why was she not allowed to join them?

In the meantime, midnight was drawing near. The boat began to rock, a soft splashing began between the clumps of plants, and beyond the reeds pale, mysterious lights appeared. The treacherous mist obscured her way, and there was a noise as if someone in the reeds were whispering, "Aha! The girl won't get away now."

But the mill, Małgosia's faithful friend, was watching over her. All of a sudden, its small-paned windows threw flames into the ring of mist, and the huge black body on its many legs began to shudder.

At the same moment the familiar, thunderous voice reached the ears of the dazed girl, calling with an excited urgency: "Małgoś! Małgoś! Małgoś! Małgoś!"

Now the girl could put down the oars, for the current alone, drawn by the great jaws of the mill, carried the boat toward the sluice gate. She lay down in the bottom of the boat like a sleepy child in a gently rocking cradle; smiling, she watched the pale flames flickering angrily in the marshes, and the cold, damp nets of the water maidens, who had tried to ensnare her. And the old mill was becoming angrier and angrier, calling, "Małgoś! Małgoś! Małgoś!" worrying about its friend. Finally, the prow of the boat knocked against the posts of the bridge.

One night, jumping out of the boat after one of her trips, she noticed her father on the bridge. He stood leaning against the handrail and staring intently at the frothing water. Małgosia's heart trembled at the thought that he, too, was watching over her, despite his apparent indifference. She ran onto the bridge and, laying her head on his shoulder, asked dreamily, "Daddy! Who were you waiting for?"

"I thought the farmers were out stealing my fish!" answered the old man and yawned. Then, scratching himself, he shuffled off slowly back to the house.

Małgosia had never felt so lonely and abandoned as at that moment, and had never wished so much that she, too, could be loved by someone. She thought of the carpenter from the town, a stingy and ugly widower who ate enough for three and who had a sunken chest and legs splayed like the prongs of a pitchfork. At this moment it seemed to her that this carpenter was an entirely adequate person. And as for the miller who leased the windmill two miles away, who laughed all the time and was generally considered an idiot, she could hardly think of him and stay calm! Even her father's boys, like long thin sacks of flour, vulgar and quarrelsome lads, seemed in her present state of mind to possess many fine qualities, even though only a few months earlier she couldn't have looked at them without feeling nauseous.

》 《

In this difficult situation the mill once again decided to come to her aid, and one day part of its workings broke with a great clatter. The flour-covered apprentices turned pale with fear, and Stawiński flung his cap to the ground. The sluice gates were hurriedly closed, and everyone began discussing what to do; then they set about stopping anyone riding across the dike. The whole house was in an uproar. The boys stood debating on the bridge, to the consternation of travelers. The old man wouldn't eat his lunch and began swearing by all the saints that he was sure to die soon. And the pigs who dwelled under the mill, seeing that no one had fed them their bran, began squealing as if the end of the world were nigh.

Amid the chaos the name of Szarak the blacksmith was mentioned at least a hundred times, and in the end one of the apprentices harnessed a horse to the cart and rode off toward the town. Małgosia was seized by the same anxiety she had experienced the day she had caught cold and waited for the healer who was going to cup her. She brushed her hair, took out her new shoes, and ran out in front of the mill, which, having brought discord to everyone, was now sprawling over the dike and baring its teeth, mightily contented!

Night came, a cold wind blew up, and the girl had to retire to her room. She had just gone to bed when there was a rattling outside and an unknown voice reached her from the direction of the mill. "Oh Lord!" thought Małgosia, and, flinging her clothes on, rushed off to pour some vodka, stoke the fire, and heat up some sausage in sauce. Within a quarter of an hour everything was ready – it would have taken the sleepy serving girl an hour or more to do it.

In the meantime, the blacksmith had looked the mill over like an old woman inspecting a sick man, and he and Stawiński came into the house. Right from the doorway the smith noticed the smell of sausage, and he smiled with pleasure at the thought that the miller had so much respect for him that he had waited for him with supper till midnight. Yet he was surprised to notice the table neatly laid in the main room, a steaming dish of food, and two chairs facing each other, but not a sign of the lady of the house.

The worried miller drank a toast to his health, invited him to eat, and himself ate in silence as was his way. Only after supper did he call, "Małgosia! We'll need to send a pillow and a blanket over to the mill. The gentleman is going to stay the night."

Małgosia came out, so red that she felt ashamed. Furious at herself, she crumpled her apron in her hands and stared at the floor. But when she looked up and saw the young, cheerful face of the blacksmith and his eyes twinkling under his dark brows, she burst out laughing and ran into the hall to give instructions to the serving girl. The blacksmith laughed, too, without knowing why, and Stawiński, still troubled, muttered, "She's a bit of a handful. She rarely meets people, that's why she giggles. She's still a foolish young thing, she's only eighteen."

The next day at dawn Szarak went to work, but before he had finished setting up the anvil and fixing the bellows by the fire, he was already served breakfast. For the first time in his life Stawiński had to admit that his daughter was a good hostess and that she looked after her guests. But his miller's heart could not but be touched when he saw how Małgosia was concerned about the mill, how she kept looking in and asking Szarak about everything. He was less happy that the blacksmith talked so much while he was working, or that he showed tricks such as grabbing hold of a white-hot piece of iron with his bare fingers. The old man said nothing, however, for he saw that the smith worked like a Trojan, and that though he might fool around for a moment, once he started hammering the earth itself groaned.

The repair took several days. During this time the blacksmith and the miller's daughter got to know each other well, and every evening they spent together, just the two of them, for Stawiński, now that his mind was at rest, went back to dealing with his business interests and paid less attention to his daughter. On the last evening, sitting on the bench outside the house, the young people held the following conversation, which was whispered, as that was the way that came most naturally to them.

"So you live on the hill half a mile from the town, Mr. Szarak?" asked the girl.

"That's right! On that hill, the one that goes down to the meadow, where there's that wattle fence and some trees," replied the smith.

"What a lovely place for a kitchen garden! I'd put in beetroot, potatoes, beans, and flowers if it were mine!"

The blacksmith dropped his head and said nothing.

"Your cottage is nice, too, Mr. Szarak. It's that one next to the well with the sweep?"

"That's the one, but I wouldn't exactly say it was nice. There's no one to look after it."

"If it were up to me," said Małgosia, "I'd whitewash it first of all, then I'd put curtains in the windows and put up window boxes, and in the living room I'd hang all the pictures I have. Why don't you do that? It would look much more cheerful."

The blacksmith sighed.

"I don't know," he said. "If we lived closer to each other, Miss Małgosia, you'd be an encouragement to me, and you could advise me on what to do and where."

"Oh, I'd even do it myself, while you were at the smithy."

"But it's so far away," continued the blacksmith, taking hold of the girl's finger, "that I expect you wouldn't want to leave your father?"

This time it was Małgosia who was silent.

"I like you awfully, Miss Małgosia, that's the truth! Damn it, now when I go home I won't know what to do with myself. But what do you care about that! No doubt you're looking for a land steward or some such?"

"I know your worth, Mr. Szarak!" retorted the girl, turning her head. "I have no thought of any stewards. I only want to . . . "

She fell silent again. This time the smith took her whole hand.

"Well then," he asked suddenly, "would you marry me, Miss Małgosia?"

She gasped.

"I'm not sure!" she answered.

At this moment Szarak seized her by the waist and kissed her parted lips.

"Let's have none of that nonsense!" she said sharply, and, breaking loose from his embrace, she ran into the house, slamming the door behind her.

That night, neither of them could sleep.

The next day the last screws were tightened, and the sluice gates were opened. The water gushed noisily onto the waterwheels, which had been drying up from boredom; they shuddered and began to turn. The mill was working perfectly!

Stawiński bit his lip so as not to show his emotion, but his hands shook with joy. He looked everything over, swore at the apprentices, and finally invited the blacksmith into the house to collect his fee, where he opened up a bottle of mead in his honor.

As Stawiński was setting out the crisp new banknotes on the table, Szarak scratched his ear and gave an embarrassed smile.

The miller noticed and asked, "What's the matter, son, are you still not happy that you're making my wallet lighter by twenty-three rubles?"

"For a repair like that I'd have thought you owed me your daughter!" murmured Józef.

"What?" cried the old man. "Would you rather have the girl than the money?"

"I'd rather have both . . . "

Stawiński looked him sharply in the eye.

"But I won't give you any money for her now, only when I die," he said.

"I'll live longer than you!" replied Szarak, and kissed his hand. "You won't give her away without a dowry, after all, and I get so bored on my own, so lonely, when the winter comes, that . . . "

Małgosia's head appeared briefly in the open window.

"Come here, girl!" called her father.

"I'm not coming in!" she answered, shielding her eyes. "Arrange things on your own, Father."

Stawiński shook his head.

"So, then, Mr. Szarak," he said, "I see you've not been wasting your time here. Hmm, well, since it's the will of God, I'll give you the girl, because you're a good workman, and I know you don't lack for money. But don't do her any wrong, because I would never forgive you."

A few weeks later Małgosia's wedding with the blacksmith was celebrated in food, drink, and dance. Two neighbors who had long been at odds with each other took the opportunity to make up, while four others had a falling out. One of Stawiński's apprentices had too much to drink and swore that he would drown himself in desperation, but he compromised and just got more drunk. However, one of the farmers, who had long been intending to give up the vodka, accidentally fell into the pond and got a vigorous talking-to from his wife. Right from the first day of the wedding, the bow-legged carpenter and the ever-grinning owner of the windmill, both of whom had competed for Małgosia, began telling friends and strangers alike that the girl had something wrong with her, that her father was a usurer – as a result of which there were ghosts in the mill – and that people's grain was stolen from the sacks. Each of the disappointed rivals declared that he never would have married the miller's daughter. And in the meantime, the newlyweds moved into the smith's house.

Here Małgosia fulfilled all of her promises. She refurbished the cottage, put up wild vine on the walls, decorated the interior with pictures and ornaments, and made a beautiful garden on the hill that led down to the meadow. Under her supervision the blacksmith's property grew bigger and better-looking; the cottage looked like a manor house. And Szarak himself purchased a new leather apron so massive that two good-sized Warsaw men could have been cut from it, and there would have been enough left over for a woman, too . . .

》 《

A year passed while the young couple were making these arrangements. In the spring the storks arrived and settled in the ancient nest on the barn; they began clattering and clattering their bills, and in the end they clattered up little Staś. On that day the blacksmith closed the smithy. Granddad Stawiński rode the journey of over a mile bareback, and he wept his eyes out when he saw his plump, pink little grandson, who was crying as if he were being skinned alive, and who on his hands and feet had as many dimples as joints.

Under similar circumstances, the fine ladies of the world cover their windows with thick curtains, hire natural and artificial wet nurses, and, resting up for a month or more in an embroidered negligee as if they had constructed the whole earth, they receive congratulations from ladies and gentlemen murmuring in French. However, since Małgosia was unfamiliar with such ways, she went back to work forty-eight hours later, and the child's grandfather fell ill for her – from joy, of course. Within a few days he had gotten to know his grandson inside and out. He had discovered great potential as a miller and was the first to confess that he had never seen such a bright child as Staś, even among the children of the gentry!

In the meantime, the newborn child was experiencing the curious and mysterious period of infancy, the indistinct memories of which we sometimes encounter in our dreams, as it were, cracking open the gates of our preconscious life.

Imagine a simple fellow who in the space of a single moment is inundated with all the affairs of society. There are artistic and industrial issues, philosophical and agricultural questions, vices and virtues, and among them many matters upon which his very life depends. He must put everything in order, separate his own affairs from those of others, in the space of one hour acquire practical skills for his needs in the next, and not collapse under the burden of work!

This was the situation in which Staś one day found himself. After the long sleep before his birth, he had been struck by a storm of impressions. The air acted on his skin and his lungs; his eyes were assaulted by colors – white, gray, blue, green, red – in all possible combinations and hues, and along with them thousands of forms both animate and inanimate. He heard people's conversations, the creaking of his own cradle, the bubbling of boiling water, the buzzing of flies, and the whining of the puppy, Kurta. He felt the tightness of his swaddling clothes, differences in the temperature, which changed every few seconds, and above all hunger, thirst, sleepiness, and the movement of his own limbs. All this, disordered, chaotic, importunate, seethed in the depths of his tiny, barely stirring existence. He couldn't say where the hunger came from, or the color white, or the banging of hammers in the smithy. The poor little thing felt only exhaustion, and whimpered, shaking with cold. His only distraction was sleep, which was constantly being interrupted – and the chance of sucking. Thus, he sucked like a leech, slept, and cried, and the adults stood and shook their heads at his helplessness! Did you hear that? They're calling helpless someone who has fallen into such a terrible turmoil and has so many things to do!

At this time Staś did not yet distinguish his mother from himself, and when he was extremely hungry he sucked his big toe instead of his mother's breast. They laughed at this, though we know grown-up people who would take someone else's two-ruble overshoes in place of their own twenty-grosz walking stick.

After working hard and amassing several months' worth of experiences, Staś achieved some remarkable results. He managed to grasp the difference between his leg and the edge of the cradle, and even between his mother's bosom and his mattress. By this time he was already very clever. He knew that hunger attacked him from the direction of his feet, that all possible noises were concentrated at certain points in his head, and all the colors at other points, and a third point was used for sucking.

Within the next few months he made even more discoveries. He could already distinguish between good and bad events, and between beautiful and ugly things. Previously laughter and crying, frowning and stretching out his hands or feet, had followed one another in no particular order; he used them like a novice uses the piano keyboard, touching the keys without knowing what will come of it. Now he laughed only at the sight of his mother, who fed him; he cried after his bath, against which all his bipedal instincts protested; he frowned at the sight of the swaddling clothes that so restricted children's movements; and he reached out his hands and feet toward the cup with his sweetened milk.

Now likes and dislikes, fears and hopes began to develop in him. He liked Kurta the dog because he was warm, licked him, and had a snout like velvet. He was afraid of the dark, in which a person could come to harm. He longed for the garden, where he could take deep breaths and where the harmonious rustle of the trees, echoing the rhythms of his mother's singing, rocked him to sleep. He did not like dull colors, which reminded him of the hard floor or his not-always-dry mattress. On the other hand, red and blue, and shiny objects, made him laugh. He knew by now that the flame of a candle, though it dances and is pretty, has a deceitful way with a child's fingers. He also remembered that his father's legs were hard, black, and bigger than Staś himself, while his mother's little legs were so short that they began and ended right near the floor.

For his mother he felt unqualified love, for she brought him the most pleasure. His father enjoyed Staś's good graces insofar as he possessed a very interesting mustache, and also the most enticing object in the world – a watch. However, his father's caresses were not enjoyable, for he played with the boy when he was hungry or sleepy, scratched him mercilessly with his rough beard, and squashed his frail young bones with his huge, clumsy hands. There was only one thing that made Staś reach out his hands and laugh when he saw his father – being given a swing. True, the child felt uncomfortable in those powerful arms, but how high they threw him, how they could make the wind rush past him, how they could blow his hair back and ruffle his shirt!

By now Staś knew how to kid and play. Sometimes his mother would take him on her lap, and his father would sit opposite and say, "Come on, Staś, come to me!"

He would make as if to go, stretch out his hands, but then would suddenly turn round and plop down on his mother's arm. And there was no sign of Staś anywhere in the house – or at least he couldn't see anyone!

Sometimes his father stood him on the table and held him by the sides, and his mother hid. She would hide behind his father's right side, and Staś would go *peepo!* lean his head to the right and find her at once. Then his mother would hide behind his father to the left, and Staś would go *peepo!* lean his head to the left and find her straight away. The child could have played like this all day long, but what of it, when father had to go to his smithy and mother to tend her cows! So the baby was put into his cradle, and such a hubbub arose in the house that it even made Kurta bark!

Staś sometimes stood on his head, but he soon observed that this is not a comfortable position and that the most appropriate activity for a human being is crawling on all fours. Thanks to this form of motion, he learned that the walls, the chairs, and the stove are not inside his eye but outside it, much farther away than arm's length.

His rapidly growing muscular strength obliged him to perform certain tasks. Most often this involved knocking over his stool, banging his spoon on the floor, or rocking his cradle. And since for some time he had shared the cradle with young Kurta, the dog, seeing the rocking, jumped onto the mattress and sprawled out like a lord. This insolent abuse of his rights drove Staś to envy, so he cried until the dog was thrown out and Staś himself was placed in the cradle.

Later he began to learn the extremely difficult art of walking. The boy was amused at how high one is above the ground; yet he also understood the dangers inherent in the pleasure, and hardly ever undertook it himself without the assistance of grown-ups. In any case, he would stand up first. Then he would raise his left arm and his right leg, bend it inward, and slap the right side of his foot down on the ground. Then he would raise his right arm and left leg, bend it in, curl up his toes, and slap the left edge of his foot down on the ground. After a number of these complex maneuvers, he had not moved a inch from where he stood, but had made his head spin, which made him fall over. At such times he thought to himself that while walking on two legs does something for human vanity, crawling on all fours has great practical value. The sight of people walking around on their two feet gave him the kind of feeling that a reasonable person must feel when he finds himself in the company of tightrope-walkers. For this reason Staś had great respect for Kurta, who operated with all four limbs, and wished only that he would someday be able to run as fast as Kurta could.

Seeing the uncommonly rapid growth of the child's spiritual and physical qualities, his parents began to think about an education for him. He was taught to say "Dada" for Daddy, "Mama," and "Kurta," who for some time was also called "Dada." They bought him a high chair with arms and a beautiful lindenwood spoon, with which Staś could, if need be, have covered his whole head. His father, copying his mother in all things, also wanted to give his only son a present, so one day he brought him a splendid cat-o'-nine-tails with a deer's-foot handle. When Staś took the expensive gift in his hand and began to gnaw on the black cloven hoof, his mother asked his father, "What did you buy that for, Józik?"

"For Staś."

"What do you mean? You're not going to beat him, are you?"

"What else am I supposed to do when he turns into a little rascal like I was?"

"Look at him!" cried Staś's mother, hugging the child. "How do you know he'll be a rascal?"

"Just let him try not to be – then I'd really give him a hiding!" replied the blacksmith good-humoredly.

Since at this moment Staś began to cry, he irked his mother and inclined her to her husband's point of view. The parents no longer disagreed; they recognized the necessity of the device and hung the whip on the wall between Saint Florian, who since time immemorial had been putting out some kind of fire, and the clock, which for twenty years had been attempting in vain to run on time.

》 《

Notwithstanding these first lessons in moral principles based on the deer's foot, the blacksmith looked for a teacher for his son.

There was a full-time schoolmaster in the village, but he was more occupied with writing denunciations and vodka-tasting than with teaching the children to read and write. The farmers and the Jews despised him, and all the more so did Szarak, who did not even think to leave the education of his son in the hands of a teacher, but went straight to the organist.

Staś is fifteen months old now, thought the blacksmith. In three years or so his mother'll teach him to read, and in four I'll hand him over to the organist.

Only four years! It was already time to win the good graces of that servant of God, who shaved like a priest, spoke in a throaty voice, and interjected Latin phrases from the liturgy into his conversations.

So, without wasting time, one day Szarak invited the organist to Szulim's for a cup of mead. The unctuous ecclesiastical artist wiped his nose on a checkered handkerchief, cleared his throat, and, pulling a face as if he were about to preach a sermon against warm alcoholic beverages, notified Szarak that today, and tomorrow, and to the end of time he was prepared to go with him to Szulim's and drink mead.

The organist was proud and oversensitive, and above all he had a weak head. Before they had finished the first bottle he had begun to talk gibberish, and as they drank the second he waxed sentimental and informed Szarak that he considered him almost his equal.

"For you see, my . . . Dear Lord! . . . it's like this. I'm the organist, and they blow the bellows for me; and you're the blacksmith, and . . . Dear Lord! . . . they blow the bellows for you, too . . . so . . . I'm sure you see what I'm getting at . . . The blacksmith and the organist are brothers. Ha, ha! Brothers . . . Me, the organist, and you, the dirty workman . . . *Misereatur tui omnipotens Deus!*"

Szarak, who was usually a cheerful fellow, became gloomy when he was in his cups. He was, then, unable to appreciate his companion's compliment, and replied so loudly that Szulim and a number of the farmers heard him, "I don't know about being brothers! A blacksmith's got more in common with a locksmith, and an organist . . . with a beggar!"

"What! I'm like a beggar?" cried the offended maestro, fixing the smith with a piercing glare.

"Sure thing! You even pray if you're paid to, and you play better when someone gives you . . . "

Szarak did not finish, for at that moment he received a hefty blow with a bottle above his temple. Glass flew right up to the ceiling, and the sticky mead ran down the blacksmith's face and over his Sunday clothes.

"Grab him!" shouted the injured man, not knowing whether to wipe himself clean or to chase after the organist, who was running away in what he considered the most direct line, though it was an extremely crooked one.

Now those present stepped between the two quarreling men. They threw the organist out and set about calming the blacksmith, who was beside himself with rage.

"I'll show you, you little piper!" called Szarak, catching sight of the more than usually solemn countenance of the organist.

"Józef! Friend! Blacksmith!" the intermediaries cried placatingly. "Calm down, now! What's the point of getting mad at a drunk? He's an idiot, he doesn't know what he's doing."

"I'll thrash that troublemaker till he's black and blue!"

"Leave off, Mr. Szarak! What's the sense in a thrashing? Not everyone should be thrashed. He's a cleric, second in rank to the priest! God might punish you."

"Nothing'll happen to me!" retorted the blacksmith.

"Maybe not you. But you have a wife and child . . . "

These last words had a miraculous effect. At the thought of his wife and child, the enraged blacksmith became calm and even tried to suppress his desire for revenge. It was true that the organist ranked next to the priest. What if he made the Lord God angry by giving the other man a beating, and He harmed his wife or his child?

He left the inn with a terribly long face.

Good grief, these children are a problem! he thought to himself. I've only got the one, and already I have to worry about finding a tutor for him, and go wasting money on mead! And that's nothing! I get abused in front of a crowd and can't fight back because I'm afraid for my child . . .

Oh, Staś, Staś, I wonder if you'll ever know how much I've suffered for you! I just hope the wife doesn't give me a dressing-down!

At home things did not go without a fuss, but from then on Szarak loved his son even more, after he had begun to think of his education so early and for this reason had had a bottle of mead broken over his head. In a few months the good blacksmith had forgotten the wrong he had suffered, but he deeply regretted having fallen out with the organist, the one man capable of overseeing the education of his son, who was already able to walk and talk and showed uncommon talents all round.

Meanwhile, the summer came, and with it the moment in which an unexpectedly happy conclusion was to be found for the blacksmith's paternal worries.

》 《

One day Staś's mother laid him in the orchard on a blanket under a pear tree. She tucked in his shirt and said, "Sleep now, son, and don't cry. You're Mummy's sweetest little love that ever God created! And you, Kurta, lie here by him and make sure that he doesn't get pecked by a chicken or stung by a bee, or that a bad person doesn't cast a spell on him. I'm going to weed the beetroot patch, and if you two don't behave yourselves here I'll take a beanpole and sort you out!"

But at the very thought of carrying out her threat, she seized hold of the boy's hand as if someone really were about to hurt him, and she hugged him, kissed him, and rocked him, saying tenderly, "As if I'd beat you with a beanpole! That good-for-nothing Kurta maybe, but not you! My little sweetie . . . my little dumpling . . . my darling little son! Don't you laugh, Kurta, you hairy mongrel! Don't narrow your eyes and wag your tail. You know I'd rather skin you alive three times over than raise the smallest stick to my dear little Staś. Go to sleep now. Hushaby!"

And Kurta tucked his tail underneath him, opened his mouth from the heat, and hung his red tongue out to one side like a hand-kerchief. He was a clever, wily dog. He was thinking to himself: You can say what you like, woman, but I know that whenever Staś's mattress has to be dried out, he gets such a spanking that you can hear it in the smithy!

That was what bold Kurta thought, but he said nothing, knowing that stronger than any reason was the fire iron which everyone in the house, starting with the mistress, used to counter his canine objections.

In the meantime, Staś wiped his eyes with his fat little fists and set his flaxen head on his mother's arm. If he had been able to talk properly, doubtless he would have said to her, "If you have to put me down, then just do it, because after a bowl of kasha and milk like that a fellow feels sleepy!"

The lad would have fallen asleep of his own conviction, but his mother believed that he needed to be helped, so she rocked him some more and sang a lullaby:

You roamed unseen
Through forests green
Yet what did this avail you here?
I laid my head
On feather bed
And won the prize of sleep so dear.

Only when he grew heavy and thrust his head between her arm and her breast did she lay him down on the blanket. Then she tugged Kurta's wet tongue, and, looking round, went off to the bottom of the garden.

The coarse blanket and the earth beneath it seemed a little cold and hard to Staś after his mother's embrace. So although his legs were sleeping soundly, his head woke up again, and he raised it on his pudgy hands. He tried to look about to see where his mother was, maybe even to cry for her. But as he was still small, he wasn't very good at looking around, and instead of gazing straight ahead he looked down, at the grass. This time good old Kurta gave him a couple of glutinous licks on his suntanned face, and began such a thorough search for lice in Staś's hair that Staś fell on his left side, his chubby elbow underneath his temple. He attempted to lift himself up again; he leaned his right arm on the blanket and tried to untangle his legs. But at this moment his fingers splayed, his cherry-red lips parted, his eyes snapped shut – and he fell asleep. At his age sleep is as powerful as a big strong farmer – it'll lay you down before you've even begun to fight with it.

Then, from the freshly mowed meadow, where the spiky, bulging sheaves mused, a wind blew up, hot as the breath of the sun. It brushed across the squat bundles, whistled through the knots in the rotten willow trees, which tried in vain to frighten it off with a wave of their branches, squeezed through the wattle fence, and blew across the blacksmith's garden. The green leaves of the beet with their crimson edges, the slender dill, and the feathery parsley began to tremble as if in a fever, probably with anger, for they are an idle nation and do not like to be touched. And the tousled leaves of the potatoes, the gaudy sunflowers, and the pale red poppies rocked like Jews in the synagogue, evidently embarrassed by the frivolity of the wind, which was driving the bees from the hives and twisting the blacksmith's wife's cap around on her head, even though, despite the fact that she was only twenty-one, she *was* Staś's mother, the lady and mistress of all that was in the garden, the cottage, the cowshed, and eight acres of fields!

"Oh, what tricks that wind is playing!" murmured the redheaded poppies, the sunflowers looking up into the sky, and the thick potato tops.

And the round leaves of the pear tree under which Staś's mother had laid him to sleep whispered like diligent nannies, "Quiet! Quiet! You'll wake the child!"

Kurta, who liked to be active and at the very least leave notches in the pigs' loppy ears, began to be horribly bored.

What kind of world is this, he thought, where children do nothing but sleep, the mistress busies herself with pulling up leaves, the trees instead of doing an honest job just sway and rustle, the stork clatters his heart out, and the master and the boys do nothing in the smithy but work the bellows and hammer! He hits the anvil with the small hammer, tap, tap, tap, and the boys strike the iron with the big hammers, bang, bang, bang, till the sparks fly. Many times I've stood before the smithy and seen it.

And in despair at the indolence of the world, the hardworking dog fell on his side so that the earth itself groaned. He sprawled out, stretched his legs in front of him, and, to emphasize his contempt for the world, closed both eyes so as not to have to look at anything.

Now, before the eyes of his tireless soul there extended a field full of his mistress's cabbages, among which there was a family of hares feeding, rubbing their paws, and pricking up their ears like fingers.

"I'll show you, you rascals!" barked Kurta, and off he ran, scattering the pests on all sides!

He chased and chased them, and the field stretched on infinitely, the hares proliferated like drops of rain in a thunderstorm, and the master, the mistress, and the apprentices, watching the chase, cried,

"My, that Kurta's a hardworking dog, he won't rest even for a minute!"

And Kurta stretched out and ran so fast that his tail, which couldn't keep up with him, got left far behind. He could barely breathe, but he ran on.

Then, over the head of the dreaming dog, a fly began to circle and berate him in a shrill voice, "You lazy little mongrel, you! You ate your fill of feed, and now, when the whole world is moving round the sun, you're lying there like a big lump and daydreaming!"

The dog woke up and snapped at the fly with his teeth.

"Look at her, the sponger! She accuses me of lying down when I've been chasing the hares out of the cabbage patch!"

And, not wanting to waste time defending his honor, he stretched out even more comfortably and returned to his former occupation. The fly went on circling him, even though he frowned and bared his claws. It squeaked, "Oh, you, you mongrel, you loafer! They told you to watch the child and you're falling asleep yourself, you lazybones!"

And from this moment on the dill and the parsley, the potato leaves, the poppies and the sunflowers, the wind in the sky, the breath of the sleeping Staś, the storks on the barn, and the hammers in the smithy all murmured in time: "Lazy Kurta! Lazy Kurta! Lazy Kurta!"

But Kurta, stretched out under the pear tree, was hard at work chasing hares!

》 《

While Staś and Kurta were sound asleep, rocked by the warm wind, Mrs. Szarak had cleaned the cabbage of pests and weeded the beets, and she was plucking lettuce leaves for lunch, collecting them in a sieve. That good vegetable dwelled in the corner of the garden, by the wattle fence that ran alongside the road. The mistress was kneeling carefully over it, and as she selected fresh leaves, she was wondering if the lettuce was pleased when it was washed in warm water to be cleaned of soil, covered with vinegar, and seasoned with lard?

She already had half a sieveful, almost all she needed, when from the road there came the sound of short, shuffling steps and the tapping of a walking stick. At the same time Mrs. Szarak heard what seemed to be a conversation.

"Damn it!" said the voice angrily. "That's how he repays me for showing him so much of the world! He would have rotted away somewhere under a fence or burned to death like a condemned soul if it wasn't for me . . . Idiot!"

There was another shuffling sound.

"You're an idiot, I tell you! You belong in company with shepherds, not with me. You'd be the clever one if you were bitten by dogs, or broken up like pigs' bones. Peg leg!"

The blacksmith's wife stood up. A few paces from the fence, on the road, she saw a doddering old woman with a tall walking stick in her hand. On her back she carried a bulging canvas. A few gray curls poked out from under her headscarf and shook along with her head.

"Who are you swearing at like that, granny? Hey, Grzybina!" called Mrs. Szarak, laughing.

The old woman turned to her.

"Oh, it's you, Mrs. Szarak?" she said, walking up to the fence. "Christ be praised! Actually, I was going to call and see you, too. I had a message from your father, and I would have gone and forgotten because of this Judas here!"

As she said this, she raised the walking stick and shook it angrily.

"What did my dad have to say?" asked Mrs. Szarak quickly.

"Well . . . He's getting tangled up around my feet. As if it weren't enough that he's not helping, he's getting in the way. This is the thanks I get for rescuing him from the filth!"

"What did my father want you to tell me?" repeated the blacksmith's wife impatiently. "Were you at the mill today?"

"You bet I was! Down, you bastard!" she went on furiously, tossing the stick against the side of the fence. "I was saying a charm to get rid of Sołtysiak's fever that he's had for two weeks now, and on the way yesterday I stopped by at the mill."

"Is Father well?"

"Oh, yes! But he asked that you come and see him tomorrow with Staś, and that your man should also come to the mill on Sunday."

The old woman seemed to have forgotten about her walking stick. She leaned on the fence and continued, "You see, that organist fellow of yours, Zawada, is buying some land, and he wants Stawiński, your dad, to lend him five hundred zlotys. He went to the mill on Wednesday to ask for it, but Stawiński said to him, 'Why should I lend you money when you injured the blacksmith and fell out with him?'"

"Quite right!" put in Mrs. Szarak.

"So the organist says to him, 'I'll make up with the blacksmith, and I'll teach his son.' And the old man says, 'So make up with him then!' And he says, 'I'm afraid to go to the smithy, because he might beat me up. I'd be less fearful at your house. I'd even bring a couple of bottles of mead to make my peace.'"

"That two-faced so-and-so!" interrupted the blacksmith's wife. "It's not long ago he was telling people that it says in the Holy Bible smiths and chimney sweeps are descended from Cain and from Ham, and that they're born to be fratricides! He can go to hell!"

"Well, if it says so in the Holy Bible then you can't blame the organist," observed the old woman.

"That's slander!" cried Mrs. Szarak excitedly. "We know what's what . . . The peasants are descended from Ham, and my man's not a peasant, and from Cain came the Turks, and he's not a Turk either. He hasn't killed anyone!"

The old crone was fond of showing off her knowledge about the descendants of Ham, but this time she maintained a discreet silence, remembering that she was dealing with a literate person, the blacksmith's wife, who also happened to be from the Stawiński family of millers.

"Come into the cottage and rest," said Mrs. Szarak suddenly and hospitably, looking at the tired old woman.

"I can't!" replied the woman, and seized her stick. "I have to go to see Mateusz's wife and treat her cow, because it's swollen. And you," she added, shaking her stick, "do your job properly for the rest of the journey, or I'll . . . "

"What are you saying?" admonished the blacksmith's wife.

"Why shouldn't I say it? This devil should hop straight forward, not drag behind like a souse."

"Your legs aren't up to it, granny. There's nothing the stick can do about it!"

"I don't know about that!" retorted the old woman, waving her hand impatiently. "They've kept going for eighty years, I don't see why they should let me down now. Stay with God!"

"Go with God!" responded the blacksmith's wife as the old lady hurried away.

When she was alone, she was again seized with anger at the organist.

How do you like that! she thought. He hurt my man and ruined his clothes, and now he wants to make up because he needs some money. "Don't you fear," she whispered, shaking her fist in the direction of the gray bell tower, "you won't get your money, and you won't buy that land, and on top of it all I'm going to give you a good talking-to in front of everyone! It's not for the likes of you that my father has five hundred zlotys. Not on your life, you beggar!"

Wanting to communicate her comments to her husband right

away, she jumped over the fence and ran to the smithy. It seemed to her that the whole world already knew about the organist's double-dealing, for even the cracked, patched bellows wheezed and breathed sparks more irately than ever.

She called her husband out and told him the news the old woman had brought.

"Thank the Lord that the organist is willing to let bygones be bygones," responded the soot-covered giant genially when he heard what his wife had to say.

The young mistress wrung her hands in horror.

"And you'd make up with him?" she shouted.

"You bet I would! Who's supposed to teach Staś? The school-master?"

"So you're going to make your peace with him after he smashed a bottle over your head?"

"It was the bottle that broke, not my head."

"After he called you a filthy workman and compared you to a chimney sweep?"

"When I haven't washed, I'm dirty. Everyone knows that, most of all you," said the blacksmith, who couldn't understand why his wife was so being obstinate.

Mrs. Szarak shook her head.

"That it should come to this," she began lamenting. "So you're a peasant? Your father served with my uncle in the army, and you have no ambitions? I'm a woman," she said breathlessly, "but I'd tear his eyes out, and you want to make up with him? You're the husband of a Stawińska, you took a wife of good birth, and you have no sense of shame?"

The blacksmith frowned.

"Of course I've got a sense of shame," he muttered.

"But you want to make up with the organist."

"Says who?"

"But you just said . . . "

"What did I say? It was you who said your father wanted it that way, and we should respect his wishes."

"Is my dad your father too? I'm the one who's supposed to obey him, not you. You shouldn't want to make up with the organist even if I wanted to, on my father's orders."

Since for the last few minutes the apprentices had been scuffling in the smithy, the blacksmith wanted to get back to work, and perhaps also to escape this troublesome discussion with his wife. So he said energetically, "Well, if that's the case, there'll be no reconciliation with the organist! Your father can want or not want what he likes, it's all the same to me. But I don't want it! I won't make up with him! I won't go to the mill on Sunday, you won't take Staś there tomorrow, and that's all there is to it!"

"I will go tomorrow, and you will come on Sunday," interrupted his wife.

"Eh?" asked Szarak, and almost burst out laughing, but just managed to stop himself.

"We'll both be at the mill, and the organist will come, but only so that he can hear in company what I have to say to him! That's right!"

Her husband looked askance at her and was even about to spit through his teeth, but he left well alone and slowly went back to the smithy, scratching his head. The boys were still tussling in there, but it was easier for Szarak to calm them down than to understand his wife for a moment.

When the blacksmith's wife returned to the garden, Staś was no longer asleep but was wrestling with Kurta. His mother kissed the lively child and left him outside in the care of the dog, while she took the lettuce she had picked and went into the house to finish the lunch. The whole of the rest of the time till nightfall she spent preparing for her journey the following day and planning her revenge. If she succeeded, the organist would be disgraced for all time!

》 《

The next day, beginning at sunrise, there was a great to-do in the blacksmith's cottage. The mistress was leaving for her father's for two whole days, so she had to arrange things at home in detail. It seemed that everything felt the impact of her impending absence. Kurta had lost his appetite and was just jumping about around Staś. The cows lowed mournfully as they were being led out to pasture, and the pigs broke the gate of the sty, so eager were they to bid the mistress farewell.

In addition she had to serve lunch early and argue with her husband, who every few minutes would come in from the smithy and mumble, "To hell with these pointless trips! If we're to make up with the organist, then let's go to the mill; if not, let's stay put. Why should we create a bigger enemy for ourselves? What if he goes and brings a curse upon us during the Consecration, and brings down fire on our home, or sickness upon us and our livestock?"

At this point the blacksmith's wife took her husband by the arm and pushed him out of the room, saying, "You keep out of this. You've got the heart of a blacksmith, but I have a gentlewoman's mind, and I'll sort the organist out so that he'll burn up with embarrassment himself rather than burning us in a fire!"

After lunch, when she had washed the pots with the maid, Mrs. Szarak once again checked all the corners of the cottage, and as a parting gift she was stung by a bee so badly that her eyes watered. Then she led the little cart into the yard, put a mattress into the cart and a pillow onto the mattress, put Staś on top, and, kissing her husband, she set off.

All these preparations were a great source of delight to Kurta, and when his mistress took the handle of the cart, the dog went crazy. First he jumped on Staś and tugged the kerchief off his head, then he almost tore the blacksmith's mustache off; berated by the smith, he threw himself impetuously at his mistress and almost knocked her down.

These violent signs of joy did not serve Kurta well, for Mrs. Szarak was reminded that she could not very well leave the house without a dog, and so she had him taken inside. Magda the maid managed with considerable difficulty to carry Kurta into the kitchen. However, as soon as she'd gotten him inside, Kurta jumped through the window into the yard and was even more pleased with himself. As a result, the poor creature was slapped across the neck with his mistress's shawl, kicked in the side by his master's heel, and hit on the head with a piece of wood by the maid, after which he was taken to the empty pigsty and the gate was fastened shut. The dog howled so terribly that more than one old woman out in the fields heard him and foretold ill fortune, and quickly said a prayer for the souls of the departed.

It was a scorching hot day. Here and there were small white clouds, which seemed to be wondering where they might go to get away from the heat. Under Mrs. Szarak's feet and the wheels of the cart the grains of hot sand crunched quietly. An unseen lark in the sky trilled a greeting to the mother and son, and from among the cornfields poppies and cornflowers stuck their heads out toward the road, as if to check whether someone they knew was coming.

Mrs. Szarak stopped and looked around. There was their cottage on the hill, draped with vines as with a robe. At this moment the sweep of the well was being lowered: Magda must have gone for water. A little man with a pony stood in front of the smithy, but the blacksmith obviously hadn't noticed him, for the hammers continued to pound, over the banging and clanging of which rose Kurta's doleful whining.

What a pretty picture! Mrs. Szarak seemed to draw strength from it, and, pulling the cart, she ran down the hill.

The road was winding and hilly. Every few dozen paces there rose ever greater hills. The biggest of them came in a birch wood, which lay down in the valley seemingly so close that you could stretch out a hand and grasp its branches. In reality, it was half an hour's walk away.

Slowly the cottage and the smithy disappeared from view, and even Kurta's dirge died away. The sand grew deeper, the sun was hotter and hotter, the little clouds stayed in one place like empty ferries by the bank of the Vistula, and new larks continued to wish the travelers a safe journey.

Mrs. Szarak felt so happy at this time that even anger at the organist left her heart. "Perhaps we should make up with him? Not on your nelly!" she muttered. "I'm not exhausting myself here in this heat just to earn five hundred zlotys for him."

In the meantime Staś lay in the cart, enchanted by new impressions. For the first time in his life, he saw before his eyes the unbounded horizon and the infinite depth of the sapphire-colored sky. He wasn't yet able to wonder what it was or to be surprised; he merely sensed extraordinary things. The earth, which up till now he had walked on, had disappeared; wherever he turned his gaze, he met the sky. He felt as if he were flying, that he was drowning in a vast thing to which he could not yet give the name "space." His soul was filled with something indefinable and peaceful.

He was like an angel made up of a head and wings; he rose over the boundless regions, not remembering the past or thinking of the future, but sensing infinity at every moment. Eternal life must also be like this.

All of a sudden the horizon was darkened by a multitude of green branches, and shade fell over the cart. They had entered the wood and were drawing close to the big hill.

The sweltering heat, the weight of the cart, and anger at the organist had their own effect on the blacksmith's wife. She began to feel tired. She felt like sitting down amid the trees and resting, but she was afraid of prolonging the journey. Besides, should she sit down in the wood? If she had been alone she would not have cared, but Staś's presence made her wary, though she didn't know exactly of what. No one hereabouts had ever heard of there being wolves or bandits, but today the woman would have been afraid of a hare if it had jumped out at her.

Oh, this wood! You could say your prayers ten times over before you reached the other side . . . If only she'd taken Kurta with her, she would have felt more cheerful . . . but there he was, crying and locked in. At this moment, even the wrong done to the dog fell like a heavy burden upon the soul of the blacksmith's wife.

If only this wood would come to an end! If she could only make it to the top of the hill. Mrs. Szarak took off her headscarf and put it on the cart. This brought her little relief. Perspiration streamed off her and took her strength away. She felt she would never make it to the foot of the hill, let alone to the top!

Just before the start of the hill, to the right of the travelers, another road came in from the middle of the wood, and from this road at this very moment came the rattle of a small carriage. Mrs. Szarak perked up: Now at least she wouldn't be alone! She quickened her pace, and soon she spotted a cariole in the form of a trap, but handsomely built and covered with a leather canopy. The trap, which was on springs, was pulled by a fine-looking bay horse. Inside sat a gentleman whom Mrs. Szarak was not able to see clearly, since at that moment the whole equipage turned onto the main road facing away from her.

If only you'd give me a lift! thought the blacksmith's wife, but she was too shy to speak to the owner of the trap, though she was walking right behind it.

This trap, built with such great craftsmanship, bore Mr. Loski, landed gentleman and district judge. He was returning home from the courts and doubtless would have given a ride to a tired and good-looking woman, if he had seen her. Unfortunately, the judge was deep in thought, and not only did he not notice Mrs. Szarak at the intersection, but he did not even hear her quickened breathing.

The travelers reached the foot of the hill. The carriage moved at walking pace; the blacksmith's wife followed step for step, pulling her burden.

The hill was about two hundred paces high and was fairly steep. In light of this, Mrs. Szarak had an idea that would bring her respite at the cost of the horse. Without much reflection, she fastened the handle of the cart onto the axle of the trap.

It was a brilliant plan. The handle was firmly fastened, the cart with Staś in it rolled along even better than before, and the woman was able to rest a little. Now if they could only make it to the top!

She walked behind the cart and, yielding to the voice of exhaustion, rested heavily with both hands on its rim. It was a huge relief for her. Walking was so much easier that she could have gone twice as far as from home to the mill. But what of it! In this world human happiness is never long-lived. They were already halfway up the hill . . . Now it was only fifty paces to the top . . . Many thanks, horse, for pulling us up here! Now it was time to unfasten the cart from the trap.

Suddenly, the horse set off at a trot; and the trap, and the cart behind it, and Staś inside it, rode off down the hill!

Mrs. Szarak was dumbfounded. Before she could shout "Stop!" the judge's trap and Staś's cart were already at the bottom of the hill.

"Help!" cried the woman, setting off downhill at a run, her arms spread. With a flash of clarity it occurred to her that if the cart so much as hit a stone it could be overturned.

But the cart was sailing along across the sand as if it were traveling on thistledown. The little wheels spun and shook like mad, and Staś was enjoying the speedy ride immensely. The judge, who knew nothing of what was going on, was cheerful all the same, and his horse, which had just been relieved of a weight, snorted with satisfaction and broke into a gallop.

For a moment Mrs. Szarak thought that she would be able to catch up with the trap, or that those inside it would at least hear her. She was wrong. She stopped, intending to shout in her loudest voice, even if it made her lungs burst; but she had just opened her mouth when her voice died. She had seen something fall out of the cart. When she ran closer, she saw that it was only her headscarf. The horse slowed down. She ran closer. She could already see Staś's head and his little arms tucked in neatly by his sides.

"Staś, my darling! Help!"

The cart rocked and moved off more quickly. She couldn't see the child's arms any longer. Now his head could barely be made out. The cart was getting smaller and smaller.

Mrs. Szarak could not understand why a wall of earth did not rise up before the horse, why heaven did not block the road, why the trees did not stand in the way of those in the trap. How many birds were there in their nests who saw her maternal despair, yet not one of them came to her assistance. If only one of the birds had called out to the gentleman: "Stop!" If only a single stone had woken from its sleep at that grievous moment. But it was no good! Everything was silent.

She looked at the sky. Above her head a squirrel was calmly gnawing a pinecone. The clouds had not moved. The sun was burning as before. She looked toward the road, and there the trap could be made out only with difficulty, while the cart was no more than a yellow spot. She felt as if on that wretched cart was her own heart, which had been torn violently from her breast and was being dragged mercilessly goodness knows where, and that it was attached to her by a thread that was growing thinner and thinner. A moment longer and the thread would break, and with it the heart and life of the poor mother!

The carriage grew smaller and slowly began to disappear in the swaying greenery. Now it was the size of a bird . . . Now it vanished completely again, now it reappeared . . . now it vanished again . . .

Mrs. Szarak wiped her eyes, which were full of dust and tears. There was nothing to be seen! She ran into the middle of the road. Nothing . . . She crossed to the other side. Something flashed in the distance but disappeared at once. Exhausted, prostrated by pain, she fell face down on the ground and, curled into a ball, began to wail like an animal whose young have been torn from her swelling breast.

At this moment, on the hill where the misfortune had befallen her, there appeared a pony in harness, and behind it the piously shaven visage of a man who sat in a small but loudly rattling gig. Mrs. Szarak did not hear the noise and did not see the traveler, but he noticed the curled-up human figure on the road, and he stopped the pony.

"Is she drunk, or is she dead?" the solemnly shaven driver asked himself. "Maybe she has the cholera, or perhaps someone murdered her? Should I go on, or should I turn back?"

The individual looking down from the vantage point of his seat upon the vale of tears that was human life was afraid of robbers, cholera, and trials, and was already tugging on the reins to turn the gig around when he remembered the reading from the twelfth Sunday after Whitsun, from chapter 10 of the Gospel according to Saint Luke, the parable of the Samaritan: "And he went to him, and bound up his wounds, pouring in oil and wine, and set him on his own beast, and brought him to an inn, and took care of him."

As the gentleman recalled this, the gig moved forward, though very slowly and cautiously, up to the woman. Then it stopped, and the Samaritan sitting in it leaned out and prodded the blacksmith's wife lightly with his whip.

"Hello there!" he called. "*In nomine Patris et . . .* "

Mrs. Szarak leaped to her feet and, looking with glazed eyes at the clean-shaven face of the traveler, whispered, "Mr. Zawada?"

"It is I!" he replied. "But what has happened?"

"My Staś is gone! Oh, God!" she groaned, and leaned against the side of the gig.

"What's that? The gypsies took him? Oh, my Lord!"

Mrs. Szarak briefly described the incident.

"Don't you worry, ma'am!" cried the organist. "It was obviously some gentleman in the trap . . . Dear Lord! . . . and such folks don't steal babies. Sit up in my gig! *Et cum spiritu Tuo.*"

"What for?"

"What do you mean, what for? Dear Lord! We'll go and look for the boy, and that's all there is to it!"

"Perhaps he's already . . . "

"Perhaps he's already what? You think he may be dead? Who would I have to teach then? If I'm supposed to teach him when he is six years old, then, dear Lord, the lad's not going to die at the age of two. *In saecula saeculorum . . .* "

The organist's logic, and above all his Latin, were so incontrovertible that the blacksmith's wife got into the gig without another word and sat humbly on the box facing the organist. But the faithful if impetuous servant of God would not allow it.

"Please . . . Dear Lord!" he called. "Please, take the seat, and I'll sit on the box. *Introibo ad altare Dei.*"

"What are you doing, sir?"

"Oh, yes! Dear Lord, I do believe I would be a man with no upbringing if I allowed you, ma'am, the wife and daughter of my friends, to sit on the box. I'm driving, so I will sit on the box. *Sicut erat in principio.*"

Mrs. Szarak obeyed the organist's instructions, not daring to look him in the eyes. After all, it was to spite him that she had set off today on her journey. But God, mindful of His servants, had crossed her plans for revenge and arranged for the organist himself to rescue her from her predicament.

"You know, Mrs. Szarak," said her noble guardian, "I, dear Lord, have a matter concerning a certain gentleman which I need to discuss with Mr. Loski, the district judge, but first I'll take you to the town, and there we'll find out from the Jews who in these parts drives a covered trap. Then we'll find Staś, then we'll go and collect him, and I'll take you and the child to the mill. *Indulgentiam, absolutionem et remissionem peccatorum nostrorum.*"

But Mrs. Szarak was no longer listening to his plans, announced in a sermonizing tone. She had laid her head on her arms and was crying her eyes out. This brought her some relief.

Half an hour later the gig drove into the town marketplace, to the accompaniment of the cracking of the whip and the Latin, which the excited organist was dishing out even more liberally than usual.

》 《

Mr. Loski was a middle-aged man, both honest and decent. He possessed considerable prudence, a large estate, and side-whiskers in the English style. A small bald patch attested to the fact that this good citizen must, in his youth, have knocked his head against many a wall and have lived a far from God-fearing life. This, however, did not undermine the respect he enjoyed among his neighbors. As for his wife, it made him even dearer to her, adding to the present happiness of their conjugal life a hint of regret for the past and uncertainty about the future.

Since being appointed to the position of district judge, Mr. Loski had held office amid universal approval. Not wishing to take people away from their work, he bought himself a stylish covered sprung trap and drove himself to the courthouse two miles away. And so whenever he came back from sittings later than usual, his wife would ask him casually, "Did you call on the neighbors?"

"Oh, no," he would reply. "I came straight from the office."

"Oh!" concluded the lady, regretting deep inside that her husband was not accompanied to that office by a coachman, or at least by a serving boy.

We will not err from the truth in mentioning that the judge's acquaintances, especially the ladies, to some extent shared Mrs. Loska's doubts regarding the innocent lifestyle of her husband. Renown, one it is acquired, lasts forever!

On the day the incident described here took place on the road, Mr. Loski was returning home around two in the afternoon. He had had few cases in court that day, and at home he was awaited by a gathering of his neighbors, so he was in a hurry. At the moment Mrs. Szarak attached the cart to his trap, he had been mulling over a dispute between two farmers over a hen; later he began to think about how he would entertain his guests. He had not the slightest idea that he would become the innocent cause of deep distress for the blacksmith's wife and an object of amusement for his neighbors.

At the edge of the wood the road to the judge's property branched off the highway to the left. Loski turned onto it without any problem and drove into open country. In one place there were a number of people digging ditches, and the judge noticed that they were nudging each other animatedly and pointing at his trap.

Later he encountered a woman with a small boy, who stopped on the road, their mouths gaping so wide it looked as if they were trying to swallow the bay horse along with the trap. These signs of admiration were immensely flattering to the judge, who was pleased to note that his beloved equipage was beginning to attract attention.

Staś, who at the beginning was delighted with the fast ride and the bouncing of the cart, had grown bored and fallen asleep, probably dreaming about Kurta's tricks and his mother's kisses. Soon the trap bumped over the frame of the gate and entered the courtyard.

Before the manor house, amid flowers, under a canvas awning, the judge's wife and the company of ladies and men were awaiting their host. The judge noticed this, and, wishing to arrive with a flourish, decided to circle the large lawn. At a tug of the reins, the horse began to toss its handsome head and to stamp its feet rhythmically. The judge, not wishing to be worse than his horse, also stretched out his legs, straightened up gracefully, and assumed the posture of a gentleman.

He did in fact achieve the intended effect. When he rounded the courtyard and found himself opposite the awning, the whole company began to applaud, shouting "Bravo!" and manifesting other signs of appreciation.

Loski pulled even harder at the reins, the horse tossed its head even more gracefully, the trap with the child's cart attached moved even more grandly, and the applause of the onlookers took on the appearance of wild gaiety. By now the judge was surprised, all the more so when he noticed his old butler was biting his lip so as not to burst out laughing.

"Bravo! Bravo! Congratulations! Ha, ha!" cried the men.

Loski got out of the trap and was astonished to see ambiguous looks on the ladies' faces, while his wife, who was blond and fair-complexioned, a real angel, had an indistinct smile on her lips and very distinct tears in her large, mild eyes.

"Take the horse to the stables!" the judge said to a manservant, thoroughly embarrassed by now.

"And what should I do with that, sir?" asked the old rascal, waving a napkin at the cart.

Loski looked around and was horrified to see an object that had so little connection with his standing as a man and a guardian of justice. This frightful matter was complicated all the more by the fact that the Loskis did not have any children of their own.

"Congratulations on your find!" called the men.

"You could at least make me a town councillor!" shouted an eighty-year-old retired colonel, an old bachelor.

In the meantime, the ladies had surrounded the cart, where Staś had woken up and begun to cry.

"What a beautiful baby!" said one.

"What fine features!"

"He must be at least a year old," added a third.

"And it so happens that it's been two years since the judge began working for the public good!" roared the colonel in a stentorian voice.

"But gentlemen, there must have been a mistake!" explained the unhappy judge in an altered voice.

"In such matters there can be no mistake!" put in the incorrigible colonel. "Though there's no denying it, the boy's pretty as a picture!"

Taking advantage of the hullabaloo, Mrs. Loska disappeared into her room. A few minutes later she emerged again, with very red eyes but otherwise somewhat calmer. After her came the fat old nurse.

When the judge's wife took Staś from his cart with trembling hands and passed him to the nurse, her poor husband asked in an exceptionally humble voice, "What do you intend to do with him?"

"Well, I'm not going to hand him over to the farmers," responded his wife quietly, and with a hint of reproach in her voice.

Hearing this, the young ladies blushed, the older ones exchanged glances, even the men grew more serious, and the colonel said, "Well, dear lady, all joking aside, it would be a good idea for you to have the boy fed; he must be hungry. In the meantime, however, the parish and the chairman of the district council should be informed, for this is clearly a misunderstanding, and the parents of this young fellow must be in a pretty pickle."

Now the nurse, who had been scrutinizing the child, murmured, "I swear to God, he's the spitting image of the master! The master looked just like that when he was a year old! I still remember him: the nose, the eyes, even that mole on his neck. The dead spit! This is no farmer's child."

To put an end to these distasteful remarks, the judge's wife pushed the old chatterbox gently onto the veranda and instructed her to feed and wash the child. The company had composed itself, and everyone began to criticize the probable carelessness of the child's nanny, who had fastened the cart to the trap, and at the same time to express sympathy for the worried parents. The judge nodded and tried to guess in which village the cart had been tied on, and when the subject changed and his wife calmed down, at least on the surface, Łoski left his guests for a moment and ran to the cloakroom.

Here the nurse had sent the servants away and was holding the child on her lap, feeding him a bottle of milk. Staś was drinking, but at the same time was looking anxiously around the unfamiliar room, as if he were seeking his mother. When the judge came in, the boy spotted the man and, his arms outstretched, threw himself forward impetuously and in his endearing little way cried, "Dada! Dada!"

"The voice of blood, I swear to God!" exclaimed the nurse. "Oh, what a smart child he is! He's the absolute image of you, sir!"

The judge came close to the little boy, looked at him intently, touched his sunburned face delicately, then, glancing to the left and right, kissed Staś. When he had done this, to the indescribable delight of the nurse, he went out to the hallway.

A strange feeling had stirred in his heart. He felt sentimental, concerned, and at once satisfied and proud. He liked Staś more than any other child he had known.

In the corridor he met his wife, but he didn't dare look her in the eye. When she noticed this, she gave him her hand and murmured, "I'm not angry anymore."

Loski took the hand and squeezed it tightly to his breast, then suddenly went out onto the veranda, worried that she might notice he was moved.

》 《

In a small town, Saturday is a day of quiet and rest. For this reason the mayor of X., his wife the mayoress, and their friend the notary went out for a stroll in the afternoon.

The mayor, a short, squat little fellow, walked in front. His right hand, in which he carried a cane, he kept behind his back; his left, bent at the elbow, he held in front of him the way an old man helping with the collection at mass carries the tray. At the same time he smiled continuously and closed his eyes. People said he did it "so as not to know where things had come from" – come into that outstretched hand, of course.

A few paces behind him came the notary, a tall, elderly bachelor who had lent his arm to the mayoress. We doubt very much if this manner of taking a walk surprised anyone in the town. Everyone had grown used to it, including the mayor, who was particularly satisfied and who was only concerned that "things should come" thick and fast.

In honor of this trio of local celebrities, by the wooden cottages of the market square stood a few Jews on their Sabbath, yawning, and next to the broken pump a dog scratched itself lazily, its clearly visible ribs offering an illustration of the town's prosperity.

Just as the group reached the edge of the market square, the organist's gig charged up and nearly knocked them over. The mayor even jumped out of the way, while the notary, evidently out of excitement, straightened his collar.

At the same moment the gig came to a stop in front of the notary.

"Have you gone crazy, galloping along like that?" asked the notary.

"*Laudetur Jesus Christus!*" responded the organist, touching his cap with his whip.

The mayor noticed the tearful Mrs. Szarak, and coming up to the gig, smiling as ever, he asked, "What is it? Has there been an accident? Did someone die? Has there been a fire?"

"Reckless fellow!" the notary said, following his own train of thought. "He almost ran us over, me and Jó . . . that is, the mayoress and I."

"My son is gone! My little Staś!" cried the blacksmith's wife, bursting into tears once again.

"Who is this?" asked the mayoress.

"I believe she would be the daughter of Stawiński the miller," explained the notary.

"That's right, Stawiński's my father, and now I'm married to the blacksmith. Oh, please help me find him, dear good people!" said Mrs. Szarak, shaking with grief on the gig.

"Tee hee!" giggled the mayor. "You do have something to cry about! A young woman like you, God'll give you ten more children!"

"*André, soyez convenable!*" the mayoress reproached him. She had attended boarding school in the provincial capital.

"Save me, please, good people!" wailed the blacksmith's wife, and, leaning over the side of the gig, she stretched out her arms as if she were trying to hug the mayoress and then her husband.

But the mayoress, who had graduated from boarding school, took a step back with a gesture of indignation, and the mayor, who was also offended, cried, "Less of this damned familiarity! Don't you know who I am?"

"Of course, I know you're the mayor, your honor. Help me find my son! I'm so unhappy, I don't know what's happened to him since I last saw him! Maybe he fell out of the cart and got run over!"

"What do I care about it?" asked the mayor. "Go and tell the watchman! She thinks I'm going to go running around looking for her brat! Did you hear that, sir?"

The word "brat" offended the blacksmith's wife. Her tears dried, the blood rushed to her face.

"What are you mayor for?" she shouted. "Not to help poor people in their misfortune? So my Staś is a brat, is he? You were just like him once, and maybe one day, if he's found, he'll be . . . "

At this point tears prevented her from continuing.

"She's a naive one!" muttered the organist, who was obviously thinking that the mayor with his hand outstretched was indeed not there to help poor people in their misfortune.

Be that as it may, as a result of the outburst by the blacksmith's wife, the situation would have become ticklish if the notary, who did business with Stawiński, had not intervened. He interrupted the argument by calling on the organist to explain what had happened to Staś.

In the meantime, a crowd of Jews had appeared from nowhere and surrounded the gig, and the organist described Staś's accident to the whole gathering as if he were delivering a sermon. When at the end, in a loud voice he asked those present if anyone knew a gentleman who owned a covered sprung trap, one of the Jews called, "I know! It's Mr. Loski, the judge."

"And the word became flesh!" cried the organist. "I was supposed to go and see him on business. Goodness knows why I came here!"

With these words he turned the gig around.

"Oh, drive as fast as you can, my good sir!" said the blacksmith's wife, tugging at the tails of the organist's long overcoat.

The Jew leaned on the gig and said, "Mrs. Szarak! Don't forget it was me who told you . . . I'll call in at the smithy tomorrow."

"What shenanigans are these now?" said the organist indignantly.

"I'm perfectly aware myself that Mr. Loski rides to court in a covered trap pulled by a bay horse."

"So why did you ask if you already knew?" exclaimed the Jew angrily.

"I don't have to explain myself to a tatterdemalion like you!" retorted the organist loftily, preparing to set off.

"Let's go now, please!" begged Mrs. Szarak.

"Oy vey! What an aristocrat!" cried the Jew, seizing the reins. "My good organist, I have a question for you: Would you mind coming to my house on Sundays to play the barrel organ for me?"

The crowd gathered around the gig burst out laughing.

The proud organist, hit at the most sensitive point of his self-esteem, turned pale, and in his eyes there appeared a vengeful glint. He stood up from the box and, straightening his long figure, he cried in a mighty, solemn voice, "You miserable Jew! I christen you . . . *In nomine Patris* . . . "

"Oy vey! You swine! You son of a bitch!" shouted the crowd, scattering across the market square.

At this moment the organist whipped the horse, and the gig slipped away in clouds of dust, accompanied by the laughter and abuse of the mob.

They rode along at a fair trot for ten minutes or so. Every few seconds Mrs. Szarak stood up and, swaying on the bouncing gig, looked down at the road.

"Sir!"

"What it is?"

"Is it far?"

"Just one more mile, we'll be there in a flash!"

The pony was strong and nimble, but even on his smooth skin broad patches of perspiration were beginning to appear.

"Gee up, boy!" shouted the organist.

At times the dust cloud trailing behind them like a tail drew level with the gig, stood in their way, and threw fine particles into three pairs of eyes. When this happened the horse dropped its head between its knees and snorted, the organist wiped his eyes with his rough sleeve, and only the poor mother went on staring at the road without even blinking.

"Sir!"

The organist already knew what she wanted to say, and without waiting for the rest he said, "Over there, between the trees. Can you see? We'll be there in ten Our Fathers."

They turned to the right. In the fields a small group of people were digging a ditch.

The gig halted.

"Hey there!" called the organist, beckoning to those digging.

One of them laid aside his spade and came toward the gig. Mrs. Szarak's pulse was beating like the hammers in the smithy, and she was trembling as if the gig were still moving, even though it was standing still.

"Has the master come home?" the organist asked the man as he approached.

"He has!"

"Did you by any chance see a cart behind his trap?"

"We sure did!"

"Was there a baby in it?"

"There musta been, 'cos there was somethin' shaking inside."

"May God repay you."

"Go with God. Is it yours?"

"Not mine. It's this lady's," answered the organist, pointing behind him with his whip.

"Sir," said the blacksmith's wife.

"What?"

"Let me down from the gig. I'll go on foot, I think I'll get there quicker that way."

"You shouldn't talk such nonsense, ma'am. Gee up, boy!"

"Oh, sweet Jesus! Will I find him?" whispered the blacksmith's wife, kneeling on the rocking floor of the gig.

The horse galloped along.

About two-thirds of a mile from the manor, the organist spotted a dark object moving quickly from one side of the road to the other. When they drew closer they saw that it was a dog, which was running ahead of the gig with its nose to the ground.

"Kurta!" cried the organist. "Look, Mrs. Szarak, it's your Kurta!"

When the dog saw the blacksmith's wife, he began to howl, bark, fling himself at the gig, and jump up at the horse, which snorted and fended him off as best it could. The faithful dog had gotten out of the pigsty and had followed the trail of Staś's cart all the way here.

"So far so good!" exclaimed the organist, and tugged at the reins.

They pulled up in front of the gate to the manor.

The blacksmith's wife got down, took a couple of steps, and suddenly leaned against the gatepost, her head spinning. The organist took her by the arm, and in this way they walked toward the manor, preceded by Kurta, who continued barking, jumping, and running in circles.

At this time the whole company was sitting on the veranda having lunch. The newcomers stopped at the fence, looking timidly toward the gentry, when all of a sudden Kurta bounded forward.

The blacksmith's wife ran after him and, breathless, with her hands raised, she knelt at the end of the table where Staś, alive, rested, and smiling, sat on the nurse's lap.

"Down, you bad dog!" cried the terrified nurse at Kurta, who was forcibly trying to jump on her.

"The mother! The mother!" exclaimed those present, as they saw the woman drop to the ground and with a cry kiss Staś's pudgy little feet.

Lunch was interrupted. Everyone stood up and gathered round the other end of the table, where an amusing scene was taking place: The two women were quarreling over the child.

Mrs. Szarak wanted to take her own child back, while the nurse wouldn't hand him over.

"He's my son! My little Staś!" cried the mother.

"And who might you be, lady?" exclaimed the nurse, wrestling with her. "How vulgar! Imagine grabbing a delicate little baby like this as if he were a lump of lard!"

"He's mine!"

"What do you mean, yours? This is our master's son, anyone will tell you! He's so pretty . . . There, you see, the master's here. Give the boy back!"

The whole company laughed unceremoniously.

"What are you laughing at?" said the nurse, her hackles up. "This is the master's son! He looks just like him. Down, you mongrel!" she shouted again at Kurta.

Mrs. Szarak, on her knees, looked up in surprise at the man who had been called Staś's father. Studying him, she said with innocent simplicity, "He wouldn't be as handsome as he is if he were your master's. He's the son of the blacksmith, Józef Szarak."

At this point the organist chimed in and in an unctuous speech confirmed that the lost child, who had received the name of Stanisław at holy baptism, was the legitimate offspring of Mr. Józef Szarak and Mrs. Małgorzata Szarak, née Stawińska.

This information, coming from such a respectable source, the judge's wife received with signs of great satisfaction, while the judge smiled the way one would smile after eating a bowl of unripe sloes.

"Well I never!" whistled the old colonel, and added, "So that's that!"

The judge grimaced even more and waved his hand casually.

"I'm delighted," he said, "that this poor little chap has found his family again so quickly!"

"That reminds me of that fable called 'The Fox and the Grapes,'" put in the colonel.

The ladies bit their lips, the judge squirmed as if he were treading on pins, the organist didn't understand a word of it, and Mrs. Szarak heard nothing, as she was busy cuddling Staś.

It would be superfluous to mention that the organist was obliged once again to tell the story of Staś's adventure.

Having already expressed their sympathy for the mother, everyone now laughed at the tale, with the exception of the nurse, who was deeply hurt that Staś was not her master's son.

"He's such a clever little boy! And he looks so much like him! He even has that mole on his neck," the old woman muttered.

》 《

For the sake of completeness we shall add that when the organist had finished the business concerning the certain gentleman with the judge, he drove Mrs. Szarak to her father's, where he told the story for the third time to a horrified Mr. Stawiński. After he left the mill, that very same day he told it a fourth time to the blacksmith and a fifth time to the certain gentleman.

On Sunday, after mass, Stawiński, his daughter and grandson, and all the apprentices turned out onto the bridge to watch the arrival from town of the single-horse gig in which, wonder of wonders, Szarak the blacksmith and Zawada the organist sat like two brothers.

The old miller gave the two reconciled foes a long and tedious speech on the need for the mutual forgiveness of grudges, which at this point was entirely unnecessary. Then he called everyone to lunch, after which he handed the organist the sum of five hundred zlotys as an interest-free loan for three years. As a result, afterward the organist would frequently repeat to people the following dictum as a moral lesson: "Dear brothers! As I look back over my life, I can see clearly that the merciful Lord God never forsakes people such as myself: the virtuous and the just. *In saecula saeculorum . . .* !"

On Monday the organist was back in the church and Szarak in the smithy; Staś was playing with Kurta in the yard under Magda's supervision, while the blacksmith's wife was working in the garden.

Around midday a wagon pulled up, and a fellow who was not from the village unloaded a fine-looking chestnut calf with a white star on its forehead. Since the young quadruped was apparently afraid of the barking dog and refused to walk, the drover put one arm around its neck, the other under its backside, and in this way brought it to an astonished Mrs. Szarak.

"What's this? Where's it from?" asked the mistress.

"It's a present from Mrs. Łoska, a dowry for your little boy," answered the man.

"Józef! Magda! Come here! Staś is going to have a cow! They sent him it from the manor," called the woman, kissing the calf, whose tail was being plucked at by a no-less-excited Kurta.

With this epilogue, Staś's little adventure came to a close.

# Michałko

Work on the railway was finished. The bookkeeper paid off those who were owed money and cheated those he could; then crowds of people began to disperse and head back to their villages.

Around the inn that stood by the tracks, up till midday there was a hubbub of voices. One man was filling his traveling basket with pretzels, a second was buying vodka to take home, while a third was getting drunk then and there. Then they made up bundles of coarse canvas and, slinging them over their shoulders, they walked off, calling, "Good health, daft Michałko!"

And he stayed behind.

He stayed behind in the gray fields and didn't even watch his own people, but instead stared at the shining tracks that ran far away, goodness knows where. The wind ruffled his dark hair, flapped his sackcloth coat, and from a long way off brought the last verse of the song the travelers were singing.

Soon the canvas sacks, sackcloth jackets, and round caps disappeared behind the juniper bushes. Eventually the song, too, faded away, while he stood with folded arms because he had nowhere to go. Just like the hare that at that very moment was hopping across the tracks, his home was in the fields, a country orphan, and his pantry was what God provided.

From beyond the sandy hill there came a whistle, a cloud of

smoke, and a rumbling sound. The workmen's train pulled in and stopped at the unfinished station. The portly engine driver and his youthful assistant jumped down from the locomotive and ran to the inn. The brakemen followed suit. There remained only the engineer, who stared pensively at the deserted surroundings and listened to the quiet hissing of the steam in the boiler.

Michałko knew the engineer and bowed to him right down to the ground.

"Oh, it's you, daft Michałko. What are you doing here?" asked the engineer.

"Nothing, sir!" replied the country boy.

"Why don't you go back to your village?"

"I've nothing to go back for, sir."

The engineer started to hum, then said, "Go to Warsaw. You can always find work there."

"But I don't know where it is."

"Get up in the wagon and you'll find out."

"Daft" Michałko jumped up into the wagon like a cat and sat on a pile of stones.

"Got any money?" asked the engineer.

"I have a ruble and forty groszes, sir, and a zloty in loose change."

The engineer started humming again and looking around, while the locomotive continued to rumble. Finally, the crew of the train hurried out of the inn carrying bottles and bundles. The driver and his assistant climbed up into the locomotive, and they set off.

After about a mile, at a bend, threads of smoke appeared, then a poor village built amid marshes. At this sight Michałko grew animated. He began to laugh and shout (though he couldn't be heard at such a distance) and wave his cap.

One of the brakemen sitting up in the brake compartment told him off. "What are you leaning out for? If you fall out you'll be in big trouble."

"That's our village, sir, right there!"

"If it's your village, then just sit still," retorted the brakeman.

Michałko sat still as he was told. But his heart grew weary, so he began to say his prayers. Oh, if only he could return to his village of clay and straw, there in the mud . . . But he had no reason to go back. They called him daft, but he understood enough to know that in the outside world you were less likely to be half-dead with hunger and had a better chance of finding a bed for the night. In the outside world the bread was whiter, you could at least see meat, there were more houses, and people didn't suffer as much hardship as the folk where he was from.

They passed through station after station, stopping longer at one, more briefly at another. At sundown the engineer told them to give Michałko something to eat, for which Michałko thanked him with a low bow.

They entered a completely different region. Here there were no brimming marshes, but hilly fields and winding, fast-flowing streams. The chicken coops and wattle barns disappeared, and there appeared fine manor houses and brick buildings that were better constructed than the churches and the inns where Michałko was from.

At night they drew to a halt near a town built on a hill. It looked as if the houses were climbing on one another, and in each one there were as many lights as there are stars in the sky. You wouldn't see as many candles as there were in that town if you attended a hundred funerals.

Some beautiful music was playing, and crowds of people were walking along and laughing, even though it was so late that in Michałko's village all you would have been able to hear was the cry of a specter and the barking of frightened dogs.

Michałko didn't sleep. The engineer had told them to give him a pound of sausage and a roll, and then they had sent him to another wagon filled with sand. It was as soft as a feather bed there, but instead of lying down Michałko squatted and ate his sausage and bread till his eyes popped out, thinking to himself: No two ways about it, there are some mighty strange things in this world!

After a halt of several hours, at daybreak, the train moved off, and they continued briskly on their way. At one station in the woods they stopped for longer than usual, and the brakeman told Michałko that the engineer would probably be going back, because a telegram had come for him.

Sure enough, the engineer summoned Michałko.

"I have to return," he said. "Are you going to carry on to Warsaw?"

"Dunno!" murmured Michałko.

"Well, you won't die if you're among people."

"Who am I supposed to die on? I don't have anyone!"

It was true. Who did he have to die on?

"Go then," said the engineer. "Right by the railway station they're building new houses. You can carry a hod and you won't die of starvation, so long as you don't take to drinking. Afterward things might get better for you. Here's a ruble for emergencies."

Michałko took the ruble, embraced the engineer round the knees, and climbed up on his wagon of sand.

Soon they moved off.

On the way, he asked the brakeman, "Sir, is it far to our station?"

"About forty miles or so. I don't know really."

"How long would it take to go on foot, sir?"

"Maybe three weeks. Actually, I have no idea."

Michałko was seized by a boundless terror. Why had he gone and let himself travel so far away that it would take him three weeks to walk home!

In the village they sometimes told of the farmhand who had been whisked up by a gale-force wind. Before he even had time to cross himself, it carried him two miles away and flung him down, dead as a doornail. Had the same not happened to him? Was this fire-breathing machine, which terrified the older people, not worse than a gale-force wind? And where would it cast him down?

At this thought, he grabbed hold of the side of the wagon and closed his eyes. Now he felt it bearing him along, roaring fearfully, the wind whipping his face and laughing: ho, ho, ho! hee, hee, hee!

This was some storm that had swept him up! Only it hadn't taken a child from his mother or his father, nor from his own house, but an orphan from the fields.

He knew that something was not well with him, but what could he do about it? Things were bad for him and would probably get worse, but since things were already bad, worse, and worst, he opened his eyes and let go of the wagon. It was God's will. As a country boy, it was his task to bear hardship on his shoulders and fear and sorrow in his heart.

The locomotive gave a shrill whistle. Michałko looked ahead and saw what looked like a forest of roofs enveloped in a shroud of smoke.

"Is there a fire somewhere?" he asked the brakeman.

"That's Warsaw!"

Michałko's heart sank once again. How would he find the courage to go into that smoke?

The station. Michałko climbed down. He kissed the brakeman's hand and set off slowly toward an establishment whose signs bore painted images of red tankards of beer and green bottles of vodka. He was drawn not by the desire to drink but by something else.

Behind the inn could be seen a house under construction, and in front of the establishment stood the bricklayers. Michałko remembered the engineer's advice and went to ask about work.

The bricklayers, fine specimens of manhood bespattered with lime and brick dust, accosted him first.

"And who might you be? Where're you from? What's your mother's first name? Who made that cap for you?" One of them tugged his sleeve, another pulled the cap down over his eyes. They spun him around a few times till he couldn't remember which direction he'd come from.

"So where are you from, my lad?"

"From Wilczołyki, sir," answered Michałko.

But because he spoke in a singsong accent and with such a troubled expression on his face, the bricklayers burst into peals of laughter.

He stood among them, and though they were bullying him somewhat, he laughed, too.

These are cheerful folks, that's for sure! he was thinking to himself.

His laugh and his honest look won people over. The bricklayers settled down and began to ask him questions. And when he said that he was looking for work, they told him to follow them.

"He's a dumb ox, but I think he's a good kid," one of the master bricklayers said.

"We should take him on," added another.

"So, will you buy yourself a job?" one of the journeymen asked Michałko.

"I don't know how."

"Stand us a jug of vodka," explained another.

"Or you'll get a hiding!" put in a third with a laugh.

After some reflection, Michałko replied, "I'd rather get something than give something."

This was also to the liking of the bricklayers. They pulled Michałko's cap over his eyes a few more times, but they didn't mention the vodka again, nor did they give him a thrashing.

Playing around like this, they arrived and set to work. The master bricklayers climbed up onto the high scaffolding while the girls and young lads began carrying bricks. As the new boy, Michałko was given the task of mixing up the lime and the sand with a trowel.

This was how Michałko became a builder.

The next day they gave him an assistant, a girl who was as poor as he was. Her entire clothing consisted of an old headscarf, a ragged skirt, and a pitiful blouse. She was not in the least good-looking. Her face was swarthy and thin, snub-nosed, with a low forehead. But Michałko wasn't choosy. She had barely come to stand by him with his trowel when he began to take an interest in her, as a lad usually will with a girl. And when she looked at him from beneath her faded headscarf, he could feel himself go all hot inside. He even plucked up enough courage to ask her, "So where are you from, miss? Are you from far away? Have you been working long for the bricklayers?"

He asked her all these questions, calling her "miss." But since she started to call him by his first name, he followed suit.

"Don't tire yourself," he would say to her. "I'll do the work for both of us."

And he toiled conscientiously till the sweat poured off him, while the girl did nothing but move the trowel back and forth across the surface of the lime.

From that time on, they went around together all day long, always with each other and no one else. Sometimes one of the journeymen would join them. He did nothing but shout at the girl and make fun of Michałko. In the evening, Michałko stayed behind and slept at the building site because he had nowhere else to go, while his companion went into town with the others, including the journeyman, who still shouted abuse at her and occasionally gave her a smack on the head.

"I don't think he likes her," Michałko thought to himself. "But what can be done? It's a journeyman's job to knock us around."

He himself did all he could to make up for the wrongs she suffered. He continued to perform both his own work and hers. At breakfast he shared his bread with her, and for dinner he would buy her some beetroot soup for five groszes, because she hardly ever had any money of her own.

When they were put to work carrying bricks up to the top of the building, Michałko could no longer help out his friend, because the master bricklayers had their eye on her.

But he followed right behind her across the rickety scaffolding, and how he worried that she would slip and spill her bricks!

When the bad-tempered journeyman saw Michałko's solicitude, he made fun of him and pointed him out to the others. They also laughed, and shouted at Michałko from up above, "Dumbo!"

One day at noon the journeyman called the girl to one side, wanting something from her and even smacking her around more than usual. After this conversation, she came to Michałko with tears in her eyes, asking if he didn't have twenty groszes she could borrow.

What would he not have given her! He quickly untied the bundle where he kept the money he still had from the train and gave her what she had asked for.

The girl took the twenty groszes to the journeyman, and from that time on scarcely a day went by without Michałko lending her money without any hope of repayment. And when he once asked timidly, "Why do you give money to that villain?" she replied, "That's just the way things are!"

One day the journeyman fell out with the manager and quit work. As if that weren't enough, he ordered the girl to do the same and to leave with him, as if she were some sort of servant.

The girl hesitated. But when the manager threatened that if she didn't stay till the evening he wouldn't pay her for the entire week, she picked up her hod again. A simple person won't look down on money, especially if it's hard-earned wages.

The journeyman flew into a rage.

"Are you coming or not, damn you?" he shouted.

"How can I go if they won't pay me? I could at least buy myself a cheap skirt for that ruble."

"So!" roared the journeyman. "I never want to see you again! If you ever cross my threshold again you're dead!"

And he headed off toward the city.

In the evening, as usual the bricklayers left. Michałko and the girl were left alone at the building site.

"Aren't you going?" Michałko asked in surprise.

"Where am I supposed to go, now that he's told me he'll throw me out . . . "

It was only now that Michałko began to understand.

"So you were staying with him?" he asked with a hint of reproach in his voice.

"That's right," she whispered, embarrassed.

"And you gave him all your wages, even though he beat you?"

"Well, yes . . . "

"Why did you do such an awful thing?"

"Because I liked him," the girl answered quietly, hiding among the poles of the scaffolding.

Michałko felt as if someone had stabbed him with a knife. It wasn't for nothing that people had laughed at him!

He moved closer to the girl.

"But you're not going to like him anymore?" he asked.

"No!" she answered, and began to cry bitterly.

"And you'll like me instead?"

"Yes."

"I won't hit you or take away your money."

"I know!"

"You'll be better off with me . . . "

The girl said nothing in reply, but only cried harder and trembled.

The night was cold and damp.

"Are you cold?" asked Michałko.

"Yes."

He sat her down on a pile of bricks, still weeping. He took off his sackcloth jacket and put it round the girl's shoulders; he himself was left in his shirtsleeves.

"Don't cry! Don't cry!" he repeated. "You only have to spend one night here. You have a ruble. Tomorrow we'll take it and rent a room, and I'll buy you a skirt from my own money. So don't cry . . . "

But the girl wasn't paying attention to what Michałko was saying. She raised her head and listened. She thought she heard the sound of familiar footsteps on the street.

The steps drew closer. At the same time, someone began whistling and calling, "Come home . . . Hey, you! Where've you gone to?"

"I'm here," cried the girl, jumping to her feet.

She ran out onto the street where the journeyman stood.

"I'm here!" she repeated.

"And you have the money?" asked the journeyman.

"Yes! Here! Here you are!" she said, handing him the ruble.

The journeyman thrust the ruble into his pocket. Then he grabbed the girl by the hair and set about beating her, saying, "Next time you do what you're told, or I won't let you in. You won't buy your way out of this with a ruble! Do what you're told! Do what you're told!" he repeated, striking her with his fists.

"Oh Lord!" the girl cried.

"Do what you're told . . . Do as I tell you . . . "

Suddenly he let go of the girl, as he felt a powerful hand take hold of him by the back of the neck. He turned around with difficulty and saw Michałko's flashing eyes.

The journeyman was a strapping Mazovian fellow, and he smashed Michałko in the head so hard that he saw stars. But the young lad didn't let go; on the contrary, he gripped the journey-man's neck even more firmly.

"If you strangle me, you piece of filth, you'll see what'll happen," the journeyman grunted in a hoarse voice.

"Then stop beating her!" said Michałko.

"All right," the other gasped, his tongue lolling out.

Michałko released his grip, and the journeyman tottered away. He took a few deep breaths, then said, "If she doesn't want me to beat her, she shouldn't be with me. She likes me, that's for sure, but I beat her because that's how I am. What use to me is a girl that I can't hit? She can go to hell!"

"Then she will. So what!" retorted Michałko.

But the girl seized him by the hands.

"Leave off now," she said to Michałko, trembling and squeezing his hands. "Don't come between us . . . "

Michałko was dumbfounded.

"And you, come home," she said to the journeyman, taking his arm. "Why should someone treat you like dirt out on the street . . . "

The journeyman tore away from her and said laughing, "Go to him! He won't beat you. He even gave you money . . . "

"Oh, do me a favor!" snorted the girl and went off ahead.

"You see, a woman needs to be handled like a dog!" said the jour-neyman, pointing at the girl. "Smack her about, and she'll follow you anywhere."

And he disappeared. Only his malicious laughter rang out in the silence of the night.

Michałko stood looking after them and listening. Then he went back to the scaffolding and stared at the place where just a moment ago the girl had been sitting.

His head was spinning, and he couldn't catch his breath. She had scarcely finished telling him that she would like only him when she left him. Just a short while ago he had been so happy, and it had been so good here with another living creature, a girl at that. Now the place was so empty and sad!

Why had she gone? Because that had been her will, that was what she had wanted! What could he have done about it, good and strong as he was? He instinctively respected her attachment to the journeyman. He wasn't angry that she had broken the promise she had made to him, and he had no thought of imposing his feelings by force. But in spite of everything he missed her, he missed her so much . . .

He wiped his eyes with his hands, disfigured from the lime, and picked up his jacket, which had been thrown down on the pile of bricks and still seemed warm. He went back out onto the street and stood a while.

Nothing could be seen; only the faint red light of the streetlamps glowed through the fog.

He went back into the cold building and lay on the ground. But instead of going to sleep he just kept sighing deeply, lonely, pining for his girl.

His girl, because she herself had told him that she would like only him!

The next day Michałko went to work as usual.

But things didn't go smoothly. He was tired, and also he had somehow taken an aversion to the building. Wherever he walked, whatever he touched, whatever he looked upon, it all reminded him of his girl and his bitter letdown. The others made fun of him too, shouting, "So, daft Michałko, now you see that the lasses are costly here in Warsaw!"

Costly they were! Michałko had spent all his savings on his girl, had gone hungry, had never bought himself anything; yet she had brought him no happiness, and on top of everything she had left him in such a shameful way. He felt bad in that place, humiliated.

So when he heard that over in central Warsaw they pay bricklayer's assistants better, he decided to go there for the first time.

He went with one of the journeymen, who had promised to take him to the street where they were building the greatest number of houses.

They set off in the early morning and for a long while they walked toward the Vistula. When Michałko saw the bridge, he gaped in amazement. At this moment he even forgot about the girl.

At the gatehouse he hesitated.

"What's wrong?" asked the journeyman.

"I don't know if they'll let me in, sir," replied Michałko.

"Don't be stupid!" the journeyman said caustically. "If anyone asks, just say you're with me!"

"Of course," thought Michałko, surprised that he hadn't come up with such a reply himself.

Then he marveled at the bathhouses, and at the barges, which didn't sink into the water even though they were so huge; and then he couldn't believe that the entire bridge was built of solid iron.

"There must be some trickery in this," he said to himself. "I don't think there's that much iron in the whole world!"

And so they walked on, the journeyman and Michałko, one after the other, across the bridge, down Nowy Zjazd, along the street. Near the royal castle Michałko took off his cap and crossed himself, thinking it was a church. In front of the Bernardine monastery he was almost run over by an omnibus. Before the figure of Our Lady by the Church of the Charity he was about to kneel and say a prayer, and the journeyman barely managed to drag him away.

On the streets there was a great din, carriages one after another, crowds of people. Michałko stepped out of some people's way, got in others', and went pale with fear that they might give him a hiding. In the end he became truly confused – and he lost the journeyman.

"Sir! Sir!" he started to exclaim desperately, and rushed down the street.

Someone stopped him, saying, "Shut up, you son of a bitch! Shouting's not allowed here!"

"But my master's disappeared!"

"What master?"

"He's a bricklayer's journeyman."

"Quite a master for you! Where do you need to get to?"

"Where they're building the house."

"What house?"

"The brick one," replied Michałko.

"You're a bright one! They're building a house down here . . . and over there . . . and that way!"

"I can't see anything."

People took him by the arm and showed him.

"Look! Over there they're building one house. Down this way there's another . . . "

"Oh, I see! I see!" said Michałko, and went over to the second house, since that way he didn't have to make a dash across the street.

When he reached the building site he asked about the journeyman. But he didn't find him there, and they sent him to another site. However, there, too, no one had heard of a journeyman called Nastazy, so Michałko had to go elsewhere.

In this way he ran down several streets and visited many unfinished houses, wondering to himself where the people lived while their homes were still being built.

Gradually he moved away from the center of the city. The streets became quieter, there were fewer pedestrians and hardly any carriages. On the other hand, there was an ever-increasing amount of scaffolding, with piles of bricks and red walls.

Michałko had given up hope of finding the journeyman and began to think about looking for work.

He went into the first building site he came across, stood among the laborers, and watched. From time to time he took part in the conversation or gave someone a hand. He helped one man to lay the bricks, handed another a hod, and told those who were mixing the lime not to do it like that but another way. And at once he demonstrated what he meant, splashing the master bricklayer from head to foot.

"What are you doing round here, you mongrel?" the manager asked him.

"I'm looking for work, sir."

"There's no work for you here."

"There isn't now, but maybe later there will be. And it'll be no loss to you if I help out."

The manager, who was a shrewd fellow, guessed that Michałko wasn't exactly loaded with money. He took out his notebook and pencil, began to cross things out and count things up, and in the end took Michałko on.

People said that he earned twenty groszes a day extra on him.

Michałko worked on this building site till the fall. He didn't die of starvation, and he didn't pay for his lodgings, but he also didn't even buy himself a pair of shoes. The only thing he did do was get drunk as a lord a few times on the day of rest. He even meant to start a fight in the inn, but he left it too late and they threw him out.

The house shot up like pepperwort. Before the bricklayers had even finished the outbuildings, the front had a roof and had been plastered, the windows had been installed, and people had even started to move in.

At the end of September heavy rains set in. Work on the building was stopped, and the mates were dismissed. Among them was Michałko.

The manager had kept something back from his wages every week, saying he would pay it in a lump sum. When the time came to settle up, however, Michałko, even though he couldn't read or write, realized that the manager had conned him. He gave him three rubles when he was owed five or even six.

Michałko took the three rubles, pulled off his cap, and stood scratching his head and shifting from one foot to the other. But the manager was so engrossed in his notebook that you could have said ten Our Fathers before he noticed Michałko and asked him sternly, "So what else do you want?"

"I must be due more than this, sir," said Michałko humbly.

The manager went red. He stepped up to Michałko, poked him in the chest, and said, "Do you have a passport? Just who are you anyway?"

Michałko was speechless. The manager went on, "Maybe you think I've diddled you, you bumpkin?"

"Well, it's just . . . "

"So go with me to the police, and I'll prove to you beyond a shadow of a doubt that you're a thief and a vagrant."

The passport and the police worried Michałko. So he said, "I wish you joy from the wrong I've been done!"

And he left the site.

And since the manager himself was apparently in no hurry to go to the police, it all went no further that Michałko's getting a scare.

Michałko now felt as if he were stranded in open country. He passed his own street, and walked down a second and a third, always looking in where he saw red walls and a few posts hammered into the ground. But either the buildings were already finished or the work was just coming to an end, and when he asked whether they could offer him a job they didn't even answer.

He wandered around like this for one whole day and then the next, avoiding policemen in case they asked him for his passport.

He couldn't find a chop house with hot food, so he lived on blood sausage, lard, bread, and herring, and washed it all down with vodka.

He had already spent a whole ruble without accomplishing anything positive. He slept by fences and longed for human company, for he had no one he could talk to.

It occurred to him that it might be better to return home, so he asked passersby how to get to the trains. He followed their directions and found a railway, but it wasn't his. He saw a huge, busy station with lots of houses around it, but there was no sign of any tracks.

He grew confused and fearful, not knowing what had happened. Eventually some kind soul explained to him that there were three other railways, but that they were on the other side of the Vistula.

Now he remembered that on his way here he had crossed the bridge. After spending the night in some ditch, then, the next day he asked the way to the bridge. They told him exactly where to go straight on, where to turn left and where to turn right. He committed everything to memory, but once he began to go straight ahead and to turn, he ended up at the Vistula but couldn't find the bridge.

He returned to the city. Unfortunately it had begun to rain. People took shelter under umbrellas, and those who had no umbrellas ran for cover. In such a rainstorm Michałko didn't dare stop anyone to ask for directions.

During the heaviest downpour he stood against a wall, hunched and frozen in his soaking jacket, and comforted himself with the thought that at least the rain would wash his bare feet.

As he stood there, pale, water dripping from his long hair down his neck, a gentleman stopped before him.

"What are you, a pauper?" asked the man.

"No."

The gentleman walked on a few paces, then came back with another question.

"Are you hungry?"

"No."

"Are you cold?"

"No."

"Bit of a fool!" muttered the man. Then he added, "But would you take ten groszes?"

"I would if you gave it to me, sir."

The gentleman gave him a zloty and went off muttering.

Then he stopped again, looked at Michałko as if he were of two minds, but finally walked off for good.

Michałko held the zloty in his fist and said to himself in surprise, "Make no mistake, there are some good gentlemen here!"

All of a sudden it occurred to him that a good gentleman like that might be able to tell him the way to the bridge; but it was too late.

Night fell, the streetlamps were lit, and the rain came down harder. Michałko looked for the streets where it was darkest. He turned this way and that. He noticed some new buildings and suddenly recognized the street where he had been working a few days ago.

Here was where the cobblestones ended. Here was the fence. Here was the coal shed, and here was his house. There were lights in several of the windows, and through the open gateway the unfinished outbuildings could be seen.

Michałko walked into the courtyard. Say what you like, he had earned the right to spend the night here. After all, he had built this house.

"Hey, you! Where do you think you're going?" a man dressed in a thick sheepskin coat called down to him from the stairs.

It must have been cold out.

Michałko turned around.

"It's me," he said. "I'm going to go and sleep in the cellar."

The man in the sheepskin coat was indignant.

"You want to spend the night here? What do you think this is, a flophouse?"

"I worked here all summer," answered Michałko anxiously.

The caretaker's wife appeared in the doorway, concerned about her husband.

"What's going on here? Who is it? Maybe he's a robber?" she asked.

"No! This kid says he worked on the building site so he has the right to spend the night here. He's a daft one!"

Michałko's eyes shone. He gave a laugh and ran up to the caretaker.

"So you're from our village?" he exclaimed, overjoyed.

"Why do you say that?" asked the caretaker.

"Because you talked to me the way they do in the village. I'm daft Michałko!"

The caretaker's wife giggled while her husband shrugged his shoulders.

"I can see you're daft," he said. "But I'm not from any village, I'm from the town. From Łapy!" he added in such a tone that Michałko sighed sadly.

"Oh! I expect it's as big as Warsaw?"

"Maybe, maybe not," replied the caretaker, "but it's always been a respectable place."

After a moment of silence he said, "In any case, get lost, you can't sleep here."

Michałko's heart sank. He looked pathetically at the caretaker and asked, "Where am I supposed to go in this rain?"

The caretaker was struck by the pertinence of this point. It was true: Where was he supposed to go in the rain?

"Hmm," he answered, "stay then, since it's raining. Just don't even think about thieving anything in the night. And in the morning, be gone at sunrise, or the landlord'll see you. Nothing gets by him!"

Michałko thanked the caretaker, went to the outbuildings, and groped his way down into the familiar cellar.

He rubbed his hands, which were numb with cold, wrung out his soaking jacket, and lay down on the fragments of brick and the sawdust he had brought down here for himself before.

It wasn't warm; on the contrary, it was even a little cold and damp. But he'd been accustomed to hardship since he was a child, and so he paid no attention to his present discomfort. He was more troubled by the question of what to do next. Should he look for work in Warsaw, or should he go back home? If he was to look for work, what kind of work should it be, and where should he look? And if he was to return home, which way should he head, and what for?

He wasn't afraid of going hungry. He had two rubles, and besides, was hunger anything new to him?

"Hmm, it's God's will," he whispered.

He stopped worrying about the next day and appreciated the present moment. Outside the rain was pouring down. How awful it would have been to sleep in the gutter, and how good it was here!

And he fell asleep, like a weary country boy who, when he dreams something, says that he has been visited by spirits.

And tomorrow . . . whatever God decided would happen!

The next morning the weather had cleared up, and the sun even came out. Michałko thanked the caretaker once again for letting him stay the night, and left. He was fresh as a daisy, though his hair was stuck together from the previous day's rain, while his sackcloth jacket had grown stiff as leather.

For a moment he stood in front of the gateway, trying to make up his mind which way to go: left or right? On the corner he saw a pub that was open, so he stepped in for some breakfast. He drank a tall glass of vodka and, feeling more cheerful, set off toward where he could see scaffolding.

Should I look for work? Should I go home? he was thinking to himself.

Suddenly, somewhere close by, there was a crashing sound like a short peal of thunder, followed by another, louder one.

Michałko looked around.

A few hundred yards away, to the right, he could see the tops of some scaffolding, and above it what looked like red smoke.

Something had happened. Michałko was seized by curiosity. He ran off toward the scaffolding, slipping and splashing through the puddles.

On an unpaved street where there was only a handful of houses a group of anxious people had gathered. They were shouting and pointing at an unfinished building in front of which lay boards, broken pillars and fresh rubble. Above it all rose a cloud of red brick dust.

Michałko ran closer. Now he could see what had happened: the new house had collapsed.

One entire side of the building had disintegrated from top to bottom, as had the greater part of another.

Window frames dangled in the remains of the walls; the great beams meant to support the ceilings had dropped, sagged, and broken like matchsticks.

Frightened women looked out from the windows of neighboring houses. But on the street, aside from the builders, there were only a few people. The news of the accident hadn't yet reached the city center.

The foreman was the first to come to his senses.

"Is anyone missing?" he asked, trembling.

"It doesn't look like it. Everyone was at breakfast."

The foreman began to number off his men, but he kept losing count.

"Are the journeymen here?"

"We're here!"

"And the mates?"

"We're here!"

"Jędrzej's missing!" called out a voice.

Those present froze for a moment.

"Yeah, he was inside . . . "

"We have to look for him!" said the foreman hoarsely.

And he set off toward the collapsed building, followed by a handful of the braver men.

Michałko instinctively went forward, too.

"Jędrzej! Jędrzej!" called the foreman.

"Watch out! That wall could come down at any moment!"

"Jędrzej! Jędrzej!"

From inside the house there came a moan in response.

At one point an opening the width of a door had appeared in the side wall. The foreman ran over, looked in, and seized his head in both hands. Then, like a madman, he rushed off in the direction of the city.

On the other side of the wall a man was writhing in agony. Both of his legs had been crushed and were pinned under a beam. Over his head the crack in a section of wall was growing steadily bigger, and the wall was threatening to come down at any moment.

One of the carpenters started to check the place over, and the petrified laborers stared at him, ready to go and help if it was possible.

The injured man jerked himself around and held himself up on his hands. He was from the country. His mouth was dark with pain, his face gray, his eyes sunken. He looked at the people standing a dozen or so yards from him; he groaned, but didn't dare call for help. He just kept repeating, "Oh my Lord! Merciful God!"

"We can't go in there," the carpenter said in a hollow voice.

The crowd retreated.

Among them was Michałko, who was perhaps even more scared than the others.

Terrible things were taking place within him! He felt all the injured man's pain, his fear and despair; yet he also felt a force that was propelling him forward . . .

It seemed to him that of all the crowd he alone was duty-bound to rescue this man, who had come here from the country to earn a living. And at that moment, while the others were saying to themselves, "I'll do it!" he was thinking to himself, "I won't do it! I refuse!"

He looked about fearfully. He stood alone before the crowd, closer to the wall than the others.

"I won't do it!" he whispered, and picked up a pole that was lying by his feet.

People began murmuring to each other.

"Look! What's he doing?"

"Quiet!"

"Merciful God, have pity on me!" the injured man cried, weeping from the pain.

"I'll do it! I'll go in!" said Michałko, and walked toward the ruins of the house.

"You'll both die!" exclaimed the carpenter.

Michałko had already reached the trapped man. He saw his crushed legs and a pool of blood, and he felt faint.

"My brother! my brother!" whispered the injured man and embraced Michałko round his knees.

Michałko slid the pole under the beam and in desperation levered it up. There was a cracking noise, and from two floors above some fragments of brick fell on them.

"It's coming down!" shouted the laborers, running for cover.

But Michałko heard nothing, thought nothing, felt nothing. With his powerful arms he pulled on the pole again, and this time lifted the beam right off the crushed legs of the man lying there.

Pieces of brick were falling from above. The red dust swirled, thickened, and filled the interior of the building. A clattering sound was heard on the other side of the wall. The injured man gave a loud groan, then suddenly fell silent.

Through the opening in the wall Michałko appeared, bent double, and with great difficulty dragging the injured man. He slowly crossed onto safer ground and stood in front of the crowd, shouting naively, "He's out! He's out! Except one of his boots got left behind . . . "

The laborers took hold of the injured man, who had lost consciousness, and carried him carefully to the nearest house.

"Water!" they cried.

"Vinegar!"

"Fetch a doctor!"

Michałko trailed after them, thinking: These are good people here in Warsaw. No two ways about it!

He noticed that he had blood on his hands, so he washed them in a puddle, and stood in front of the gateway to the house where the injured man had been taken. He didn't try to go inside. After all, was he a doctor? Would he know what to do?

In the meantime, more and more people were gathering on the street. Inquisitive folks ran up, dorozhkas galloped there, and from far off could even be heard the bells of the fire brigade, whom someone had summoned.

A new crowd, by now composed of sensation-seekers, gathered at the gateway, and the more enthusiastic drove a path through with their fists so they could see the bloody spectacle.

Michałko bumped into one of these men, who was standing by the doorway.

"Out of the way, nosey!" shouted this individual, seeing that the barefoot country boy wasn't yielding to the pressure of his hand.

"Why?" asked Michałko, taken aback by this outburst.

"Who do you think you are, you impudent pup?" roared the man. "What, are there no police here to clear the place of idlers like you?"

Uh oh! This doesn't look good, thought Michałko, and began to worry that he'd be thrown in jail for what he'd done.

And, wishing to avoid trouble, he pushed his way back into the crowd . . .

A few minutes later, they began to call from the gateway for the person who had pulled the injured man from the collapsed building.

No one answered.

"What did he look like?" people asked.

"He was from the country. He had a white coat, a round cap, and he was barefoot."

"Isn't there anyone like that on the street?"

They began to look.

"There was someone here before," a voice shouted, "but he left!"

The police and the laborers searched high and low, but no one could find Michałko.

# The Barrel Organ

Every day around noon, on Miodowa Street you could meet a middle-aged gentleman who was on his way from Krasińskich Square to Senatorska Street. In the summertime he wore an elegant dark blue overcoat, gray trousers from a first-rate tailor, shoes that shone like mirrors, and a slightly discolored top hat.

This gentleman had a ruddy face, graying side-whiskers, and mild gray eyes. He walked with a stoop, his hands in his pockets. In good weather he had a cane under his arm; on cloudy days he carried an English silk umbrella.

He was always deep in thought and moved along slowly. As he reached the Capuchin church he would touch the brim of his hat religiously, then cross to the other side of the street to check the barometer and thermometer at Pik's. Then he would return to the right-hand sidewalk, stop in front of Mieczkowski's display, look at the photographs of Modrzejewska, and walk on.

As he walked he gave way to everyone, and when someone bumped into him he would smile benevolently.

If he saw a beautiful woman, he would put on his pince-nez to take a good look. But since he did this in a phlegmatic sort of way, he usually met with disappointment.

The gentleman's name was Mr. Tomasz.

Mr. Tomasz had been walking down Miodowa Street for the last thirty years, and he often thought that many things had changed there. Miodowa Street could have thought the same about him.

When he had still been a defense lawyer, he used to move along so quickly that no seamstress hurrying home from her fashion shop could have kept up with him. He was cheerful and talkative; he bore himself straight, and had a full head of hair and a mustache that curled up sharply. Even in those days he was impressed by the fine arts, but he had no time to spend on them, for he was mad about women. True, he was lucky with them, and there was constant talk of marriage; but what of it, since Mr. Tomasz could never find a single moment to propose, being busy either with his practice or with his assignations. From Frania he would go off to the courts, from the courts he would run to Zosia, whom he would leave toward evening to have supper with Józia and Filka.

When he became a partner, as a result of intense mental exertion, his forehead spread up toward the top of his head, and a few silver hairs appeared in his mustache. Mr. Tomasz had already lost his youthful ebullience; he had acquired wealth, and a reputation as a connoisseur of the arts. And since he still adored women, he began to think of marriage. He even took a six-room flat, put in parquet floors, had the place wallpapered, bought some beautiful furniture – and began to look for a wife.

But it is difficult for a mature person to make up his mind. This one was too young; another he had admired for too long. A third was charming and of the right age but had the wrong kind of temperament; a fourth had grace, youth, and the necessary temperament, but without waiting for the lawyer's proposal she married a doctor.

Mr. Tomasz was not concerned, however, since there was no shortage of young ladies. Over time he decorated his flat, taking ever more care that each detail should be of artistic worth. He changed the furniture, moved the mirrors around, and bought paintings.

In the end, his domestic decor became famous. Though he himself did not quite know when it happened, he created an art gallery in his own home, which was seen by increasing numbers of curious visitors. And since he was hospitable by nature, he organized splendid receptions. He knew many musicians, and so ended up having concert evenings in his flat, which even society ladies honored with their presence.

Mr. Tomasz enjoyed it all; and, observing in the mirror that his hairline had reached the crown of his head and was moving back toward his snow-white collar, he reminded himself more and more often that come what may, he must marry, especially as he was still well-inclined toward women.

Once, when he had a larger than usual gathering of guests, one of the young ladies looked over the salons and exclaimed, "What beautiful pictures, and how smooth the floors are! I expect your wife will be very happy."

"If smooth floors will be enough to make her happy," murmured one of the lawyer's close friends.

Everyone in the salon laughed. Mr. Tomasz smiled, too, but from that moment, whenever anyone mentioned marriage to him, he would wave his hand dismissively, saying, "I think not!"

It was at that time he shaved off his mustache and grew sidewhiskers. He continued to speak of women with great respect and was most forbearing when it came to their faults.

No longer expecting anything of the world, since he had also given up his practice, the lawyer directed all his moderate emotions toward the arts. A beautiful painting, a fine concert, a new theatrical production became, as it were, the mileposts on the road of his life. He never grew enthusiastic or became enraptured; he merely enjoyed things.

At concerts he would choose a seat far from the stage, so as to be able to listen to the music without hearing other noises and without seeing the performers. When he went to the theater, he first acquainted himself with the work in question, so as to be able to follow the action without any feverish sense of curiosity. He studied paintings at times when there were the fewest visitors in the art gallery, and spent hours there.

If he liked something, he would say, "You know, this really is rather pretty."

He was one of those few people who are the first to spot talent. But he never condemned mediocre works.

"Just you wait, maybe he'll amount to something yet," he would say when others criticized the artist.

Thus he was always tolerant of human imperfection and never even mentioned vices.

Alas, no mortal being is devoid of some eccentricity, and Mr. Tomasz was no exception. His problem was that he could not abide barrel organs and organ-grinders.

When the lawyer heard a barrel organ on the street, he would quicken his pace and would be out of sorts for several hours. Normally a calm man, he would get excited; usually quiet, he would begin to shout; and though always mild, he would become enraged at the first tones of the barrel organ.

He made no secret of his weakness, and even offered an explanation.

"Music," he would say agitatedly, "is the subtlest flesh of the spirit; yet in a barrel organ that spirit is diluted and turns into a machine and an instrument of robbery. For organ-grinders are nothing but bandits!

"Besides," he would add, "those organs irritate me. I only have one life, and I can't waste it listening to such disgusting music."

One malicious person, knowing about the lawyer's loathing for musical devices, thought up a tasteless practical joke and sent two organ-grinders to play under his windows. Mr. Tomasz fell ill with wrath, and when he discovered who was responsible challenged him to a duel.

They even had to convene a court of honor to prevent bloodshed over such an apparently trivial matter.

The building in which Mr. Tomasz lived had changed hands a number of times. It goes without saying that each new owner felt it his bounden duty to raise the tenants' rent, first and foremost Mr. Tomasz's. The lawyer paid each increase without protest, but only on the condition, expressly written into the lease, that no barrel organs were to be allowed to play in the building.

As well as the clause in the contract, Mr. Tomasz would summon every new caretaker and conduct more or less the following conversation with him:

"Listen, my good fellow . . . What's your name now?"

"Kazimierz, sir."

"Listen now, Kazimierz! Every time I come home and you open the gate for me, you'll get twenty groszes, understand?"

"I understand, sir."

"And besides that, you'll receive ten zlotys a month from me, but do you know what for?"

"I can't imagine, sir," the caretaker would answer with gratitude.

"For never letting barrel organs into the courtyard. Got it?"

"Yes, sir."

The lawyer's flat comprised two parts. The four larger rooms had windows onto the street while the two smaller ones overlooked the courtyard. The state rooms were for guests. Parties took place there, clients were received, and friends and relatives of the lawyer's from the country stayed there. Mr. Tomasz himself rarely appeared here, and then it was only to check whether the parquet had been waxed, whether the place had been dusted, and whether the furniture had not been damaged.

But when he wasn't out and about, he would spend whole days

sitting in the study on the courtyard side. There he would read, write letters, or examine documents brought to him by acquaintances who had asked him for advice. And when he didn't wish to strain his eyes, he would sit in the armchair by the window and, lighting a cigar, lose himself in thought. He knew that thinking is an important activity in life which should not be neglected by those who care about their health.

On the other side of the courtyard, directly opposite Mr. Tomasz's windows, was a flat that was rented by less well-off tenants. For a long while an elderly lawyer's clerk lived there, but when he lost his job he moved to Praga. After him a tailor took the little rooms, but he sometimes liked to get drunk and raise a ruckus, so his lease was terminated. After that an old retired lady, who was forever arguing with her maid, moved into the flat.

But on St. John's Day the old lady, who had become quite senile but was rather wealthy, was taken to live with her relatives in the country, and the flat was rented by two ladies with a young girl of about eight.

The women worked for a living. They made stockings and vests on sewing machines, one doing the sewing and the other finishing them off. The younger and prettier of the two the little girl called Mummy while she addressed the older one as Ma'am.

Both the lawyer's windows and those of the new tenants were open all day long. So when Mr. Tomasz sat in his armchair, he could clearly see what was going on at his neighbors'.

The furniture there was modest. The tables, chairs, sofa, and chest of drawers were draped with cloth for sewing and balls of cotton for stockings.

In the early morning the women swept the flat themselves, and around midday a hired help would bring them a meager dinner. In general, the two women hardly ever stepped away from their rattling machines.

The girl usually sat in the window. She had dark hair and a pretty little face, though it was pale and somehow immobile. Sometimes she would sit fastening a belt of colored threads with two pieces of wire. Occasionally she played with a doll, which she dressed and undressed slowly, as if with difficulty. And at other times she didn't do anything, but just sat in the window listening to something or other.

Mr. Tomasz never saw the girl singing or running about the room, and never even saw a smile on her pallid lips and her motionless face.

"What a strange child!" the lawyer said to himself, and began to observe her more closely.

One day (it was a Sunday), he noticed that her mother had given her a little posy of flowers. The girl became a little more animated. She separated the flowers and put them back together again; she kissed them. In the end she tied them back together, put them in a glass with some water, and, sitting in her window, said, "This place is sad, Mummy, isn't it?"

The lawyer was shocked. How could it be sad in a building where he had been so contented for so many years!

One day the lawyer found himself in his study around four o'clock. At this hour the sun was opposite his neighbors' flat, and today it was shining and very hot. Mr. Tomasz looked over to the other side of the courtyard, and evidently saw something extraordinary, for he hurriedly donned his pince-nez.

This is what he saw:

The poor little girl, leaning her head on her arm, was lying almost on her back in the window, and with her eyes wide open, she was staring right at the sun. On her normally still face there now played feelings that looked something like joy, and something like regret.

"She can't see!" whispered the lawyer, dropping his pince-nez. At that moment his eyes began to sting at the very thought that someone could stare at the sun, which burned with a open flame.

Indeed, the girl had been blind for two years. When she was six she had fallen ill with some kind of fever; for several weeks she had remained unconscious, and subsequently grew so weak that she lay as if she were dead, neither moving nor speaking at all.

They had given her wine and broth, and slowly she had regained consciousness. But on the first day, when they propped her up on a pillow, she asked her mother, "Mummy, is it nighttime?"

"No, darling. Why do you say that?"

But the little girl was sleepy and didn't answer. Yet the next day, when the doctor came, again she asked, "Is it still night?"

Then they realized that she was blind. The doctor examined her eyes and declared that she would have to give it time.

But the more the sick girl recovered her strength, the more she became concerned about her handicap.

"Mummy, why can't I see you?"

"Because something's happened to your eyes. But they'll get better."

"When will they get better?"

"Soon."

"Might it be tomorrow, Mummy?"

"In a few days, sweetheart."

"When it gets better, make sure you tell me straight away, because I'm so sad!"

Days and weeks passed in perpetual waiting. The girl began to get up. She learned to feel her way around the room. She could dress and undress herself slowly and carefully.

But her sight did not return.

One day she said, "Mummy, my dress is blue, isn't it?"

"No, dear, it's gray."

"Can you see it, Mummy?"

"I can, darling."

"Just like in the daytime?"

"Yes."

"Will I be able to see everything, too, in a few days? Well, maybe in a month . . . "

But since her mother didn't answer, she went on:

"Mummy, it's day all the time outside, isn't it? Are there trees in the garden, like before? And does that white kitten with the black paws still come and visit us? Mummy, isn't it true that I used to be able to see myself in the mirror? Is there a mirror here?"

Her mother gave her a mirror.

"You have to look here, where it's smooth," said the girl, pressing the mirror against her face. "I can't see anything!" she said. "Can you not see me in the mirror either, Mummy?"

"I can see you, my love."

"How is that?" cried the girl plaintively. "If I can't see myself, there ought to be nothing at all in the mirror. And what about the little girl in the mirror – can she see me or not?"

But her mother burst into tears and ran from the room.

The blind girl's favorite pastime was taking small objects in her hands and identifying them by touch.

One day her mother brought her a china doll, in nice clothes, which had cost a whole ruble. The girl never put her down; she touched her nose, mouth, and eyes, and cuddled her.

She went to bed late, still thinking about her doll, which she had laid in a little box lined with cotton wool.

In the night her mother was wakened by a rustling noise and a whispering. She jumped out of bed, lit a candle, and in the corner she saw her daughter fully dressed and playing with the doll.

"What are you doing, dear?" she cried. "Why aren't you asleep?"

"But it's daytime, Mummy," answered the blind girl.

For her day and night had merged into one and lasted forever.

Gradually the memory of visual impressions began to fade for the girl. A red cherry became for her a smooth, round, soft cherry, and a shiny coin was a hard and resonant disc on which there were some signs in relief. She knew that the room was bigger than she was, that the building was bigger than the room, and the street bigger than the building. But everything somehow seemed to contract in her imagination.

Her attention was directed toward the senses of touch, smell, and hearing. Her face and hands became so sensitive that a few inches away from the wall she could already feel a slight chill. Distant events affected her only through hearing, and so she would spend entire days listening.

She grew to recognize the ambling step of the caretaker, who spoke in a high-pitched voice as he swept the courtyard. She knew when the wagon from the country had arrived to bring wood, she knew when there was a dorozhka or the carts that took the refuse away.

The slightest rustle, smell, chilling, or warming of the air did not escape her attention. With inconceivable rapidity, she noticed these subtle things and drew conclusions from them.

Once her mother called the maid.

"Mrs. Janowa isn't here," said the blind girl, sitting in her usual place in the corner. "She's gone to get water."

"How do you know?" asked her mother in amazement.

"How? Well, I know she took the jug from the kitchen, then she went through into the other courtyard and pumped the water. And now she's talking to the caretaker."

Indeed, from over the fence there came the murmur of a conversation between two people, but it was so faint that it could only be made out with an effort.

But even her increased abilities in the lesser senses could not replace the girl's sight. She became aware of the lack of impressions and began to pine.

She was allowed to walk around the whole building, and this brought her some relief. She trod every stone in the courtyard, and touched every gutter and barrel. But her greatest pleasure came from journeys to two completely opposite worlds: the cellar and the attic.

In the cellar the air was cold and the walls damp. The muffled noise from the street could be heard overhead; other sounds died away. This was night for the blind girl.

In the attic, on the other hand, especially in the window, everything was different. Up there there was more noise than in her flat. The girl could hear the rumble of carriages from several streets, and all the shouts from the entire building gathered there. A warm wind fanned her face. She could hear the chirping of birds, the barking of dogs, and the soughing of the trees in the garden next door. For her this was day.

That was not all. The sun shone more often on the attic than on her flat, and when the blind girl turned her dead eyes toward it, she thought that she could see something. The shadows of forms and colors stirred in her imagination, though so indistinctly and fleetingly that she couldn't remember anything.

It was at this time that her mother decided to live with her friend and move into the building where Mr. Tomasz lived. Both women were pleased with the new flat, but for the blind girl the move was truly a misfortune.

She had to stay in the flat and wasn't allowed to go to the attic or the cellar. She couldn't hear birds or trees, and in the courtyard there was a terrible silence. Neither secondhand dealers, nor tinkers, nor rag-and-bone men ever came in. They didn't admit the women who sang religious songs, or the old man who played the clarinet, or organ-grinders.

Her only pleasure was staring at the sun, which didn't always shine and which quickly dropped behind the buildings.

The girl began to pine again. Her health declined in the space of a few days, and her face assumed the expression of despondency and lifelessness that had so surprised Mr. Tomasz.

Not being able to see, the blind girl wanted at least to be able to listen to all sorts of different new sounds. But it was so quiet in the building.

"Poor child!" Mr. Tomasz often whispered to himself as he observed the sorry little thing.

Perhaps I could do something for her? he thought, seeing that she looked more and more poorly, and that she was wasting away from one day to the next.

It so happened that at this time one of his friends had a court case, and as usual, seeking Mr. Tomasz's advice, had given him the papers to look over. Mr. Tomasz no longer appeared in court himself, but as an experienced practitioner he was always able to indicate the best line of action and to offer useful comments to the lawyer he had recommended to his friend.

The present case was a complicated one. The more Mr. Tomasz became engrossed in the papers, the more excited he grew. The lawyer stirred in the retired man. He stopped going out of his flat and no longer checked whether the drawing rooms had been dusted; he stayed in his office and did nothing but read documents and make notes.

In the evening Mr. Tomasz's old butler came with his daily report. He informed him that the doctor's wife had left with her children for their summer house, that the water pipes had broken, that the caretaker, Kazimierz, had gotten into a fight with a policeman and had been sent to prison for a week. Finally he asked, "Does sir not wish to see the new caretaker?"

But the lawyer, lost in his papers, was smoking a cigar and blowing smoke rings; he did not even glance at his faithful servant.

The next day Mr. Tomasz continued to study the documents; around two o'clock he ate lunch and went on working. His ruddy face and graying whiskers against the sapphire-blue background of the wallpaper recalled a study from life. The mother of the blind girl and her companion, who was making stockings on her sewing machine, marveled at the lawyer and said to each other that he looked like a hale old widower in the habit of dozing at his desk all day long.

In reality the lawyer, though he had in fact closed his eyes, was not dozing but was thinking about the case.

Citizen X had bequeathed his farm to his sister's son in 1872, and in 1875 had left his apartment building to the son of his brother. The latter claimed that citizen X was mad in 1872, while the former sought to prove that he had not gone insane till 1875. Furthermore, the husband of the man's sister had offered convincing evidence that X had acted like a madman both in 1872 and 1875, and that as early as 1869, when he had still been of sound mind, he had left his entire estate to his sister.

Mr. Tomasz had been asked to determine when citizen X had really gone mad, and then to help reconcile the three parties in conflict, none of whom would hear of compromise.

As the lawyer immersed himself in the complex issues, a strange, incomprehensible thing happened.

From the courtyard, right under Mr. Tomasz's window, there came the sounds of a barrel organ!

If the late citizen X himself had risen from the grave, regained consciousness, and come into the study to help him solve the case, Mr. Tomasz would not have experienced the feeling that he did now when he heard the barrel organ!

And if it had at least been an Italian organ, with pleasant flute notes, well-constructed, and playing nice music! Nothing of the kind! As if to add insult to injury, the organ was broken; it played vulgar waltzes and polkas out of tune, and it was so loud that the windows rattled. To top it all, the horn that sounded from time to time roared like a rabid beast.

The effect was stunning. The lawyer was flabbergasted. He didn't know what to think or what to do. He even wondered if, while reading the posthumous instructions of the mentally ill citizen X, he himself had gone mad and was suffering from hallucinations.

But no, these were no hallucinations. It was a real barrel organ, with broken pipes and a deafening horn!

In the heart of the lawyer, that indulgent, mild-mannered man, there stirred violent instincts. He felt resentful toward nature that it had not made him the king of Dahomey, who had the right to put his subjects to death, and he thought of the pleasure it would give him to end the life of the organ-grinder!

And since for people of Mr. Tomasz's mettle it is extremely easy to move from bold plans to the most terrible acts, the lawyer leaped to the window like a tiger with the intention of abusing the organ-grinder with the worst words he could find.

He leaned out and had already opened his mouth to cry, "You idle good-for-nothing!" when he heard a child's voice.

He looked across.

The little blind girl was dancing around the room, clapping her hands. Her pale face had become flushed; there was a smile on her lips, and yet from her unseeing eyes there came a stream of tears.

It was so long since the poor thing had had so many sensations in that silent building! The discordant notes of the barrel organ were a beautiful experience for her. The blast of the horn, which had almost reduced the lawyer to apoplexy, was to her a glorious sound.

The last straw came when the organ-grinder, seeing the child's delight, began to stamp his great heel on the ground and from time to time whistle like a locomotive when two trains meet.

Oh, how lovely that whistle was!

The lawyer's faithful butler burst into the study, dragging the caretaker with him and exclaiming, "Sir, I told this imbecile to throw the organ-grinder out at once! I told him he'd get paid regularly, and that we have a contract. But this oaf! He only arrived from the country a week ago and he doesn't know our ways. Listen now!" shouted the butler, shaking the bewildered caretaker by the arm. "Listen to what my master has to say to you!"

The organ-grinder was already playing his third tune, as shrill and as jarring as the first two.

The blind girl was enraptured.

The lawyer turned to the caretaker and said with his customary composure, though he was somewhat pale, "Listen, my dear fellow. What's your name?"

"Paweł, sir."

"Well, Paweł, I'm going to pay you ten zlotys a month, but do you know what for?"

"For never letting any organ-grinders into the courtyard!" the butler put in quickly.

"No," said Mr. Tomasz. "I'll pay you if every day you let in a barrel organ. Do you understand?"

"What are you saying?" cried the butler, emboldened by this incomprehensible instruction.

"Until I talk to him again, he is to let organ-grinders into the courtyard every day," repeated the lawyer, putting his hands in his pockets.

"I don't understand, sir!" said the butler, with an offensive expression of astonishment.

"That's because you're a fool, my good fellow!" said Mr. Tomasz to him good-humoredly.

"Now, off to work," he added.

The butler and the caretaker left, and the lawyer noticed his faithful servant whisper something in his companion's ear and tap his forehead.

Mr. Tomasz smiled, and as if to confirm his servant's gloomy suspicions, he threw the organ-grinder a ten-grosz piece.

Then he took the city almanac, found the listings of doctors, and

copied out onto a sheet of paper the addresses of several ophthalmol-
ogists. And since the organ-grinder had now turned to his window
and, in response to the ten groszes, had begun to stamp and whistle
even louder, which sorely irritated the lawyer, he took the paper with
the addresses of the doctors and left, murmuring to himself, "That
poor child! I should have done something for her long ago . . . "

# Antek

Antek was born in a village on the Vistula.

The village lay in a small valley. To the north it was encircled by steep hills overgrown with pinewoods, and to the south by hills that were rounded and covered with hazelwood, blackthorn, and hawthorn. It was there that the birds sang loudest and the village children most often went picking nuts or bird's-nesting.

When you stood in the middle of the village, you had the impression that both ranges of hills were moving toward each other and would meet when the red sun rose in the morning. But this was only an illusion.

For beyond the village the valley ran between the hills, cut in two by a stream and carpeted with green meadows.

There the cattle grazed, and thin-legged storks hunted for the frogs that croaked in the evening.

To the west the village had a dike; beyond the dike was the Vistula, and beyond the Vistula more hills, this time of bare limestone.

Each farmer's cottage was roofed with dark thatch and had a little garden where plum trees grew. Behind them appeared a soot-blackened chimney and a fire ladder. These ladders had only recently been introduced, and people believed that they would protect the cottages from fire better than the previous stork's nests. So that when some building caught fire, they were mightily surprised, though they didn't try to save it.

"The Lord clearly had it in for that farmer," they would say to each other. "His place burned down even though he had a new ladder, and he'd paid a fine for the old one that had some broken rungs."

It was in this village that Antek was born. He was laid in an unpainted cradle that had been left after his brother had died, and he slept in it for two years. Then a new sister, Rozalia, came into the world, so he needed to make way for her, and, as someone who is already grown up, he had to sleep on the bench.

Throughout that year he rocked his sister, and throughout the next he explored his world. Once he fell in the river, on another occasion he was struck with a carter's whip for almost getting trampled on by his horses, while a third time he was bitten so badly by some dogs that he lay by the stove for two weeks. In this way, he experienced a great deal. In return, in his fourth year his father handed down to him his cloth shirt with a brass button, and his mother told him to look after his sister.

When he was five, he was already being sent to mind the pigs. But Antek didn't watch over them too closely. He preferred to look across to the other bank of the Vistula, where, from behind one of the limestone hills, something tall and black kept appearing over and over again. It emerged from the left as if it had come from inside the earth, rose up, then dropped to the right. The first one was followed at once by a second and third that were just as tall and as black.

In the meantime, the pigs, as is their wont, had wandered into the potato patch. When Antek's mother noticed, she whacked him on his shirt so hard that Antek could scarcely catch his breath. But since he bore no rancor in his heart, because he was a good child, once he'd had a shout and scratched at his shirt, he asked his mother, "Mummy! What's that black thing moving there on the other side of the river?"

Antek's mother followed his pointing finger, shaded her eyes with her hand, and replied, "Over the Vistula there? Can't you see that's a windmill? And next time keep an eye on those pigs, or I'll thrash you with nettles."

"Oh, a windmill! And what sort of thing is that, Mummy?"

"You're a daft one!" answered his mother, and ran off to her chores. How was she supposed to find time to give explanations about windmills!

But the windmill wouldn't give the lad any peace. Antek could see it every day. He even saw it at night, in his dreams. And he developed such a huge curiosity that one day he slipped away onto the ferry that carried people over the river and crossed to the far bank of the Vistula.

He got off the ferry, climbed up the limestone hill right by the place where there was a sign saying not to climb, and saw the windmill. The building looked to him like a bell tower, though it was wider, and where a bell tower has a window, it had four hefty sails in a cross. To begin with, he couldn't understand a thing – what was it and what was it for? But soon some shepherds explained it all to him, and he found out about everything. First about how the wind blows on the sails and sets them spinning like leaves; then about how in the windmill corn is ground into flour; and finally about the miller who sits by the mill and beats his wife, and is so clever that he knows how to drive rats from barns.

After this introductory lesson Antek returned home the same way he had come. The ferrymen gave him a clip on the ear in recognition of his bloody exertions, and his mother also clouted him on the back, but it didn't make any difference: Antek was happy because he had satisfied his curiosity. And so, though he went to bed without any supper, he dreamed the whole night either about the windmill that ground corn or about the miller who beat his wife and drove rats from barns.

This trivial incident had a big influence on the boy's whole life. From that moment on, from sunrise to sunset, he whittled sticks and tied them together in a cross. Then he made a tower; he tried and tried, shaping and constructing, till he had built a little model windmill that turned in the wind like the one across the Vistula.

What joy it brought him! All he needed was a wife he could beat, and he'd be a real miller!

By the age of ten he'd gone through four penknives, but he had carved some wonderful things with them. He made windmills, fences, ladders, wells, even whole cottages. It made people think, and they would tell his mother that he'd either be a master craftsman or a complete wastrel.

During this time another brother, Wojtek, was born, his sister grew up, and his father was crushed to death by a tree in the woods.

Rozalia was an extremely useful person to have around the cottage. In the winter she swept the floor, brought water, and even cooked barley soup. In the summer she was sent to mind the cattle with Antek, because he was busy with his whittling and didn't pay enough attention. They beat him, begged him, wept over him; he shouted, promised, and even shed tears along with his mother, yet he carried on as before, and the cattle were forever wandering off and causing damage.

It was only when his sister tended the cattle with him that things got better: he whittled sticks and she watched the cows.

At times their mother, seeing that the girl had more sense and goodwill than Antek, even though she was younger, would wring her hands in despair and lament to her cousin Andrzej, "What am I to do with Antek, the little changeling? He's no help at all around the house, he doesn't mind the cattle properly, all he does is carve sticks as if he were possessed. Oh Andrzej, I don't think he'll make a farmer, or even a farmhand; he'll be nothing but a loafer, a laughingstock, and an offense in the eyes of the Lord!"

Andrzej, who as a young man had been a raftsman and had seen the world, comforted the widow with these words: "There's no way he'll be a farmer; he doesn't have the common sense for it. You should send him to school to begin with, then apprentice him to a craftsman. He'll get some book learning, pick up a trade, and so long as he doesn't go completely to the dogs, he'll make a living."

To which the widow replied, still wringing her hands, "What are you saying, cousin! It's a crying shame for a farmer's child to learn a trade and do work that anyone can order."

Andrzej blew smoke from his little wooden pipe and said, "Sure it's a shame, but it can't be helped."

Then, turning to Antek, who was sitting on the floor by the bench, he asked, "So tell me, young rascal, what do you want to be? A farmer or an apprentice?"

To which Antek replied, "I'm going to build windmills that grind corn."

That was how he always responded, even though they shook their heads at him, and sometimes their brooms.

One day when he was ten his sister Rozalia, who was then eight, fell seriously ill. After she went to bed at night, in the morning it was hard to wake her. Her body was hot, her eyes were glazed, and she talked nonsense.

At first her mother thought she was faking, so she gave her a few hard whacks. When this failed to work, she rubbed her down with vinegar, and the next day gave her water and absinth to drink. Nothing helped; in fact, it made things worse, because after the girl drank the liquor purple blotches appeared on her skin. Then the widow, rummaging among all the clothes in the chest and the cubbyhole, came up with six groszes and sent for Mrs. Grzegorzowa, a great healer woman, to come and help.

The wise old woman looked the girl over carefully, spat on the floor around her in the required fashion, and even smeared lard on her, but to no avail.

Then she said to the mother, "Light the bread oven, cousin. The girl needs to sweat it out."

The widow immediately lit the oven and raked out the embers, awaiting further instructions.

"Right," said the healer woman. "Now put the girl on a pine board and put her in the oven for three Hail Marys. She'll be up and about in no time!"

And so they put Rozalia on a pinewood board (Antek watched from the corner of the room) and put her into the oven feet first.

When she felt the heat, the girl came to.

"Mummy, what are you doing to me?" she cried.

"Quiet, silly, it's for your own good."

The women had already slid her halfway in when the girl began thrashing about like a fish in a net. She struck the healer woman, threw her arms around her mother's neck, and screamed, "You'll burn me, Mummy!"

The women slid her all the way inside, boarded up the oven, and began to recite three Hail Marys.

"Hail Mary, full of grace . . . "

"Mummy! Mummy dear!" the poor girl wailed. "Oh, Mummy!"

"The Lord is with thee, blessed art thou among women . . . "

Now Antek ran up to the oven and seized hold of his mother's skirts.

"Mummy!" he cried tearfully. "It'll hurt her to death in there!"

But all he got was a smack on the head for interrupting the prayer. For some reason the sick girl had also stopped banging the board, tossing about, and shouting. The three Hail Marys were said and the oven door unboarded.

Inside the oven lay a corpse with reddened skin that was peeling off in places.

"Oh Lord!" cried the mother when she saw her daughter, who no longer even looked human.

And she was so seized by grief for the child that she was barely able to help the healer woman carry the body to the couch. Then she knelt in the middle of the cottage and, beating her head against the dirt floor, she cried, "Oh, Mrs. Grzegorzowa! What have you gone and done?"

The healer woman was morose.

"You'd be better off holding your tongue. I suppose you think the girl went red from the heat? That was the sickness leaving her body. It's just that it went a little too quickly and it finished her off. It's all God's will, after all."

In the village no one knew the cause of Rozalia's death. The girl had passed away. Too bad. It must have been fated. After all, children died in the village every year, and still there were always so many of them!

Two days later they put Rozalia into a freshly planed little coffin with a black cross; the coffin was placed on a dung cart and was drawn by two oxen beyond the village, to a place where rotten crosses and silver birches stood guard over sunken graves. On the uneven road the little coffin twisted to the side a little, and Antek, clinging to the folds of his mother's skirt as he walked behind the cart, thought to himself: Rozalia must be uncomfortable in there if she's straightening herself and turning on her side . . .

Then the priest sprinkled holy water on the coffin, four farmhands let it down on straps into the grave and shoveled earth onto it, and that was all.

The hills with the rustling woods and those where bushes grew were still there. The shepherds continued playing their pipes in the valley and life went on, went ever on as it does, though now there was one fewer girl in the village.

For a week people talked about her; then she was forgotten and her grave was left alone with only the wind to sigh over it and the crickets to chirrup by it.

Then, later still, the snow fell and frightened even the crickets away.

In the winter the farm children had classes. And since Antek's mother looked upon him as more of a hindrance than a help, she conferred with cousin Andrzej and decided to send the lad to school.

"Will they teach me how to build windmills at school?" asked Antek.

"Certainly! They'll even teach you to write in a book as long as you show willingness."

So the widow took forty groszes in a bundle and Antek by the hand, and went in trembling to see the schoolmaster. As she entered his cottage, she found him darning an old sheepskin coat. She bowed to the ground before him, handed over the money she had brought, and said, "With my deepest respects, sir, I wish to ask you to be so good as to take on this rascal and teach him, and not spare him your hand any more than his natural-born father would."

The respected sir, straw poking out of the holes in his shoes, took Antek under the chin, looked into his eyes, and patted him on the back.

"A good-looking lad," he said. "How much do you know already?"

"You're right, sir, he is good-looking," repeated the mother with satisfaction, "but I don't think he actually knows anything at all."

"How is that? You're his mother and you don't know what he knows and how much he's learned?" asked the teacher.

"How am I supposed to know how much he knows? I'm a woman, those things are none of my business. As for what he's learned, this Antek of mine, I know that he's learned to watch the cattle, chop wood, draw water from the well, and that's all, I think."

In this way Antek started school. But as his mother begrudged the forty groszes she had paid, to put her mind at rest she summoned a few of the neighbors to her house and asked them whether she had done the right thing in sending Antek to school and laying out such an expense on his behalf.

"Well," said one of the farmers, "the schoolmaster's supposed to be paid by the district council, so if you'd been stubborn you could have not given him anything. But he always drops hints, and the ones who don't pay something extra, he teaches them worse."

"Is he a good teacher?"

"For sure! When you talk with him, he sounds like a bit of a moron, but there's nothing wrong with his teaching. This is only the third year that my lad's been going to him, and already he knows his whole alphabet from beginning to end and back again."

"The alphabet's not much use," another farmer put in.

"I'll say it is," said the first. "How often have you heard the chairman of the council say that if he only knew his alphabet, he'd make more than a thousand rubles a year off this district, as much as the clerk!"

A few days later Antek went to school for the first time. It seemed to him almost as impressive as the room in the inn where the counter was; the benches were set up in rows like in church. The only thing was that the stove was broken and the door didn't close properly, so it was a little cold. The children's faces were red and they kept their hands thrust into their sleeves, while the schoolmaster wore a sheepskin coat and hat. And Jack Frost lurked in the corners of the school, staring at everything with his glittering eyes.

Antek was given a seat among the children who didn't yet know their letters, and the lesson began.

Nagged by his mother, Antek had promised himself that he would make his mark.

The schoolmaster took a piece of chalk in his stiff fingers and wrote a sign on the rickety blackboard.

"See, children!" he said. "This letter is easy to remember, because it looks like someone doing a cossack dance; you say it *A*. Quiet, you little monkeys! Repeat: A . . . A . . . A . . . "

"A! A! A!" the first group of pupils cried in unison.

Antek's voice sounded above the entire squeaking mass. But the schoolmaster still didn't notice him.

The boy was a little hurt by this; his pride had been spurred.

The schoolmaster drew another sign.

"This letter," he said, "is even easier to remember, because it looks like a pretzel. Have you ever seen a pretzel?"

"Wojtek has, but I don't think we ever saw one," offered one boy.

"So then, remember that a pretzel looks like this letter, which is called *B*. All together: B! B!"

The chorus cried: "B! B!" But this time Antek managed to stand out. He curved his hands into a trumpet and lowed like a yearling heifer.

The class burst out laughing, while the schoolmaster literally shook with rage.

"What?" he shouted at Antek. "So you're such a fine fellow, eh? You'd turn the schoolroom into a cattle shed? Give him here so I can warm him up!"

The boy was so taken aback he couldn't move. Before he knew what was happening, the two strongest boys had grabbed him by the arms, dragged him into the middle of the room, and laid him out.

Antek still hadn't figured out what was going on when he felt several heavy blows and heard a warning: "Don't you be crying, you little so-and-so! Don't you be!"

They let go of him. The boy shook himself like a dog climbing out of cold water and went back to his place.

The schoolmaster drew a third and a fourth letter, the children called out their names all together, and then came the exam.

Antek was the first to be called on.

"What's this letter called?" asked the schoolmaster.

"A!" replied the boy.

"And this next one?"

Antek said nothing.

"The next one is called B. Say it, you blockhead!"

Antek still said nothing.

"Say it, blockhead: B!"

"I'm no fool!" murmured the boy, remembering the schoolmaster had said, "Don't you *be*."

"So, you little good-for-nothing, you're stubborn, eh? Let's warm him up!"

And the same boys as before grabbed him and laid him down, and the teacher administered the same number of strokes of the rod, this time admonishing him: "No being stubborn! No being stubborn!"

A quarter of an hour later the senior group began their lesson, and the juniors went off for a break to the schoolmaster's kitchen. There, some of them peeled potatoes under the supervision of the housekeeper, while others brought water or fed the cows, and in this way passed the time till noon.

When Antek returned home, his mother asked him, "So? Did you study?"

"Yes."

"And did you get anything?"

"Oh yes – twice!"

"For your lessons?"

"No, as a warm-up."

"That's just a beginning, you see. Later on you'll get something for your studies!" his mother consoled him.

Antek fell into worried thought.

"Oh well, too bad," he said to himself. "He beats us, but at least he'll show us how to build windmills."

From that day on, the children in the junior group kept on learning the first four letters, then went to the kitchen and the yard to help the schoolmaster's housekeeper. There was no mention of windmills.

One day, the frost was milder outside and the schoolmaster's heart also seemed to have thawed, so he decided to explain to his youngest charges the value of literacy.

"You see, children," he said, writing the word *house* on the board, "what a clever thing writing is. These five signs are so small and take up hardly any space, yet they mean *house*. As soon as you look at this word, you can see right away the whole building before you: the door, the windows, the porch, the rooms, the stoves, the benches, the pictures on the wall. In a word, you see the house and everything it contains."

Antek rubbed his eyes, leaned forward, and stared at the word written on the blackboard, but he couldn't make out a house at all. In the end he nudged his neighbor and asked, "Can you see the house that sir is talking about?"

"No," replied his neighbor.

"I think he must be telling a lie!" concluded Antek.

The schoolmaster heard this last phrase and exclaimed, "What lie? What's a lie?"

"That there's a house on the blackboard. There are some chalk marks, but there isn't any house," Antek answered naively.

The schoolmaster seized hold of him by the ear and pulled him into the middle of the schoolroom.

"Warm-up!" he cried, and the whole ceremony, which the boy knew so well, was repeated down to the smallest detail.

When Antek went home, red, tearful, and restless, his mother asked him again, "Did you get anything?"

"What makes you think I wouldn't, Mummy?" groaned the boy.

"For what you learned?"

"Not for what I learned, but as a warm-up."

His mother waved a hand.

"Hmm," she said after a pause for reflection, "you must have to wait a while longer, then they'll give you something for what you learn, too."

Then, as she added wood to the fire in the hearth, she murmured to herself, "That's how it always is for a widow and an orphan in this mortal life. If I'd had half a ruble to give the schoolmaster instead of forty groszes, he would have taken my boy on right away. As it is, he's just messing around with him."

When Antek heard this, he thought to himself, "Uh oh! If he's just messing around with me now, I hate to think what'll happen when he actually starts to teach me!"

Fortunately or unfortunately, the boy's fears were never to be realized.

One day, about two months after Antek had first started school, the schoolmaster came to his mother and after the customary greetings asked, "So then, my woman, what's to become of this lad of yours? You gave forty groszes for him, but that was at the beginning; he's entering his third month now, and I've not seen another penny! That can't be; pay even just forty groszes, but every month."

To which the widow responded, "Where can I get that sort of money? I simply don't have it! Every penny I earn goes to the district council. I don't even have enough to buy clothes for the kids!"

The schoolmaster rose from the bench, put his hat on while he was still in the room, and replied, "If that's the case, then Antek has no business coming to school. I'm not going to strain my arm on him for free. Teaching like mine isn't for the poor."

He gathered himself up and left, and the widow, watching him go, thought to herself, "Never a truer word. Since the dawn of history the children of the masters have been going to school. Yet a common person doesn't stand a chance!"

She sent for cousin Andrzej again and the two of them set about quizzing the boy.

"So then you little rascal, what have you learned in these two months?" Andrzej asked him. "After all, your mother spent forty groszes on you."

"That I did!" put in the widow.

"How was I supposed to learn anything there!" replied the boy. "They peel potatoes in school just like at home, and they feed the pigs the same way. Except that a couple of times I cleaned the schoolmaster's shoes. Also, they tore my clothes during those, those warm-ups."

"So didn't you get any of that learning then?"

"Who gets anything there!" said Antek. "When he teaches so you can understand he tells lies. He writes some sign on the blackboard and tells us it's a house with a room, a porch, and pictures. A person has eyes, you can see it's not a house. And when he teaches us school learning, you can't make head or tail of it! There were a few of the older children that knew how to sing some school songs, but the younger ones are lucky if they learn to swear a bit."

"Mind your language, you, or you'll have me to answer to!" put in his mother.

"And how about farming, lad? You'd never fancy taking that up?" asked Andrzej.

Antek kissed his hand and said, "Please, send me where they teach you how to build windmills."

As if upon command, the grown-ups shrugged their shoulders.

That wretched windmill, grinding corn on the other side of the Vistula, had so taken root in the boy's soul that no force on earth could remove it.

After a long discussion they decided to wait. So they waited.

Week after week, month after month went by. The boy finally reached the age of twelve, but he still did few jobs on the farm. He whittled his sticks, and even carved bizarre figures. It was only when his penknife broke and his mother wouldn't give him the money to buy a new one that he found himself work. For one farmer he minded some horses in a meadow, where he would lose himself in thought in the gray evening mist, or stare at the stars. For another he led the oxen during the ploughing. Sometimes he would go to the woods to pick berries or mushrooms and sell the whole basketful to Mordko the innkeeper for a few groszes.

At home things were not going well. A farm without a farmer is like a body without a soul, and of course it had been several years since Antek's father had gone to rest on the hill where the cheerless crosses look down on the village through a fence overgrown with red berries.

The widow hired a hand to help with the farm; the rest of her money she had to give to the district council, and feed herself and her boys with what little was left.

So every day they would eat beetroot soup with bread and potatoes, sometimes porridge and dumplings, more rarely peas, and meat only at Easter. Sometimes there was not even that much in the cottage, and at such moments the widow, having no fire to mind, would darn her sons' little coats. Young Wojtek would cry, and Antek would spend dinnertime catching flies out of boredom; then after this feast he would go back outside to carve his ladders, fences, windmills, and saints. For he also made saints, though if the truth be told, to begin with they had no faces or hands.

Finally, cousin Andrzej, the faithful friend of the orphaned family, found Antek a place with the blacksmith in the next village. One Sunday he, the widow, and the boy went there. The blacksmith received them reasonably well. He examined the boy's arms and back, and seeing that he was pretty strong for his age, he took him on as an apprentice without pay, and only for six years.

Antek was frightened and sad as his weeping mother and old Andrzej said good-bye to him and disappeared beyond the orchards on their way home. He was even sadder when he spent his first night away from home, in a small barn, with the blacksmith's other boys, whom he didn't know and who ate his supper and also gave him a couple of whacks with their fists before bedtime as an advance on a close friendship.

But in the morning, when the whole group of them went to the smithy at the crack of dawn, when they lit the fire and Antek began to operate the cracked bellows while the others, singing "At the dawning, in the morning," set about hammering the red-hot iron, a new spirit awoke in the boy. The sound of the metal, the rhythmic banging, the song which the very woods answered with an echo – all this intoxicated the lad. It seemed as if the angels of heaven had touched strings in his heart that were not known to other country children, and that those strings only sounded now, with the wheezing of the bellows, the pounding of hammers, and the sparks flying from the iron.

Oh, what a splendid blacksmith he would become, and maybe even more . . . Because the lad, though he was mightily fond of his new work, was still thinking about his windmills.

The blacksmith, Antek's new guardian, was a mediocre fellow. He forged iron and filed it neither well nor badly. Sometimes he hit the boys so hard they swelled up; his biggest concern was to prevent them from learning their craft too quickly. Because a youngster who left his apprenticeship could open up a smithy right next to his own master and force him to do a better job!

And it needs to be mentioned that the master had one other habit.

At the other end of the village lived the blacksmith's great friend, the village councillor, who on normal days hardly ever left his work. But when some money came his way through his official business, he would abandon his farm and walk past the smithy to the inn. This would happen once or twice a week.

The councillor would come by with the money he had earned on his way to the building with the pine ridgepole; he would wander accidentally into the smithy.

"Christ be praised!" he would call to the blacksmith from the threshold.

"Christ be praised!" the blacksmith would reply. "How are things on the land?"

"Nothing new," the councillor would say. "And how are things in the smithy?"

"Nothing new," the smith would say. "It's a good thing you got away for once."

"Right," the councillor would answer. "I've been talking so much in that office that I need to wet my whistle. Maybe you could come with me and take a break from all this dust for a while?"

"By all means I could. There's nothing more important than a man's health," the blacksmith would answer, and, without taking off his apron, he would accompany the councillor to the inn.

And once he had left, the boys knew for sure they could put the fire out. However urgent the work was, even if the world had been coming to an end, neither their master nor the councillor would leave the inn before evening, unless some official business came up for the councillor.

They would return home only late that night.

Usually the councillor would lead the blacksmith by the arm, and the latter would be carrying a bottle of "mouthwash" for the following day. The next day the councillor was totally sober and went on farming till the next time his position brought him something, but the blacksmith kept on looking into the bottle he had brought back until the bottom came into sight, and in this way a single trip gave him two days' rest.

For a year and a half Antek had been working the bellows in the smithy, and very little else it seemed, and for a year and a half the master and the councillor had been regularly wetting their whistles beneath the pine ridgepole of the inn. Then something happened.

The councillor and the blacksmith were sitting in the inn, when after the first half-pint they were suddenly told that someone had hanged himself, and the councillor was dragged away from the table.

The blacksmith no longer had the necessary company and so he was obliged to stop drinking, but he bought the requisite bottle, picked it up, and set off slowly home.

In the meantime, a farmer had brought his horse to the smithy for shoeing. When the apprentices saw him, they called, "The master's not here, today he's having a tipple with the councillor."

"And none of you can shoe an old nag?" grumbled the farmer.

"None of us can," answered the oldest apprentice.

"I'll do it for you," said Antek suddenly.

A drowning man will grasp at straws, so the farmer agreed to Antek's offer, though he didn't really trust him, and to make matters worse the other apprentices laughed at him and called him names.

"Look at that runt!" the oldest one said. "He's never had a hammer in his hand since the day he was born, all he does is work the bellows and put coal on the fire, and now he's going to shoe a horse!"

But it was clear that Antek had held a hammer before, because he set to work and before very long he had forged some nails and a horseshoe. True, the horseshoe was too big and not quite the right shape, but even so the apprentices stood open-mouthed.

At this very moment the master came back. They told him what had happened and showed him the nails and the horseshoe.

The blacksmith stared and rubbed his bloodshot eyes in disbelief.

"And where did you learn to do this, you thief?" he asked Antek.

"In the smithy," answered the boy, pleased by the compliment. "When you were at the inn and the others went off somewhere, I'd forge things out of lead or iron."

The master was so taken aback that he even forgot to beat Antek for using up his materials and his tools. He ended up going to his wife for advice, which resulted in Antek being taken out of the smithy and set to work in the blacksmith's garden.

"You're too clever for your own good, son!" the blacksmith would say to him. "You'd learn your trade in three years and then you'd be off. Don't forget your mother gave you to me to serve for six years."

Antek stayed with the blacksmith for another six months. He dug the garden, weeded it, chopped wood, rocked the children, but he never set foot in the smithy again. In this regard everyone kept a watchful eye on him: the master, his wife, and the other boys. Even Antek's own mother and cousin Andrzej, though they knew about the blacksmith's decree, never said a word against him. According to their agreement and to the custom, it was only after six years that the boy had the right to have a go at smithery on his own. And if he was unusually quick and, without being taught by anybody, had learned the craft on his own within a year, then so much the worse for him!

As for Antek, he'd had enough of this way of life.

"If I'm to dig and chop wood, I'd rather do the same thing for my mother," he said to himself.

He thought about this for a week, a month. He couldn't make up his mind. But in the end he ran away from the blacksmith and went back home.

Those two years had changed him for the better. He had grown taller and more manly, had gotten to know more people than those in his valley, and above all had become familiar with more crafts-man's tools.

Now, living at home, he sometimes helped around the farm, but mostly he made his devices and carved figures. Now, though, as well as a penknife he had a small chisel, a file, and a gimlet, and he was so good with them that Mordko the innkeeper even began to buy some of his work. Quite what for Antek didn't know, though his windmills, cottages, imitation chests, saints, and carved pipes found their way around the whole district. People were impressed by the abilities of the unknown, self-taught artist, and Mordko was paid respectable sums for the pieces, but no one asked about the boy, much less thought of giving him a helping hand.

For who cultivates the flowers of the field, wild pear trees and cherry trees, though it should be common knowledge that if they were looked after carefully they would produce more?

In the meantime the boy grew up; the girls and women of the village looked more and more favorably upon him, and more and more often said to each other, "He's a handsome creature, there's no denying it!"

Antek really was handsome. He was well-built and graceful, and he held himself straight, not like the farmers, whose arms dangle down while their feet shuffle along from their toilsome labor. His face was also different from everyone else's. His features were regular, his skin fresh, his expression intelligent. He had curly blond hair, dark eyebrows, and deep blue, dreamy eyes.

The men admired his strength and complained that he wasted his time. But the women preferred to look into those eyes.

"When that creature sets his gaze on you," one of the women said, "it gives you gooseflesh. He's still a kid, but he looks at you like a fully grown gentleman!"

"That's not it at all!" objected a second. "He looks just like any other young bloke, but he has a sweetness in his eyes that's irresistible. I know what I'm talking about!"

"I think I know better," retorted the first. "After all, I served at the manor . . . "

And while the women were arguing about his eyes, Antek wasn't looking their way at all. He cared more for a good file than for the best-looking woman.

At this time the chairman of the district council, an old widower who had married off his daughter from his first marriage and still had several small children at home from his second, took a third wife. And since bald men usually have all the luck, he found himself a young, beautiful, rich wife from across the Vistula.

When this couple stood at the altar, people began to laugh; even the priest shook his head somewhat, because they really didn't go together.

The chairman shook like an old man leaving the hospital, and the only reason he didn't have more gray hair was that he was as bald as a coot. His wife had the spark of life in her; she was a full-blooded gypsy with cherry-red lips slightly parted, and black eyes in which her youth burned like a fire.

After the wedding the chairman's house, which was usually a quiet place, livened up greatly, because there was a constant stream of guests. First the watchman, who had business with the district council more frequently than usual; then the district clerk, who clearly didn't get enough of the chairman in the office and so visited him at home; then the government fusiliers, who up till now had hardly ever been seen in the village. Even the schoolmaster himself, when he went to collect his monthly salary, flung his sheepskin coat in the corner and dressed like a magnate, so that a number of the villagers began to call him the Lord of the Manor.

And all these watchmen, fusiliers, clerks, and schoolmasters were drawn to the chairman's wife like rats to a mill. One of them had barely left when another could already be seen over the fence, and a third was coming in from the far end of the village, while a fourth was hanging around the chairman himself. The lady in question enjoyed it all, laughing and offering the guests food and drink. Though sometimes, too, she would drag one of them out by the hair, because her mood changed easily.

Finally, after what seemed like a six-month wedding party, things settled down a little. Some guests grew bored, others were chased away by the chairman's wife, and only the aging schoolmaster, eating meagerly himself and starving his housekeeper, with each monthly salary would buy himself some fancy article of clothing and sit on the threshold of the chairman's house (for he'd been banned from going in), or curse and sigh in the lanes between the cottages.

One Sunday Antek went to high mass as usual with his mother and brother. The church was already crowded, but there was still a little room for them. Antek's mother knelt among the women to the right and Antek and Wojtek with the men on the left, and each of them prayed as best they were able. First to the saint in the main altar, then to the saint who hung above the first one, then to the saints in the side altars. He prayed for his father, who had been crushed by a tree, and for his sister, whose sickness had left her too quickly in the oven, and for the merciful Lord God and His saints from all the altars to bring him happiness in life, if that was their will.

All at once, as Antek was repeating his prayers for the fourth time, he felt someone step on his foot and lean heavily on his shoulder. He raised his head. Pushing through the throng, above him stood the chairman's wife, her face dark and red, out of breath from hurrying. She was dressed like a peasant woman; from under the kerchief draped across her shoulders could be seen a blouse of fine linen and strings of amber and coral rosary beads.

They looked into each other's eyes. She left her hand on his shoulder; he knelt and gazed at her as at a miraculous apparition, afraid to move in case she suddenly disappeared.

People began to whisper.

"Out of the way, friend, the chairman's wife is coming through ... "

They moved out of the way, and the chairman's wife passed on right up to the main altar. On the way she seemed to trip and looked at Antek again, and her gaze made the boy go all hot. Then she sat in the pew and prayed from her prayer book, occasionally raising her head and gazing around the church. And when during the Elevation things went so quiet you could hear a pin drop, and the pious fell on their faces, she closed her book, turned back again to Antek, and fixed her fiery pupils on him. A shaft of light fell from the window onto her swarthy face and her rosary beads, and to the boy she looked like a saint before whom people fall silent and turn to dust.

After the service everyone crowded out on their way home. The clerk, the schoolmaster, and a distillery owner from two villages away stood around the chairman's wife, and Antek wasn't able to see her again.

At home, the boys' mother made them an excellent barley soup whitened with milk and some big pierogi with groats. But even though Antek liked all this, he barely nibbled at his food. Then he left the house, ran up into the hills, and, lying down at the highest point, looked down at the chairman's house. Yet all he could see was a thatched roof and a thin trail of light blue smoke rising slowly from the whitewashed chimney. As a result, for some reason he grew so melancholy that he hid his face in his old coat and burst into tears.

For the first time in his life he felt the extent of his hardship. Their cottage was the poorest in the village, their land the worst. His mother, though she owned her own place, had to work like a tenant and dressed almost in rags. He himself was looked upon in the village as a lost cause who for some unknown reason sponges off other people. How many times had they knocked him about, and even set their dogs on him!

How far he was from the schoolmaster, the distillery owner, and even the clerk, who whenever they wanted could go into the chairman's wife's house and talk to her. He didn't want much. All he wished was that just one more time, one last time in life, she would rest her hand on his shoulder and look into his eyes like that moment in church. Because in her gaze he had glimpsed something extraordinary, like a lightning bolt which for a split second had illuminated heavenly depths full of secrets. If someone were to study them well, they would know everything there is to know on this earth and would be as rich as a king.

In the church, Antek had not looked closely at what he had glimpsed in her eyes. He had been unprepared, dazzled, and had missed his opportunity. But if she deigned to look at him once again! . . .

He dreamed that he saw happiness sailing past him and yearned for it terribly. His trembling heart had awoken and had begun somehow, painfully, to grow. Now the world seemed completely different to him. The valley was too narrow, the hills not high enough, and the sky might even have lowered a little, for instead of drawing him to itself, it had begun to weigh on him. He came down from the hill intoxicated, and without knowing how found himself by the bank of the Vistula. As he watched the swirling waters, he felt that something was pulling him toward them.

Love, which he was not able even to name, fell upon him like a storm, stirring up in his soul fear, sorrow, surprise, and he did not know what else.

From then on he went to high mass at church every Sunday and waited with heart aflutter for the chairman's wife, thinking that as before she would place her hand on his shoulder and look into his eyes. But things don't happen twice, and besides, the chairman's wife's attention was now taken up with the distillery owner, a healthy young fellow who traveled from two villages away just to come to the service.

Then Antek had an original idea. He decided to make a beautiful cross and give it to the chairman's wife. Maybe then she would look upon him and cure him of the longing that was sapping his life.

Outside the village, at the crossroads, there stood an unusual cross. Round its base it was swathed in bindweed; higher up there was a lattice with a spear and a crown of thorns; while at the top, on the left branch, was one of Christ's arms, for someone had stolen the rest of the figure, probably for purposes of sorcery. Antek took this cross as his model.

So he carved and remodeled his cross, starting afresh over and over again, trying to make it beautiful and worthy of the chairman's wife.

At this time disaster struck the village. The Vistula overflowed, broke through the dike, and flooded the fields along the riverbank. People lost a great deal, but Antek's mother was the worst hit. In their cottage they began to starve. They had to earn some money, so the poor woman went looking for work herself and found Wojtek a job as a shepherd. But it wasn't enough. Antek, who wouldn't work on the farm, was a real burden to her.

Seeing this, old Andrzej set about trying to persuade the lad to go and seek his fortune.

"I mean, you're a bright kid, you're strong, handy. Go to the town. You'll learn new skills there, and in addition you'll be able to help your mother out. Here you're taking the last morsel of bread from her mouth."

Antek went pale at the thought of leaving the village without even seeing the chairman's wife at least one more time. Yet he understood that there was no other way, and asked only that he be given a few days.

During that time, with redoubled zeal he went on with his cross, and when he finished it it was very fine, with the bindweed at the bottom, the instruments of torment, and Jesus' arm on the left-hand branch. But when he had completed the work, he absolutely could not summon the courage to go to the chairman's cottage and give the chairman's wife her gift.

In the meantime, his mother patched his clothes, borrowed a ruble from Mordko for the journey, tried to get some bread and cheese for his traveling basket, and cried a lot. But Antek dallied, from one day to the next delaying his departure.

This irritated Andrzej, who one Saturday called the boy out of the cottage and said sternly to him, "When are you going to come to your senses, lad? Do you want your mother to die from hunger and overwork because of you? With her old hands she can't feed herself and a strapping fellow like you who lazes around all day long!"

Antek dropped to Andrzej's feet.

"I'd go right away, Andrzej, it's just I'm so terribly sorry to leave my family!"

But he didn't say who he was most sorry to leave.

"Come on!" exclaimed Andrzej. "Are you a suckling child that you can't manage without your mother? You're a good lad, there's no denying it, but you have an idler in you who'd live off your mother till your hair turned gray. I tell you what: Tomorrow's Sunday, we're all free, so we'll see you off. After church you'll have dinner and leave. There's no sense in sitting around here any longer doing nothing. You know yourself that I'm right."

Humbled, Antek went into the cottage and said he would leave the next day to look for work and learning. His poor mother, choking back her tears, set about preparing him for the journey. She gave him an old basket, the only one in the house, and a sackcloth bag. In the basket she put some victuals, and in the bag the files, hammer, chisels, and other tools with which Antek had for so many years been making his trifles.

Night fell. Antek lay on his hard bench, but he couldn't get to sleep. Raising his head, he stared at the dying coals in the hearth and listened to the distant barking of the dogs or the chirruping of a cricket in the cottage, singing over his head like the grasshoppers that sang over the untended grave of his little sister Rozalia.

Suddenly he heard another sound in the corner of the room. His mother, who could not sleep either, was weeping quietly . . .

Antek buried his head in his coat.

The sun was high when he awoke. His mother was already up and was putting the pots on the oven with trembling hands.

Then they all sat down to breakfast at the table, and after the small meal they went to church.

Antek had his cross against his breast, beneath his coat. Every other minute he would squeeze it, looking round anxiously to see if he could see the chairman's wife, and wondering nervously how he would hand her the gift.

The chairman's wife was not in church. Kneeling in the middle of the church, the boy recited his prayers automatically, but had no idea what he was saying. The organ music, the singing, the pealing of bells, and the suffering of his own soul fused together into one great turmoil. He felt that at this moment the whole world was shaking at its foundations, when he was to leave this village, this church, and all those whom he loved.

Yet the world was calm, and it was only within him that sorrow raged so.

Suddenly the organ fell silent, and people bowed their heads. Antek started and looked up. Just as before, so today it was the Elevation, and as before on the pew by the great altar sat the chairman's wife.

The boy moved from his place through the throng, crawled on his knees right up to the pew, and found himself at the feet of the chairman's wife. He reached into his coat and took out the cross. But all his courage deserted him, his voice dried up, and he couldn't utter a single word. So instead of giving the cross to the woman for whom he had devoted several months of work, he took his creation and hung it on a nail hammered into the wall by the pew. At this moment he offered God his wooden cross, and along with it his secret love and his uncertain future.

The chairman's wife heard the commotion and looked curiously at the boy, just as before. But he saw nothing, for his eyes were blinded with tears.

After the mass the mother and her children returned to their cottage. They had barely finished their potato soup and a few dumplings when cousin Andrzej arrived and, after greeting them, said, "Come on then, lad! Get ready! No time like the present."

Antek belted his coat with a strap, and slung the bag over one shoulder and the basket over the other. When they were all ready to leave, the boy knelt, crossed himself, and kissed the dirt floor of the cottage as he would the church floor.

Then his mother took him by one arm, his brother Wojtek by the other, and his loved ones led him like a bridegroom to the edge of the big wide world.

Old Andrzej trailed along behind them.

"Here's a ruble, Antek," said his mother, pressing a bundle full of copper coins into the boy's hand. "Don't buy carving tools with it, save the money for a rainy day, when you get hungry. And if you ever make up the money, pay for a mass so that the Lord God may bless you."

And they walked slowly along, up the gully, till the village vanished from sight; they could hear only the quiet playing of a fiddle and the sound of a drum and bells from the inn. Eventually this, too, died away; they found themselves up on the hill.

"Let's turn back now," said Andrzej. "You, lad, go straight ahead and ask for the town. Your place isn't in the country but in the town, where people prefer the hammer to the plough."

At this the widow said tearfully, "Cousin Andrzej, let's at least stay with him up to the shrine, where we can bless him."

Then she lamented, "Whoever heard of a mother leading her own flesh and blood to his doom? Sure, boys have left the village to join the army, but that was because they had to. It's never happened that someone of his own free will left the village where he was born and where the holy earth should receive him again. Oh, my miserable fate! That I should be seeing a third person leave the house and should still be alive myself! Did you put the money somewhere safe, son?"

"I did, Mummy."

They reached the shrine and began to say their good-byes.

"Cousin Andrzej," said the widow, sobbing, "you've seen so much of the world, you were in the brotherhood, please, bless this orphan, and do it well, so that the Lord God will take good care of him."

Andrzej looked at the ground, recalled a prayer for travelers, took off his cap, and laid it by the shrine. Then he raised his hands to the heavens, and when the widow and her two sons knelt, he spoke:

"O Holy God, Our Father, who led Thy people out of slavery in the land of Egypt, who feedest every creature that moves, who returnest the birds of the air to their ancient nests, we beseech Thee, have mercy on this poor and heartsore traveler! Watch over him, Holy Lord, when he suffers misfortune comfort him, when he is sick heal him, when he is hungry feed him, when he is afflicted bring him succor. Be Thou merciful, Lord, toward him amongst strangers, as Thou wast toward Tobias and Joseph. Be Thou father and mother to him. Give him Thine angels for his guides, and when he has accomplished that which he has intended, return him safely to our village and to his home."

In this way the farmer prayed in a temple where the wild grasses were fragrant, where the birds sang, where beneath them the huge bends of the Vistula glistened, and above them the old cross spread its arms wide.

Antek fell at his mother's feet, then at Andrzej's, kissed his brother, and set off.

He had barely gone a few dozen paces when his mother called after him, "Antek!"

"What is it, Mummy?"

"If you're unhappy there among strangers, come back to us. God bless you!"

"Stay with God!" responded the boy.

He walked on a few more yards and again his mother called out sorrowfully, "Antek! Antek!"

"What is it, Mummy?" asked the boy.

His voice was fainter now.

"Don't forget us, son! God bless you!"

"Stay with God!"

And he walked on and on, like the boy who went to collect the pledge that had been issued upon his own soul. Finally he disappeared over the hill. The agonized moan of his mother rang out across the fields.

Toward evening clouds covered the sky and a fine rain fell. But as the clouds were not thick, the rays of the setting sun broke through. It looked as if a golden dome covered with mourning crape were suspended over the dull land and the muddy clay of the road.

Across that dull, silent, treeless land, on the muddy road, the weary boy walked slowly along in his gray coat, the basket and the bag on his back.

In the intense silence it seemed as if the raindrops were murmuring the wistful melody of a familiar song:

Across the field, across the dale,
A young lad marches down the trail.
His marching song rings in the air
While wind and rain sing with him there.

》 《

One day you may meet a country boy looking to earn a livelihood and to get some learning he couldn't find among his own people. In his eyes you will see something like the reflection of the sky gazing at itself on the surface of calm waters; in his thoughts you will discern an innocent simplicity, and in his heart a secret and barely conscious love.

If you do, offer a helping hand to this child. It will be our little brother Antek, who outgrew his native village and went out into the world, giving himself over to the care of God and of good folk.

# Him

A few years ago, around midday, on one of the quieter streets of Berlin, two men, one an army officer and the other a civilian, were going slowly along.

The officer was walking, or rather strolling, in front, the civilian a few paces behind him. The civilian wore a stylish beaver fur coat and a glistening top hat, and trod like a general on parade. He had light-colored gloves, gray eyes that darted here and there, and the expression of a man who is permitting the world not to fall at his feet. On his mobile features could be seen pride and an untiring vigilance, the object of which was his military companion. At times it seemed as if the man in the fur coat possessed the invaluable gift of being able to prick up his ears, thanks to which he could hear not only the officer's every cough but even the secret whisper of his thoughts, which rose and fell like the waves of the Baltic Sea.

This vigilance, however, did not prevent the civilian from grimacing if someone passed him without gaping in amazement, nor from smiling at the soldiers who stood taut as strings before his companion, their hands to their temples and their eyes popping out.

The officer, who was shuffling on ahead, was a man of towering size. He wore a long cloak with a cape and a peaked forage cap. It was hard to see his face, as it was obscured by the peak of the cap and by his raised collar. Only when the collar dropped a little could you see bulging eyes with drooping lids, a graying blond mustache, which also drooped, and cheeks that were furrowed with wrinkles as if hewn out of sandstone.

While his companion in the top hat seemed most concerned that all of Berlin should see and admire him, the officer was utterly indifferent. He trod heavily, rattling his great spurs. He didn't respond to bows, and didn't even glance at the infantry unit which, as it marched past him, gave a drumroll and presented its standard, filling his companion with such pride that he had to use all his strength to prevent his fur coat from bursting wide open.

Ordinary folk, busy with their Christmas shopping, passed them by indifferently. Occasionally, however, some more observant individual would notice the huge man in the cloak and step out of his path, doffing his cap. One person was even so surprised that instead of getting out of the way he simply gaped at the officer as if he were a ghost. While a couple of elderly Berliners, obviously husband and wife because they sported identical hare-skin collars and cotton gloves, noticed the giant and nudged each other simultaneously.

"Look, it's *him!*" whispered the husband.

"Look, Fritz, it's *him!*" said the wife.

At this sight the civilian in the fur coat began to smile even more radiantly, nodding his head and pricking up his ears as if he were delighted at their powers of observation, and wanted to say, "Yes, that's him, and this is me!"

But the elderly couple in the hare-skin collars didn't notice these friendly signals. Their eyes were riveted on the magnificent figure of the officer. When he disappeared around the corner, they gazed reverently at the pavement his gigantic feet had stepped upon.

At the corner, the man in the fur coat turned once more toward the old folk and nodded to them in a most kindly way, as if to say, "Yes – this is me!"

The officer moved along heavily, like a man whose massive shoulders bore the fate of forty-five million people. Yet although he was breathing with difficulty, tired by the long walk, it seemed that if he had wished, his cloak could have turned into a pair of immense wings that would carry him away and take him to a place where nations look like anthills.

This street was busier. There were many stores, and crowds of pedestrians. The officer stirred himself, and his protruding eyes, which up till now had been looking goodness knows where, focused on the throng. In a single glance he took in thousands of people. Here he noticed a cluster of women haggling over a fatted goose with the woman who was selling it; over there a few factory workers, pale and soot-blackened, who were marching along like soldiers. He saw a wife trying unsuccessfully to drag her husband out of a pub, and further on a group of people walking down the middle of the street carrying bundles. One of these people was crying, while the others were saying to each other that they must get a move on or they'd miss the train to Hamburg, and the boat would leave for America without them . . .

The giant knitted his bushy eyebrows and turned in a different direction. And suddenly his hitherto expressionless face lit up: he saw three tiny young boys, one of whom had a sword, one a toy rifle, and one a knapsack and a cardboard pickelhaube. The vague thought came to him that although a few people had given up hope and were leaving for America, in their place these very children would grow up to be new conquerors.

All of a sudden the civilian in the fur coat leaped forward so rapidly that his top hat rocked. Something unheard-of had happened. He, the secretary, confidant, and biographer of the great man, had failed to notice that his master had stopped in the street.

He had come to a halt and was standing and staring, and the secretary couldn't even figure out what he was staring at. True, there was a delicatessen here, but surely *he* was familiar with cinnamon, nutmeg, even coconuts? Then what was he looking at?

At this moment the giant gave a gentle sigh. Heavens! *He* had sighed? The secretary couldn't believe his ears. He rounded his master from the side and saw on his face the unmistakable signs of emotion. Could he have been moved by some cinnamon?

"Oh!" the biographer almost cried aloud, seeing at the back of the shop a Christmas tree decorated with gingerbread. *He* had been sent into a daydream by the sight of a Christmas tree put up by the poor. What a poetic soul! So long as he doesn't come up with a new tax to aid poor children!

Finally the giant walked away from the shop as if he found it hard to tear himself away from the Christmas tree.

"Now we'll go home," the secretary thought to himself, pleased in his heart that one of the most interesting chapters of the biography had just been added. *He* had grown dreamy over a Christmas tree! Is that not a splendid subject? Memories of childhood, rising over the bloody trail from Saarbrücken to Paris . . . There's not a publisher who wouldn't pay for that chapter with its weight in hundred-mark notes!

The secretary, who was accustomed to correctly guessing his master's public and private plans, already had the whole concept worked out. *He*, tired after working all through the night, had gone out for a walk around midday. He was a little out of sorts and so more susceptible than usual to human emotions. The sight of the pre-Christmas crowds affected him even more, and the Christmas tree provided the final touch.

I'm sure, thought the secretary, that that Christmas tree will become the inspiration for a multitude of new projects for the working classes . . . and perhaps even a Christmas bonus?

"Oh, these great people," whispered the secretary. "They have no idea how easily their intentions can be divined by those who have made a detailed study of the mechanisms of genius!"

At this point the secretary couldn't resist paying homage to his own perspicacity. At the same time he cast an eye over Berlin and noticed that his master had gotten away from him again. True, it was only a few paces, for a person cannot get farther away from his secretary and biographer.

This time the officer was standing at a booth with toys for sale, where an emaciated, frozen merchant was singing the praises of his wares to a group of curious listeners: "This railway train goes on its own – four marks! This elephant walks and trumpets – two marks! You wind it up by turning the tail . . . This clown is twenty pfennigs!"

Only grown-ups could see the train and the elephant, because they were moving about on the tabletop. But the clown hung above. Its costume was of blue, crimson, and yellow patchwork; it had a pointed cap and two cymbals in its hands. When the merchant pulled a string, the clown did the splits, banged the cymbals together, rolled its eyes, and stuck out its tongue.

"Oh, how lovely he is!" said a little child's voice at this moment.

The officer looked across and saw a little blond-haired boy who, head tipped back and arms folded, was gazing at the clown as if it were something miraculous. Every time the clown kicked its leg harder or stuck its tongue out farther, the boy burst out laughing, clapped his hands, and cried, "Oh gosh! How lovely he is!"

The child's delight was so great and so genuine that it infected the whole crowd of onlookers. Even the giant officer smiled beneath his mustache and took his coin purse from his pocket.

He's going to buy the boy the clown! thought the secretary in the fur coat, who was then unable to refrain from composing a few words of appreciation for his own uncommon abilities, which had enabled him to read the slightest intentions of this nineteenth-century sphinx.

Yet at the same moment the officer's face clouded over again. He quickly put the coin purse back in his pocket and walked away from the booth.

He meant to buy the lad a clown for Christmas, but he realized that he had been recognized, and so he decided against it. Oh, the dangers of fame.

Yet I, continued the secretary to himself, am entitled to write that the clown was bought and given to the child with the words: "Here you are, son, this is a Christmas gift from Germany!" Though I won't publish that till after his death . . .

Half an hour later the military gentleman and his secretary were already in the former's office. The secretary stood at the desk while the officer sat in a high-backed armchair smoking a pipe.

It was the kind of moment at which biographers are entitled to ask indiscreet questions. The secretary took advantage of it.

"Today will be a memorable day for me. It's been a long time since I last saw Your Highness in such a festive mood."

"Yes!" the officer replied slowly. "That walk reminded me of a number of matters. I'm starting to encounter emigrants to America not just in reports but also on the streets."

Save the talk of emigrants for others! thought the secretary. You can't hide your feelings from me!

And he added aloud, "I expect the sight of that Christmas tree brought back to Your Highness some pleasant childhood memories."

The prince raised his head.

"What Christmas tree?"

"The one . . . in the delicatessen," answered the shrewd biographer, looking discreetly at the floor.

The prince blew out a huge cloud of smoke and shifted restlessly in his armchair.

"Oh, yes!" he sighed. "That store and our emigrants leaving home at Christmas offer an interesting illustration of the situation in Germany. Every store of that kind is a countinghouse in which Holland extorts money from us. It's a funny thing that in Germany one can't even have a stick of cinnamon on which England or Holland has not first put its seal.

"Holland! It's smaller than Brandenburg, and yet it decided that it wanted to have colonies almost four times larger than the whole of Germany! And it has them, and one fine morning we would have to drink chicory for breakfast instead of coffee if it so pleased the Dutch."

So he was moved not by the Christmas tree but by the Dutch colonies? thought the secretary morosely.

The giant fretfully puffed several times at the curved stem of the pipe, but slowly the bulging veins in his forehead grew paler, and he calmed down.

"I noticed," said the secretary, "that Your Highness liked the look of that little boy watching the clown?"

"Oh, yes! He was a well-built young lad!" replied the prince with the smile of a connoisseur of cannon fodder.

"I even had the impression that you were about to buy him the clown?"

"But I didn't," replied the giant.

"Does Your Highness believe that Christmas presents are not appropriate for German children?"

"Quite the opposite. Besides, I gave him the best present he could receive."

The secretary looked at him expectantly.

"I gave him unfulfilled desire," answered the prince, and then added, "The more desires of that kind there are, the better for us!"

"And yet eleven years ago, at Versailles, Your Highness was kinder to that little French girl, to whom you gave a doll."

"Well, you see, the more fulfilled desires there are *there*, the better for us!"

When he had finished, the prince turned and fixed his eyes on a map of the Dutch colonies that hung on the wall. The secretary grew sad, surmising, probably correctly, that in a country where a little boy longs in vain for a clown and a great chancellor for the Dutch colonies, secretaries can expect for Christmas not a bonus, but the gift of unfulfilled desires . . .

# The Waistcoat

Certain people have a bent for collecting curios of greater or lesser value, depending on their pocket. I, too, own a collection, though it's a modest one, as is usual at the beginning stages.

It includes the play I wrote back in grammar school, during my Latin classes. There are a few dried flowers, which will have to be replaced with new ones. There is . . .

I don't believe there is anything else, other than a certain tattered old waistcoat.

Here it is: faded at the front, worn at the back. It's covered in stains, some of the buttons are missing, and there's a hole in the side that was probably made with a cigarette. But the most interesting things are the adjustable straps. The strap with the buckle has been shortened and sewn onto the waistcoat in an unprofessional fashion, while the other has marks from the teeth of the buckle along almost its entire length.

Looking at it, it's easy to guess that the owner of the garment was probably losing weight daily, until he finally got to the stage at which the waistcoat was no longer of any use, but instead he was very much in need of a dress coat from a funeral parlor, fastened up under his chin.

I confess I'd be glad to pass this rag on to someone else; it's creating a bit of a problem for me. I don't have a cupboard for my collection, and I don't fancy keeping this wretched item among my own things. And yet there was a time when I bought it for a price greatly exceeding its value, and I would have given even more if the seller had known how to barter. There are times in life when one likes to surround oneself with objects associated with sorrow.

That sorrow did not dwell in my home but in the flat of my next-door neighbors. Each day I could look from my window into their little room.

Right up till April there were three of them: the gentleman, the lady, and a little maid, whom I believe slept on a trunk next to the wardrobe. The wardrobe was of dark cherry wood. In July, if my memory serves me rightly, only two of them were left, the gentleman and the lady, for the maid had gone to work for a family who paid her three rubles a year and who ate a hot dinner every day.

By October, the lady was alone. Or rather, not entirely alone, for the room still contained a lot of furniture: two beds, a table, the wardrobe. However, at the beginning of November the unneeded items were auctioned off, and of all the mementos of the lady's husband, she kept only the waistcoat that is now in my possession.

But one day at the end of November she called a secondhand dealer to the empty flat and sold him her umbrella for two zlotys and her husband's waistcoat for forty groszes. Then she locked up the flat, slowly crossed the courtyard, handed the key to the caretaker, stared for a short while at what used to be her window, on which small snowflakes were falling, and then she walked through the gate and disappeared.

The secondhand dealer remained in the courtyard. He lifted up the great collar of his cloak, thrust the umbrella he had just bought under his arm, and, wrapping the waistcoat around his hands, which were red from the cold, he grunted, "Goods for sale, gentlemen! Goods for sale!"

I called him to my flat.

"You have something to sell, good sir?" he asked as he came in.

"No, I want to buy something from you."

"No doubt the umbrella you want?" responded the Jew.

He threw the waistcoat on the ground, shook the snow from his collar, and set about strenuously opening the umbrella.

"Nice job!" he said. "Just the thing for this snow. I know that you, sir, maybe have a pure silk umbrella, even two. But they only good in the summer!"

"What do you want for the waistcoat?" I asked.

"What waistcoat?" he replied, surprised, probably thinking I meant his own.

But he quickly realized what I was talking about and picked the item up from the ground.

"For this waistcoat? You asking about this waistcoat, sir?"

And then, as if his suspicions had been aroused, he asked, "What you want with such a waistcoat, good sir?"

"How much do you want for it?"

The yellowish whites of the Jew's eyes flashed, and the tip of his elongated nose turned even redder.

"You have it for one ruble!" he replied, holding the garment out before me to display all its fine qualities.

"I'll give you half a ruble."

"Half a ruble? For such a clothing? That's not possible!" said the dealer.

"Not a penny more."

"I wish you healthy joking, sir!" he said, slapping me on the shoulder. "You can see yourself how much a thing like this is worth. After all, it's not a child clothing, it's for grown-ups."

"Well, if you can't sell it for half a ruble, then off you go. I won't give you any more."

"No need to get angry, sir!" he put in, softening. "By my own conscience, I can't sell for half a ruble, but I trust your judgment.

You say how much it's worth, and I agree. I rather come out at a loss, so long things turn out the way you wish."

"The waistcoat's worth fifty groszes, and I'm giving you half a ruble."

"Half a ruble? All right then, let it be half a ruble," he sighed, thrusting the waistcoat into my hands. "Let it be my loss, just so long as I don't break my word. My, that wind!"

And he pointed at the window, outside of which there was a swirling cloud of snow.

As I reached for the money the dealer, evidently remembering something, snatched the waistcoat back and began quickly rummaging through the pockets.

"What are you looking for?"

"Maybe I leave something in the pocket, I don't remember!" he answered in the most natural tone of voice, and as he handed back my new acquisition he added, "Throw in another ten groszes at least, kind sir!"

"Mind how you go!" I said, opening the door.

"Your humble servant! I also have good-quality fur coat at home . . . "

And even after he had crossed the threshold he poked his head around the door and asked, "Perhaps you like me to bring some sheep's-milk cheeses?"

A minute or two later he was already back in the courtyard and once more was calling, "Goods for sale!" and when I stood in the window he bowed to me with a friendly smile.

The snow began to fall so densely that it was almost like night. I put the waistcoat on the table and began to think about the lady who had walked out of the gate and gone goodness knows where, and about the flat that stood deserted next to mine, and also about the owner of the waistcoat, who was being covered by an ever thicker coat of snow.

It had only been three months before, one fair September day, that I had heard them talking to each other. In May the lady once even hummed a song, while the gentleman laughed as he read the Sunday newspaper. Whereas today . . .

They moved into our building at the beginning of April. They got up quite early, drank tea from a tin samovar, and left for town together, she to give lessons, he to his office.

He was a low-ranking clerk who looked upon his departmental superiors with the same admiration that a traveler looks upon the high Tatra Mountains. He had to work long hours, for days on end. I would even see him at midnight, bent over the table by the lamp.

His wife usually sat by him and sewed. Sometimes she would look at him, break off from her work, and say reproachfully, "Come on, that's enough now, go to bed."

"When are you going to bed?"

"I'm . . . just going to finish off a few more stitches."

"Well then, I'll just write a few more lines."

They both lowered their heads and got on with their work. Then once again, after a while, the lady would say, "Go to bed . . . go to bed . . . "

Sometimes, in response to her words my clock would strike one o'clock.

They were young and neither good-looking nor ugly; they were quiet people. If I remember correctly, the lady was considerably slimmer than her husband, who was quite heavily built. I would even have said that he was too portly for such a low-ranking clerk.

Every Sunday, around midday, they would go out for a walk arm in arm and would return home late in the evening. They probably ate dinner in town. I once met them at the gate between the Botanical Gardens and Łazienki Park. They had bought themselves two mugs of first-rate mineral water and two large gingerbread cakes, and had assumed the untroubled expressions of townspeople who are in the habit of eating hot ham and horseradish sauce, washed down with tea.

In general, the poor need little to maintain their spiritual equilibrium. Some food, a lot of work, and ample good health. The rest seems to take care of itself.

My neighbors, it seemed, did not want for food, and certainly were not short of work. But their health was not all that it might have been.

Somehow the gentleman caught a chill in July, though it was not very serious. By a strange coincidence, however, at the same time he began to bleed so badly that he lost consciousness.

Night had already fallen. The lady, wrapping her husband in blankets on the bed, called the caretaker's wife into the room and ran off herself to fetch a doctor. She tried five different doctors, but found only one, and that by accident, on the street.

The doctor, looking at her by the flickering light of a streetlamp, concluded that above all she needed to be reassured. And since she stumbled from time to time, probably from exhaustion, and there was no dorozhka to be found on the street, he gave her his arm and as they walked he explained that bleeding alone meant nothing.

"The bleeding may come from the larynx, the stomach, the nose; it's only rarely that it's from the lungs. Besides, if the person has always been healthy, and has never had a bad cough . . . "

"Oh, only from time to time!" whispered the lady, halting to catch her breath.

"From time to time? That still doesn't signify anything. He may have a slight touch of bronchitis."

"Yes . . . it's bronchitis!" repeated the lady, aloud this time.

"He's never had pneumonia?"

"Yes, he has," replied the lady, pausing again.

Her legs shook under her slightly.

"Yes, but I expect that was a long time ago?"

"Oh, a long, long time ago!" she agreed hurriedly. "Right back in the winter."

"A year and a half ago."

"No . . . but before the New Year. Such a long time ago!"

"Ah. How dark this street is! Especially as it's rather cloudy tonight," said the doctor.

They entered the building. The lady anxiously asked the caretaker whether anything had happened and heard that nothing had. In the flat the caretaker's wife also said that nothing had changed, and the sick man was dozing.

The doctor woke him gently and examined him, and he also declared that it was nothing.

"I said right from the beginning that it was nothing!" put in the sick man.

"Yes, nothing!" repeated the lady, holding his hands, which were wet from perspiration. "Of course, I know that bleeding can come from the stomach or the nose. With you it's probably from your nose. You're so stout, you need exercise, and you spend all day sitting down. Isn't that right, doctor, that he needs exercise?"

"Yes, indeed! Generally speaking, exercise is necessary, but your husband must rest up for a few days. Is it possible for him to go and stay in the country?"

"I'm afraid it isn't," whispered the lady sadly.

"Well, never mind! He'll stay in Warsaw. I'll be visiting, and in the meantime he should lie in bed and rest. If the bleeding should recur . . . ," added the doctor.

"Then what, doctor?" asked the wife, turning as white as a sheet.

"Well, not to worry. If your husband gets plenty of rest, things will heal up in there."

"In there . . . in his nose?" said the lady, clasping her hands before the doctor.

"That's right. In his nose! Of course. You stay calm, ma'am, and entrust the rest to the Lord. Good-night."

The doctor's words reassured the lady so much that, after the anxiety she had suffered for the last few hours, she became almost merry.

"So what's all the fuss about!" she said, laughing and crying at the same time.

She knelt by the sick man's bed and kissed his hands.

"What's the fuss!" the man repeated, and smiled. "Think how much blood a man can lose in a war, and yet afterward he's fine!"

"Don't talk any more now," the lady begged him.

Outside dawn was breaking, for in the summer the nights are very short.

The illness lasted much longer than had been expected. The husband stopped working at the office. This was not such a problem for him because, as a contract worker, he didn't need to take leave and could return to work whenever he wanted – and whenever he could find a job. Since he felt better when he stayed at home, the lady took on even more lessons each week and in this way provided for their daily needs.

She usually left for town at eight in the morning. Around one she would come back home for a couple of hours to cook lunch for her husband, and then she would run out again for a time.

The evenings, however, they spent together; though in order not to be idle, the lady took in a little more sewing.

Around the end of August it somehow transpired that the lady met the doctor on the street. For a long while they walked together. Finally, the lady seized the doctor's hand and said imploringly, "But either way, please come and see us. Perhaps God will have mercy! He always calms down so much after your visits."

The doctor promised, and the lady returned home, looking as if she had been crying. The man, through having to stay at home, had become somewhat irritable and despondent. He began to try to persuade his wife that she shouldn't be so concerned, that he would die anyway, and in the end he asked her, "Didn't the doctor tell you that I wouldn't live more than a few months?"

The lady froze.

"What are you talking about?" she said. "Where did you get an idea like that?"

The sick man grew angry.

"Come here to me, here!" he said abruptly, grabbing her by the hands. "Look me straight in the eye and answer me: Didn't the doctor say that to you?"

He fixed his feverish gaze on her. It seemed as if under this scrutiny even a wall would whisper its secrets, if it possessed any.

A strange calm appeared on the woman's face. She smiled gently, not flinching from that fierce stare. Her eyes just seemed to glaze over.

"The doctor said," she replied, "that it's nothing, you just need to rest a little."

The husband suddenly let go of her, shivered, laughed, then with a wave of his hand said, "There, you see how edgy I am! I'd gotten it into my head that the doctor had given up hope for me. But . . . you've convinced me. I feel reassured now!"

And, more and more cheerfully, he laughed at his imaginings.

In fact, such an attack of suspicion never occurred again. His wife's gentle calm was the best indication for the sick man that his condition was not serious.

For why should it be?

He did have a cough, but that was from the bronchitis. Sometimes, from the long periods of sitting, there was bleeding – that came from his nose. And he also had what seemed to be a fever, but really it wasn't a fever – just nerves.

Overall, he felt better and better. He had an overwhelming desire to go on long trips, though he didn't quite have the strength. There even came a time when during the day he didn't want to lie in bed, but instead would sit in the armchair, fully dressed, ready to go out if only this temporary weakness would pass.

There was only one detail that worried him.

One day, as he was putting on his waistcoat, he felt that it was somehow very loose.

"Can I really have lost so much weight?" he whispered.

"Of course, it's natural that you must have become a bit thinner," answered his wife. "But we mustn't exaggerate."

Her husband looked at her intently. She didn't even lift her eyes from her work. No, that calm couldn't be dissembled! His wife knew from the doctor that he was not so very sick really, and so there was no reason to worry.

At the beginning of September the nervous attack, which resembled a fever, occurred more acutely, lasting almost all day.

"It's nothing serious!" the sick man said. "When summer is turning to autumn even the healthiest person can be off-color, everyone feels out of sorts. The only thing that surprises me is that my waistcoat feels looser and looser. I must have lost an awful lot of weight, and I won't get better until I put some back on."

His wife listened carefully and had to agree that her husband was right.

The sick man got up every day and dressed, even though without his wife's help he was unable to put on any of his clothes. The only thing she managed to persuade him to do was to wear an overcoat instead of a frock coat.

"It's hardly surprising," he would often say, gazing in the mirror, "it's hardly surprising that I have no strength. Just see how I look!"

"Well, it's always the face that changes the most," put in his wife.

"That's true, but I'm losing weight all over."

"Are you quite sure you're not imagining it?" asked his wife, with an expression of great doubt.

He fell to thinking.

"Hmm, maybe you're right. For even . . . the last couple of days I've had the impression that . . . my waistcoat . . . is a bit . . . "

"Oh, come on!" interrupted his wife. "You're not trying to tell me that you've put on weight!"

"Who knows? From what I can tell from my waistcoat, it . . . "

"In that case you should be getting your strength back."

"Oh yes, you want it to happen all at once. First of all I have to put at least a little weight back on. And even then, you know, I won't get my strength back straight away. What are you doing behind the wardrobe?" he suddenly asked.

"Nothing. I'm looking for a towel in the trunk, but I'm not sure . . . whether it's clean."

"Don't strain so much, even your voice is different. That trunk is heavy."

The trunk must indeed have been heavy, for it had brought a flush to the lady's cheeks, but she was calm.

From then on, the sick man paid more and more attention to his waistcoat. And every few days he would call his wife and say, "There, just look at that. See for yourself: yesterday I could get my finger in here, right here, and today I can't. I really am beginning to put on weight!"

But one day the sick man's joy knew no bounds. When his wife returned from her lessons, he greeted her with shining eyes and said excitedly, "Listen, I'll tell you a secret. You know, I was cheating a bit with that waistcoat. In order to keep you from worrying, each day I shortened the strap, and that was why the waistcoat was tight. Yesterday, I pulled the strap right to the end. I was beginning to worry that my secret would be out, but today . . . Do you know what? Today, I give you my solemn word, instead of tightening the strap, I had to loosen it a little! It really was genuinely too tight for me, even though yesterday it was a little loose.

"So now I too believe that I'll get better. I do! The doctor can think what he wants."

This long speech cost him such an effort that he had to go across to the bed. There, however, as a man who without tightening any straps was beginning to put on weight, he didn't lie down, but as in the armchair he leaned on his wife while she put her arms around him.

"Well, well!" he whispered. "Who would have thought it? For two weeks I deceived my wife by saying that the waistcoat was too tight, and today it really is too tight! Well, well!"

And they spent the whole evening in each other's arms.

The sick man was affected as never before.

"Dear Lord!" he whispered, kissing his wife's hands. "And I thought that I would just go on losing weight like that till . . . the end. This is the first time in the last two months that I've believed I can get better again."

For everyone lies to a sick man, most of all his wife. But a waistcoat – that will never lie!

》 《

Today, looking at the old waistcoat, I can see that two people had been at work on the straps. The gentleman moved the buckle along each day to set his wife's mind at rest, while each day the lady shortened the strap to raise her husband's spirits.

"Will they ever meet again, to tell each other the whole truth about the waistcoat?" I wondered, staring at the sky.

It could scarcely be seen anymore above the earth. There was only snow falling, so dense and cold that even human ashes froze in their graves.

And yet who will say that beyond those clouds there is no sunlight?

# The Sins of Childhood

I was born at a time when everyone had to have a title, whether it was deserved or not.

For this reason the lady of the manor was called the countess, my father was called her plenipotentiary, and I was rarely called Kazio or Leśniewski, but rather rapscallion while I lived at home and moron when I went to school.

As you would have looked in vain for the name of the lady of the manor in the register of aristocratic families, I believe the radiance of her noble coronet extended no farther than the plenipotentiary powers of my late father. I even recall that the title of countess was my father's way of commemorating the joyful occasion when his salary was increased by one hundred zlotys a year. Our lady received the honor accorded her in silence; then a few days later my father was promoted from steward to plenipotentiary and was given, in lieu of a diploma, a suckling pig of uncommon proportions, after the sale of which I was bought my first pair of shoes.

My father, my sister Zosia, and I (for I no longer had a mother) lived in a stone outbuilding a hundred yards or so from the manor house. In the manor itself lived the countess with her daughter Lonia, who was my age, her governess, the old housekeeper Salusia, and a multitude of tirewomen and chambermaids. These girls spent all day sewing, from which I concluded that ladies were there to tear up clothing and serving girls to repair it. I had no idea of other purposes for well-born ladies and poor serving girls. In my father's eyes, this constituted my only good point.

The countess was a young widow whose husband had early on plunged her into inconsolable sorrow. As far as I know from tradition, no one called the deceased gentleman count, and no one was known as his plenipotentiary. In fact, the neighbors, with a unanimity rare in our parts, called him half-wit. In any case, he was a remarkable man. He rode his saddle horses into the ground, trampled the farmers' crops when he went hunting, and fought duels with his neighbors over dogs and hares. At home he tormented his wife with jealousy and the servants with a pepper-colored pipe stem. After this eccentric died, his saddle horses were sent to pull manure carts and his dogs were given away. He left the world a little daughter and a young widow. Oh, sorry, there was also a portrait in oils of the deceased, wearing a signet ring that bore the family crest and holding the aforementioned pipe stem, which from misuse had grown as bent as a Turkish sword.

I barely knew the manor house, first because I preferred running about the fields to falling over on its slippery tiled floor, and second because the servants wouldn't let me in, since during my first visit I was unlucky enough to break a large Saxon vase.

Before I left to go to school, I had played with the countess's daughter only once, when we were not quite ten. I had wanted to take the opportunity to teach her the art of climbing trees, and I sat her down on a metal fence in such a way that she began screaming to high heaven. Then her governess set about me with a blue parasol, saying that I could have caused Lonia permanent harm.

From this moment I conceived a dislike of little girls, not one of whom was capable of climbing trees, or swimming with me in the pond, or going horse riding, or shooting a bow and arrow, or firing stones with a catapult. And as far as fighting was concerned – and how could you really have fun without a fight! – virtually every one of them started sniveling and ran off to tell on you.

Since my father wouldn't let me play with the boys from the farm, and my sister spent just about the whole day at the manor, I grew up and educated myself alone, like the young of a bird of prey abandoned by its parents. I bathed under the mill or sailed about the pond in a leaky rowboat. In the park belonging to the manor, I chased squirrels through the branches of the trees with the agility of a cat. Once the boat capsized, and I spent half the day on a little floating clump of plants no bigger than a bathtub. Once I climbed through a skylight out onto the roof and got into such a pickle that they had to tie two ladders together to get me down. Another time I spent twenty-four hours wandering through the woods. On yet another occasion a saddle horse that had belonged to the late count, recalling better times, bore me across the fields for a whole hour and in the end, probably unintentionally, gave me a broken leg, which, by the way, healed up fairly quickly.

Having no companion, I lived with nature. In the park I knew every anthill, in the fields every hamster den, in the garden every mole trail. I knew the birds' nests and the hollows in trees where young squirrels were being reared. I could distinguish the rustling of each lime tree by the house, and I could sing the song that the wind played in the trees. At times I heard ancient footsteps through the wood, though I didn't know whose they were. I would gaze upon the twinkling stars and converse with the silence of the night, and not having anyone to kiss, I kissed the farmyard dogs. My mother had long since lain in her grave. By now beneath the stone that lay on top of her there had opened up a crevice that probably extended right down into the grave. Once, when I'd been given a hiding for something or other, I went there. I called to her and strained my ears to see if she'd respond . . . But she didn't say anything. I could tell she really was dead.

At that time I was forming my first ideas about people and the relationships between them. For instance, in my imagination a plenipotentiary had to be a little stout and have a ruddy face, a drooping mustache, thick eyebrows over grayish eyes, a bass voice, and at least the same ability to shout as my father. A person called countess I was unable to imagine any other way than as a tall lady with a beautiful face and mournful eyes, walking soundlessly through the park in a trailing white gown.

Whereas I had no notion of a person called count. Such a person, even if he existed, seemed to me less important than a countess, quite useless and unseemly in fact. To my mind, it was only in a loose-fitting gown with a long train that the stateliness of nobility could dwell, while all other garments – those that were short, tight, and especially those that consisted of two parts – could only be worn by bookkeepers, distillery owners, or at best plenipotentiaries.

Such were my legitimistic beliefs, based upon my father's injunctions, as he ceaselessly enjoined me to love and honor the countess. Of course, if I ever forgot these rules, all I had to do was to look in the red cabinet in my father's office, where alongside the receipts and notes, on a nail there hung a five-tailed scourge, embodiment of the principles of social order. For me it constituted a sort of encyclopedia, the sight of which reminded me that I mustn't scuff my shoes or pull foals' tails, that all authority came from God, and so on.

My father was indefatigable in work, unimpeachably honest, and even very easygoing. He never laid a finger on any of the farmers or the servants, merely shouting at them. If he was rather strict with me, it was probably because he had good reason to be. Our organist, into whose snuffbox I once put some poisonous hellebore, as a result of which he sneezed through the entire mass instead of singing and kept playing the wrong notes, often used to say that if he had had a son like me he would have shot him in the head.

I clearly remember that utterance.

The countess my father called an angel of goodness. It was true that in her village no one went hungry, no one was in rags, and no one suffered wrongs. Whoever was treated badly went to her with their grievance; whoever was ill got medicine from the manor; whoever had a baby asked the lady of the manor to be the godmother. My sister was educated with the countess's daughter, and I myself, though I avoided aristocratic relations, nevertheless had an opportunity to be convinced of the countess's exceptional lenience.

My father owned a number of weapons, each of which served a different purpose. The massive double-barreled shotgun was for killing the wolves that slaughtered the countess's calves, the flintlock pistol was to be used in defense of any of the countess's other property, while the broadsword was for defending her honor. His own property and honor my father would probably have defended with a common staff, because this whole arsenal, oiled every few months, lay somewhere in a corner in the attic, so that even I couldn't find it.

One way or another I had learned about these weapons and I hankered after them. I often used to dream that I would do something so noble that my father would allow me to use the huge pistol. In the meantime, I crept away to the gamekeepers and learned to "loose" their single-barreled shotguns, which were constructed in such a way that when they were fired they caused injury only to my own jaw, not touching any other living creature.

One day, during the oiling of the shotgun for killing wolves, the flintlock for the protection of the countess's property, and the broadsword for defending her honor, I managed to steal from my father a handful of gunpowder, which, to the best of my knowledge, was not for doing anything in particular. When my father left to go to the fields, I seized the massive key to the granary, which had a opening like a gun barrel and a little hole in its side, and I went hunting.

I half-filled the great key with gunpowder, tipped in a few pieces of broken button from an unmentionable item of clothing, and rammed it all down properly with tow. To create the explosion I had a tinderbox and matches.

I had barely left the house when I saw a group of crows attacking some ducklings that belonged to the manor. Right before my eyes one of the aggressors seized a duckling and, finding it difficult to carry, alighted for a moment on the cattle shed.

At this sight, the blood of my ancestors, who had taken part in the Relief of Vienna, stirred within me. I crept up to the cattle shed, lit some tinder, aimed the key at the crow's left eye, blew on the tinder, and touched the key. There was a crashing sound as if lightning had struck. The duckling, already dead, rolled off the cattle shed onto the ground; the crow, gripped with mortal fear, fled to the highest lime tree; while I was astonished to observe that in my hand, all that was left of the great key was the handle, whereas from the straw roof of the cattle shed a small column of smoke was beginning to rise, as though someone were smoking a pipe.

A few minutes later the cattle shed, which was worth some fifty zlotys, was engulfed in flames.

People came running, my father galloped up on horseback, and then, in the presence of all these brave and good people, the construction "burned right into the ground," as the owner of the distillery put it.

During this time, indescribable things were happening within me. First of all I ran home and put the handle of the ruined key in its rightful place. After this I ran away to the park with the intention of drowning myself in the pond. A moment later I changed my plans radically: I decided to lie like the bookkeeper and deny all knowledge of the key, the explosion, and the shed. Then, when I was caught, I confessed to everything straight away.

I was taken to the manor. On the terrace I could see my father, the countess in her trailing gown, her daughter in a rather short dress, and my sister, these two crying; then there was the housekeeper Salusia, the valet, the footman, the downstairs boy, the cook, the scullion, and a whole bevy of chambermaids, tirewomen, and serving girls. When I turned my gaze in the opposite direction, beyond the buildings I could see the green tops of the lime trees, and a little farther away a yellowish-brown column of smoke rising, on purpose it seemed, over where the fire had been.

At this moment I remembered the words of the organist, who had spoken of the necessity of shooting me in the head, and I drew the conclusion that if ever I was to meet a violent death, today would be the day. I had burned down the cattle shed and destroyed the key to the granary. My sister was crying, the entire servant body had gathered in front of the manor, so what else could all this mean? I quickly checked to see if the cook had his rifle, because it was his job to shoot rabbits and any domestic animals who fell incurably ill.

I was led to the countess herself. She looked at me with sorrowful eyes, while I, clasping my hands behind me (as I used to do automatically in the presence of my father), tipped my head back, because the countess was tall.

We looked at each other like this for a moment or two. The servants were silent, and there was a smell of burning in the air.

"I have the impression, Mr. Leśniewski, that this boy is of a somewhat lively disposition?" the countess asked my father in a melodious voice.

"The little scoundrel! Arsonist! He destroyed my granary key!" replied my father, then added quickly, "On your knees before the countess, you rascal!"

And he gave me a slight push forward.

"If you're going to kill me, then do it, but I'm not going down on my knees to anyone!" I answered, not taking my eyes off the countess, who had a curious effect on me.

"What! Lord Jesus . . . ," lamented Salusia, shocked, and folded her arms.

"Calm down, child, no one's going to hurt you," said the countess.

"Oh, sure! No one! As if I didn't know that you're going to shoot me in the head. I mean, that's what the organist promised me!" I retorted.

"What! Lord Jesus . . . ," cried the housekeeper again.

"He's brought shame on my old age!" said my father. "I'd skin him alive three times over and put salt on him if your ladyship hadn't taken him under her wing."

The cook, who was standing in the corner of the terrace, put his hand over his mouth and laughed till he turned blue. I couldn't take it anymore, and I stuck my tongue out at him.

A hum of amazement came from the servants, and my father, grabbing me by the arm, exclaimed, "What are you up to now? Poking your tongue out at her ladyship?"

"I was poking my tongue out at the cook, because he thought he was going to shoot me like an old nag."

The countess became even more sorrowful. She brushed the hair back from my forehead, looked deep into my eyes, and said to my father, "Who knows, Mr. Leśniewski, where life will lead this boy?"

"To the gallows!" my worried father said bluntly.

"Who knows?" replied the lady, smoothing down my tousled hair. "He ought to be sent to school, he'll go wild here."

Then, as she was leaving to go into the drawing room, she murmured, "There's material there for a decent person, Mr. Leśniewski. He just needs to be taught."

"It will be as you wish, your ladyship!" replied my father, thumping me on the back of the neck.

Everyone left the terrace, but I remained there, motionless as a stone, staring at the door through which the lady of the manor had disappeared. It was only then that I thought ruefully: Why hadn't I fallen on my knees before her? And I felt a choking sensation in my chest. If she had so commanded, I would willingly have laid down in the smoldering remains of the cattle shed and roasted myself slowly for her. Not because she hadn't had me shot by the cook or beaten, but because she had such a sweet voice and such a melancholy gaze.

From that day on I had less freedom. The countess had no desire to see the rest of her buildings go up in flames, my father resented not being able to settle up with me over the burnt-down cattle shed, and I myself had to prepare for school. The organist and the distillery owner took turns at teaching me. It was even suggested that the governess from the manor would instruct me in some subjects. But when that lady, upon making my acquaintance, observed that my pockets were full of knives, stones, shot, and caps, she grew so afraid that she refused to see me again.

"I don't give lessons to such bandits," she told my sister.

Yet I had in fact grown considerably more serious in that time. Just once I thought about hanging myself, as an experiment. But then something else came up, so I didn't do myself any harm.

Finally, at the beginning of August, I was driven to school.

I passed the entrance examination with flying colors, thanks to letters of recommendation from the countess, after which my father found me lodgings with a family, including private lessons and every convenience for two hundred zlotys and five bushels in kind annually. Then he bought me a school uniform.

I was so taken by the new outfit that I couldn't get enough of it during the day, so I got up quietly in the middle of the night, and in the dark I donned the frock coat with the red collar and the cap with the red stripe, and I thought I'd sit like that for a few minutes. But the night was rainy, there was a slight draft from the door, and apart from the frock coat and cap I was in my nightclothes. As a result I drifted off and slept till morning in my uniform.

This way of spending the night was a great source of amusement to my roommates, but it made the landlord of the lodgings suspicious that he might have a terrible rascal on his hands. He hurried off as fast as he could to the inn where my father was staying and told him that he wouldn't have me in his lodging house for all the tea in China – unless perhaps my father threw in another five bushels of potatoes a year. After some hard bargaining, they settled on three bushels, but my father bid me farewell in such a demonstrative fashion that I didn't mind that he left, and I didn't miss home, where I could expect such displays more frequently.

There were no memorable incidents in my first-form education. Today, looking back on those days from the historical distance that everyone knows is essential if one is to form an objective judgment, I can see that in its general outline my life changed but little. At school I spent somewhat more time indoors, whereas at home I had run about outside rather more. I had exchanged everyday clothes for a school uniform, and the people who were at work on the harmonious development of my physical and spiritual properties used a birch instead of a scourge.

And that was all.

As is common knowledge, school, because of its communal nature, prepares boys for life in society and teaches them skills they would not have learned had they been brought up alone. I discovered this truth a week after I first entered the school, when I learned the art of applying "cheese-presses," which require the collaboration of three people at least and therefore cannot exist outside of society.

It was only now that I discovered within myself the true talent that prevented me from getting stuck in theory and propelled me toward collective action. I was one of the foremost players of bat and ball; I was captain in our battles; I organized extracurricular excursions called "rides"; I led the class in mass foot-stampings or belchings, which all sixty of us occasionally indulged in for relaxation. But when I found myself alone in the face of grammatical rules, exceptions, declensions, and conjugations, which of course constitute the foundation of philosophical thought, I would rapidly sense an emptiness in my soul, from the depths of which would emerge sleepiness.

If, with my gift for not learning, I answered in class without too much hesitation, it was only thanks to my good eyesight, which permitted me to read from a book two or three desks away. Occasionally I would answer something completely different from what had been asked, but at these times I had recourse to the classic excuse in such situations: I would say that I had misheard the question, or that I "got nervous."

Generally speaking, I was a pupil of the future: not just because I incurred the displeasure of the older teachers who were set in their ways and was liked by the younger ones, but also because good marks in certain subjects, and with them hope of advancing to the next class, I saw only in my dreams, which extended far beyond the present.

My relations with the masters were mixed.

The Latin teacher gave me fairly good marks, because I tried hard at gym, which he also taught. The priest who taught religion didn't give me any marks at all, because I was forever belaboring him with troublesome questions, to which his only response was: "Into the corner, Leśniewski!" The master who taught art and penmanship supported me as an artist but condemned me as a calligrapher; yet, since to his mind the art of handwriting was the most important subject in school, after debating with himself, he came down on the side of calligraphy and gave me E's and the occasional D.

I had a good grasp of arithmetic, because those classes were based on the object-lesson principle: you got your hand smacked for not paying attention. The Polish teacher foresaw a great future for me, since once, on the occasion of his name day, I succeeded in writing him a poem in praise of his strictness. Finally, my marks in other subjects depended on whether my neighbors whispered the right answers to me, or whether the book on the desk in front of me was open to the right page.

My most familiar relationship, however, was with the deputy head. This gentleman had grown so used to my being summoned from class during lessons, and to seeing me after school, that he was genuinely concerned if during a particular week he was not reminded of my existence.

"Leśniewski!" he called one day, seeing that I was on my way home after classes. "Leśniewski! Why aren't you staying behind?"

"But I haven't done anything," I replied.

"What do you mean – you don't have detention?"

"I swear to God I don't!"

"And you answered everything correctly?"

"Nobody called on me to answer today!"

The deputy head thought for a moment.

"There's something amiss here," he murmured. "You know what, Leśniewski, stay here for a while."

"Please, sir, I haven't done anything wrong! I swear by my father! I swear to God!"

"Aha, so you're swearing, are you, you little oaf? Come here this minute! And if you really haven't been up to anything, this'll count toward the next time!"

Generally speaking, I had unlimited credit with the deputy, which won me a certain popularity in the school, the more so because no one else felt like competing with me.

Among the several dozen first-formers – one of whom was already shaving with a real razor, while three others spent the entire day playing cards under the desk, and the rest were as fit as fiddles – there was a cripple by the name of Józio. He was a hunchback, much too small for his age, sickly looking, with a small bluish nose, pale eyes, and lank hair. He was so frail that he had to take a rest on his way to school in the morning, and so timid that when he was called on in class to answer he grew speechless with fright. He never fought with anyone and asked others not to fight with him. When someone once jumped on his arm, which was thin as a rake, he fainted, but when he came to he didn't tell.

Both his parents were alive, but his father had thrown his mother out of the house and had kept Józio at home with him, wishing to supervise his education. He intended to take his son to school himself, to go on walks with him and coach him, but he did nothing, out of lack of time, which passed uncommonly quickly in the purchase of spirits and oat beer at Moszka Lipa's pub.

In this manner Józio was not looked after by anyone, and I sometimes used to think that even God in His heaven looked down unfavorably on such a puny little fellow.

In fact, Józio had his own money, six or ten groszes a day. He was supposed to use it to buy himself a couple of rolls and some smoked sausage during the break. But because everyone bullied him, he wished to try and protect himself at least a little, and he would buy five rolls and give them to his strongest classmates, so they would treat him kindly.

These dues were of little help, because beside the five allies stood three times as many implacable enemies. They bullied him ceaselessly. One of them pinched him, another pulled his hair, a third jabbed him, a fourth gave him a clip on the ear, and the least bold called him a hunchback.

Józio just smiled at these friendly jokes. Sometimes he said, "Leave me alone," and sometimes he said nothing, but just leaned on his thin arms and cried.

Then his friends called out, "Look, his hump is shaking!" and bullied him even more relentlessly.

To begin with, I didn't pay much attention to this hunchback, who didn't strike me as being all that interesting a character. But one day the big boy who shaved with a razor sat on Józio and set about boxing his ears. Józio was howling, while the class rocked with laughter. At this moment something tugged at my heart. I grabbed hold of an open penknife, and jabbed it into the hand of the lout who was hitting Józio, up to the bone, shouting that I'd do the same to anyone else who laid a finger on him. Blood gushed from the bully's hand; he turned as white as a sheet and looked as if he were about to pass out. The entire class suddenly stopped laughing and then began to shout: "Serves him right, he shouldn't be bullying a cripple!" At this point the teacher came in, and learning that I had stabbed my classmate with a knife, he was about to summon the deputy head with the usher and the birch. But everyone pleaded for me, even the injured bully himself, so the bully and I shook hands, then the bully and Józio, then Józio and I – and I got off scot-free.

I noticed that through the entire lesson Józio kept turning to me and smiling, probably because throughout that time he wasn't hit once. No one bothered him during the break either, while several boys declared that they would protect him. He thanked them, but came running to me to give me a roll with butter. I wouldn't accept it. He became somewhat embarrassed, and then said quietly, "You know, Leśniewski, I'll tell you a secret."

"Out with it, then," I replied, "but be quick about it."

Józio was disconcerted, but then he asked, "Do you have a friend already?"

"What would I need a friend for?"

"Well, you know, if you want, I could be your friend."

I looked down on him. He grew even more uncomfortable and

asked in a high-pitched, muffled voice, "Why don't you want me to be your friend?"

"Because I won't have anything to do with losers like you!" I answered.

Józio's nose turned bluer than usual. He was on the point of walking away when he turned to me again and said, "Maybe you'd like me to sit next to you? You know, I always pay attention to what the teachers ask. I could do the exercises for you. I'm good at whispering answers."

This struck me as being a serious point. After giving it some thought, I let Józio sit by me, and my previous neighbor agreed, for the price of five rolls, to give up his place.

That same afternoon Józio moved next to me. He was my most devoted helper, confidant, and admirer. He chose words for the exercises and did all my translations, he wrote down the examples given, and he carried my inkpot, pens, and pencils as well as his own. And how he knew how to whisper answers! During my time at school many boys had whispered answers to me, and some had even been sent to the corner for it; but none of them could hold a candle to Józio. He was a master of the art. He was able to speak through clenched teeth, and as he did so he would assume such an innocent expression that not one of the teachers suspected a thing.

Whenever I was given detention, Józio secretly smuggled me bread and meat from his own lunch. And when I got into bigger trouble, Józio, tears in his eyes, assured our classmates that I wouldn't take it lying down.

"Ha!" he would say. "Kazio's strong. He'll grab the usher by the arms and hurl him to the ground like a feather. Don't you worry!"

And indeed, my classmates were not worried in the slightest. Poor Józio did the worrying for both of us.

When he didn't need to pay attention in a particular class, he would compliment me. "Heavens! I wish I were as strong as you! Heavens! I wish I were as clever. You know what, if you wanted to, within a month you could be top of the class."

One day, out of the blue, the German teacher called me to the front. A terrified Józio barely had time to whisper to me that all feminine nouns, for example, *die Frau*, "the lady," belong to the fourth declension.

I marched out and declared confidently that all feminine nouns, for example, *die Frau*, "the lady," belong to the fourth declension. But here my knowledge ended.

The teacher looked me in the eye, nodded his head, and told me to translate. I read the German text through once fluently and loudly; then again, even more fluently; but when I began to read the same passage for a third time, the teacher told me to return to my desk.

As I walked back, I noticed that Józio was watching the teacher's pencil intently, and that he had a troubled look.

I asked him automatically, "Do you know what mark he gave me?"

"I would have given you an A," said Józio. "Well, a B at any rate . . . "

"But what did *he* give me?" I asked.

"I think it was an E . . . But he's an idiot, what does he know!" replied Józio with profound conviction.

Despite his frailty, he was a bright and hardworking lad. I used to read adventure stories in class, and he would listen to the lecture and afterward explain things to me.

Once I asked him, "What did our zoology teacher talk about this time?"

"You know," said Józio with a mysterious look, "he said that plants are just like animals."

"He must be stupid," I replied.

"But he's right," said Józio. "I kind of understand what he meant."

I started to laugh and said, "If you're so smart, tell me: How is a willow tree like a cow?"

The boy thought a moment, and began slowly, "Well, a cow grows, and a willow tree also grows."

"And what else?"

"Well, a cow feeds, and a willow feeds on juices from the soil."

"What else?"

"A cow is feminine gender in Polish, and so is a willow tree," explained Józio.

"But a cow flicks its tail!" I told him.

"And a willow waves its branches!" he retorted.

This series of arguments shook my faith in the difference between animals and plants. The idea itself appealed to me, and from this moment I developed an interest in zoology as summarized in Pisulewski's book. Thanks to Józio's explanations, I began to get A's in that subject.

One day Józio didn't come to school, and the following morning I was told that "someone wanted to see me." I ran out into the corridor, a little apprehensive as usual on such occasions, but instead of the deputy head, I found a burly man with a crimson face, purple nose, and red eyes.

The stranger said in a rather hoarse voice, "Are you Leśniewski, boy?"

"I am."

He shifted weight from one leg to the other, as if swaying, and went on, "Come and visit my son Józio, the hunchback, you know? He's sick. He kind of got run over the other day."

He swayed once again, looked at me distractedly, and left, his footsteps thudding on the floor. I felt as if someone had thrown hot water over me. I thought that I should have been the one to be run over, not that poor Józio, who was so good and so frail . . .

In the afternoon we had a break. I didn't go home to eat lunch but ran straight to Józio's.

He and his father lived on the outskirts of town in two rooms of a single-story building. When I entered, I found Józio lying on a short cot. He was all alone, without anyone. He was breathing with difficulty and shaking from the cold, because the stove had not been lit. His pupils were so dilated that his eyes were almost black. It was damp in the room, and drops of melted snow fell from the roof.

I leaned over his bed and asked, "What's wrong with you, Józio?"

He stirred and opened his mouth as if to smile, but only moaned. He took me by the hand with his own thin little hands, and spoke.

"I think I'm going to die . . . But I'm afraid . . . on my own . . . so I asked you to come. It'll . . . you know . . . not be long, and I'll be a little more at ease."

Józio had never shown himself to me as he did that day. It seemed that the cripple was growing into a giant.

He began to moan softly and coughed till a pink foam appeared on his lips. Then he closed his eyes, breathing heavily, and at times not breathing at all. If I hadn't felt the pressure of his burning hands, I would have thought that he was dead.

We sat like this for one hour, two, three, in silence. I had virtually lost the power of thought. Józio spoke infrequently and with great difficulty. He told me that a carriage had run him over from behind, that the small of his back had caused him terrible pain, though it had stopped hurting now, that his father had thrown their servant out the day before, and that today he had gone to look for a replacement.

Then, without letting go of my hand, he asked me to recite all my prayers. I did so, but as I began, "When the sunrise starts the day," he interrupted me.

"Say 'All our daily affairs' again," he said. "I don't think I'll wake up tomorrow."

The sun went down and a gray night set in, for the moon was shining through the clouds. There was no candle in the house, and besides, I had no thought of lighting one. Józio was increasingly restless; he was delirious, and only from time to time did he become lucid again.

It was late when the gate of the building rattled noisily. Someone crossed the courtyard and, whistling, opened the door of the flat.

"Is that you, Daddy?" moaned Józio.

"It's me, son!" answered the newcomer hoarsely. "How are you? I expect you're better! That's how things should be! Keep your pecker up!"

"Daddy, it's dark," said Józio.

"Who needs light! Who's this?" he exclaimed, bumping into me.

"It's me," I replied.

"Aha! Mrs. Łukaszowa? Good! Get some sleep tonight, and tomorrow I'll buy you some snares. I'm the governor! Jamaica rum!"

"Good-night, Daddy! Good-night!" whispered Józio.

"Good-night, good-night, son!" answered the newcomer, and leaning over the bed, kissed me on the head.

I sensed that he had a bottle under his arm.

"Get a good night's sleep," he added, "then it's off to school with you tomorrow! Left-right-left! Jamaica rum!" he exclaimed, and went into the other room.

There he sat down heavily, on a trunk by the sound of it, knocked his head against the wall, and a moment later there came a steady gurgling noise, as if someone were drinking.

"Kazio," whispered the sick boy, "when I'm . . . over there, come and visit me sometimes. You can tell me what the lessons were about . . . "

From the other room the newcomer roared, "To the health of the governor! Hurrah! Me, the governor! Jamaica rum!"

Józio started to shiver and began speaking ever more agitatedly.

"It aches so much! Are you sitting on me, Kazio? Kazio! Stop hitting me, boys!"

"Jamaica rum!" came the cry from the other room. There was another gurgle, and then the bottle fell to the floor with a terrible clatter.

Józio pulled my hand to his mouth, took my fingers between his teeth, and then suddenly let go. He had stopped breathing.

"Sir!" I called. "Sir! Józio's dead!"

"What are you talking about?" muttered a voice from the other room.

I jumped up from the bed and stood in the doorway, looking into the darkness.

"Józio's dead!" I repeated, trembling all over.

The man bounced up and down on the trunk and shouted, "Get out of here, you clown! I'm his father, I know whether he's dead or not! Long live the governor! Jamaica rum!"

I panicked and ran away.

I was unable to sleep properly all night long. I shivered and was tormented by terrible nightmares. In the morning the landlord of our lodging house looked me over and declared that I had a fever, that I'd probably caught it from Józio after his accident, and ordered them to set a dozen cupping glasses on my lower back. After this treatment my illness, as the landlord said, came on so strong that I had to stay in bed for a whole week.

I didn't go to Józio's funeral, which was attended by our whole class with the teachers and the priest who taught catechism. I was told that Józio had a black velvet-lined casket hardly bigger than a violin case.

His father wept bitterly, and at the cemetery he seized hold of the casket and wanted to follow it. Despite this, they buried Józio, and his father was led from the cemetery by a police officer and a constable.

When I first returned to school, I was told that someone had been asking for me every day. And indeed I was called out.

I stepped out of the classroom. Outside was Józio's father. His face was pale purple and his nose gray. He was stone cold sober, though his head and hands were shaking.

He took me by the chin and stared for a long time into my eyes, then said all of a sudden, "You stood up for Józio when the other boys were bullying him?"

Has the old man gone mad? I wondered, but I didn't answer.

With both hands he took hold of me by my neck and kissed me several times on the head, whispering, "May God bless you. May God bless you!"

He let go of my head and asked again, "You were there when he died? Tell me the truth, did he suffer a lot?"

Then he drew back and said quickly, "No . . . don't say a word! Oh, no one knows how unhappy I am!"

He began to cry. He seized his head in his hands, turned from me, and ran toward the stairs, exclaiming, "Pity me! Pity me, pity me . . . "

He was shouting so loudly that some of the teachers came out of their rooms into the corridor. They watched him go, shook their heads, and told me to go back to my own classroom.

That evening a messenger came to the lodging house with a large trunk for me, along with a card that said simply: "From poor Józio: a memento."

In the trunk was a host of splendid books that had belonged to Józio, including *The Book of the World*, Cesare Cantú's *Universal History*, *Don Quixote*, *The Dresden Gallery*, and many others. These books stirred in me a passionate desire to do some reading of a more serious nature.

It was almost springtime when I first went to visit Józio's grave. It was as small and as crooked as he himself had been. I noticed that someone had decorated it with fresh sprays. A few yards away, in the grass, I found several bottles labeled Jamaica Rum. I stayed there for an hour or so, but I didn't tell Józio what the classes had been about, because I didn't know, and he didn't ask.

A week later I went back to the cemetery. Once again I saw fresh sprays laid on Józio's grave, and once again I found a number of whole and broken bottles.

At the beginning of May some dramatic news spread around town. One morning, by Józio's grave, they had found the dead body of his father. To the side lay a half-empty bottle with a label saying Jamaica Rum.

The doctors said he had died of an aneurism.

These events had a curious effect on me. From this time on, I found the company of my classmates tiresome, and I was bored by their noisy games. I buried myself in the books that Józio had left me, or I fled the town and went wandering through ravines overgrown with bushes, thinking about goodness knows what. At times I asked myself why Józio had come to such a sorry end, and why his father had been so forlorn that he'd had to cling to his son's grave. I felt that the greatest misfortune was loneliness, and I understood why the poor boy had wanted a friend.

Now I needed a friend, too. But I somehow didn't like the look of any of my classmates. I thought about my sister. No! A sister can't take the place of a friend.

My classmates told me that I'd gone wild, and the landlord of the lodging house was by now totally convinced that I'd turn into a major criminal.

The formal certificate arrived in which the deputy head declared to the whole world that I had been promoted to the second form. This event filled me with a joyful surprise. I suddenly began to believe that although there were many higher forms in the school, none was as excellent as the second. I assured my friends that boys in all the other forms, from the third to the seventh, do nothing but go back over what they learned in the second. But in my soul I was afraid that after the holidays the teachers would suddenly realize that it was only by accident I had been promoted and would put me back into the first form.

The very next day, though, I came to terms with my good fortune, and as I traveled back home for the holidays, the whole way I kept explaining to the driver that I was the only one in my class who had deserved to be promoted, and that my promotion had been the most outstanding one. I produced such convincing arguments that he began to yawn. Yet when I fell silent, I was frightened to realize that I myself was filled with doubts.

The next day, as I drew close to home, I met my sister Zosia on the way; she had run out to meet me. I lost no time in telling her that I was already in the second form, and that my friend Józio had died because he'd been run over. She, on the other hand, informed me that she had missed me, that her chicken had had ten chicks, that there was a gentleman who visited the countess twice a week, that they had a governess who was in love with the bookkeeper, and that she, Zosia, couldn't care less about Józio because he'd been a hunchback, though she was sorry he'd died.

She said this with the air of a grown-up young lady.

I saw my father that afternoon. He greeted me warmly, and told me that for the holidays he'd give me a horse and let me use the big pistol. Then he added, "You hurry on up to the manor and pay your respects to the countess. Although . . . "

At this point he waved his hand dismissively.

"What is it, Father?" I asked, like an adult, and took fright at my own boldness.

Unexpectedly, my father replied without anger, but with a touch of bitterness, "She has no use anymore for an old plenipotentiary.

Before long there'll be a new master here, and he'll be able to manage on his own."

He broke off, and, turning away, muttered through his teeth, "Losing your fortune at cards . . . "

I began to realize that during my absence there had been great changes here. In any case, I went to pay my regards to the countess. She greeted me graciously, while I noticed that her sorrowful eyes had taken on an entirely different expression.

On the way back, I met my father in the courtyard, and said that I'd never seen the countess looking so happy. She had been dancing about, clapping her hands, just like one of her chambermaids.

"Bah! Any woman's going to be in a good mood before her wedding," my father said as if to himself.

At this moment, a small cariole pulled up in front of the manor, and out jumped a tall man with a black beard and flaming eyes. It seemed that the countess had run out onto the veranda, because through the door I could see her stretching out both arms to him.

My father walked ahead of me, laughing quietly and muttering, "Ha, ha! All the women have gone crazy! The lady's fallen for a dandy, and the governess for a bookkeeper. Salusia has to choose between me or the priest . . . Ha, ha!"

I was twelve, and I'd already heard a great deal about love. My classmate, the one who shaved and who had spent three years in the first form, sometimes told us about his feelings for a certain young lady whom he saw several times a day on the street or from his window. I myself had read a number of magnificent romantic novels, and I remember well how I suffered on behalf of their heroes.

For this reason, my father's allusions left an unpleasant taste in my mouth. I felt sorry for the countess, and even for the governess, and hostile toward the man with the beard and the bookkeeper. I would never have said it out loud, and would not have had the courage even to think it explicitly, but it seemed to me that both the countess and the governess would have done much better to fall for me.

In the course of the next few days, I ran the length and breadth of the village, the park, and the stables; I went horse riding and rowing; but I realized I was starting to get bored. True, my father often now spoke to me as to a grown-up, the distillery owner invited me over for a glass of mature rye vodka, and the bookkeeper sought out my friendship and even promised to recount to me his sufferings at the hands of the governess; but none of this interested me. I would gladly have exchanged both the distillery owner's vodka and the bookkeeper's confessions for a single good friend. But when I mentally reviewed those who had finished first form with me, I saw that none of them matched up to my present state of mind.

Sometimes, from the depths of my soul, the sorrowful spirit of my dead friend Józio would come to me and speak of mysterious things in a voice quieter than the breath of a summer's wind. At such moments I was seized with a kind of melancholy, and I yearned, though for what I didn't know. One day, when, under the influence of such phantasms, I was wandering along the overgrown paths in the park, my sister Zosia suddenly stood in my way and asked, "So why is it you don't play with us?"

I flushed.

"With who?"

"Me and Lonia."

It will remain an eternal mystery to me why at this moment I associated Lonia's name with Józio's ghost and why I blushed so deeply that my face burned and beads of sweat appeared on my forehead.

"What is it? Don't you want to play with us?" asked my sister in surprise. "During Easter there was a third-former here, and he wasn't a bit standoffish like you. He played with us all day long."

Now, for no reason at all, I hated that third-former, whom I had never met. Finally, I replied rudely, though in my heart I didn't bear Zosia any ill will, "I don't know Lonia."

"What do you mean you don't know her? Don't you remember how you got a hiding from the last governess because of her? Have you forgotten that Lonia cried for you and begged them not to do anything to you when you burned down that, that cattle shed?"

Of course I remembered everything, most of all Lonia herself. I have to confess, though, that Zosia's total recall irritated me. It seemed a matter unworthy of my school uniform that people in the country, and especially adolescent girls, should have such good memories.

Under the influence of these feelings, I replied brusquely, "Leave me alone, you and that Lonia of yours."

And I went off to the far end of the park, annoyed both by my sister's inopportune reminiscences and by the fact that I wasn't playing with the girls. I don't even know myself what I wanted, but I was so angry that when Zosia and I met up at home I wouldn't talk to her.

My sister was upset and tried to keep out of my way, but then I went looking for her, sensing that I was missing something, that I'd handled the matter of playing together altogether wrongly. In order to rectify the situation, when Zosia, who was still upset, sat down to do some darning, I grabbed the nearest book to hand and, after flipping the pages for a few minutes, tossed it down on the table and said as if to myself, "All girls are stupid!"

I thought this aphorism would be very clever, but the moment I had uttered it, I felt there was something distasteful about it. I felt sorry for my sister, and ashamed. Without saying any more, I kissed Zosia on both cheeks and went off to the woods.

Oh, how miserable I was that day. And that was only the start of my sufferings.

I don't wish to conceal anything. I dreamed of Lonia all night long, and from that time on instead of poor Józio it was her spirit that haunted me. I felt that she was the only one who could be the friend I had needed for so long. In my daydreams I talked to her as long and as eloquently as in the romantic novels, and I was as courteous as a certain viscount. In reality I couldn't even bring myself to go to the park when the girls were playing there; from behind the fence I listened to their happy laughter, mingled with the admonitions of the governess.

I well remember that place, where the refuse from the manor was thrown out and where there grew nettles and burdocks. I stood there an hour or more just in order to catch a few indistinct phrases and the crunch of little shoes on the path, and to see Lonia's dress flash by as she played skipping games.

A moment later everything fell silent in the park, and then I felt the burning heat of the sun, and heard the endless buzzing of the flies over the rubbish heap. Then the sounds of laughter and running reached me again, dresses flashed past the hole in the fence; and once more there was only the rustle of the trees and the chirping of the birds, the heat, and the pesky flies, which all but flew into my mouth.

Suddenly there was a shout from the manor.

"Lonia! Zosia! Come to the drawing room."

It was the governess. I would have hated her if I hadn't known that she, too, had her sorrows.

During one of my trips to the fence I noticed that I was not alone. From the mound I could see in a green clump of burdock a straw hat that had turned gray with age, through the missing crown of which could be seen a mop of bright flaxen hair.

When I took a few steps in their direction, the hair and the hat rose above the burdock and there appeared a boy of seven or eight in a long, dirty shirt tied at the neck with string. I spoke to him, but he jumped up and ran away with the speed of a hare toward the fields. The red collar of my uniform and the silver buttons generally made a strong impression on the village children.

I went off slowly toward the farm, and as I did the boy moved closer to the fence. When I disappeared behind the building, he climbed onto the rubbish heap and put his eye to the same hole through which I had been peeping into the garden. I doubt very much whether he could actually see anything, but he kept looking.

When I arrived at my post the following day to observe the young ladies, I noticed once again the gray hat in the burdock with the shock of flaxen hair on top, and beneath the torn brim a pair of eyes staring at me. The sun was scorching, so the boy quietly tore off a large leaf and shaded himself with it as if it were a parasol. Now I could no longer see either his hat or his hair, just the dirty shirt open on his chest.

When I left, he ran onto the rubbish heap again and, like the day before, he pressed his eye to the hole, no doubt thinking that perhaps this time I had missed some of the interesting things to be found in the park.

It was at this moment that I realized how ridiculous my actions were. I'd have been in a fine mess if my father, or the distillery owner, or even Lonia herself had seen me, a second-form pupil, in my school uniform, standing by a fence on a rubbish heap and taking turns with some would-be shepherd boy who may never in his life have worn a clean shirt.

A feeling of shame came over me. Did I not have the right to go openly into the park, without skulking in the bushes like the kid with the battered hat?

I was disgusted by the rubbish heap and the hole in the fence, but at the same time my curiosity was piqued. Who was this boy? Children of his age were already tending geese, while he was wasting the best years of his childhood roaming around outside the farm spying on other people's business, and when he was spoken to, instead of answering politely, he ran like a rabbit from the newcomer.

You just wait, I thought to myself, you won't see me around here any longer, but I'll find out what manner of child you are!

I remembered that in those romantic novels, alongside the heroes and heroines, there were also mysterious strangers with whom you have to be on your guard in order to foil their schemes in time.

Within a few days, without asking anybody, I knew everything about the mysterious stranger. He was no schemer. His name was Walek, and he was the son of the scullery maid at the manor. Everyone knew him and no one took care of him. For this reason the boy had a great deal of free time and, as I had learned firsthand, he made use of it in ways that were not always pleasant for others.

Walek had never had a father, a fact everyone exploited to nettle his mother, a rather hotheaded woman. She responded to the other servants' gibes with shouts and abuse, and, as this was clearly not enough, she took the rest out on Walek.

When the boy was still crawling around on all fours, his shirt tied up in a knot around his neck (which created the impression that he had no shirt at all), people were already calling him a foundling.

"Was it you who found him?" his mother would retort, and then would shout, "I hope God punishes you for the wrong done to me! I hope he cuts off your arms and legs! I wish you were dead, you little sod!"

This last desideratum was addressed to Walek, who immediately thereupon received a kick below the knot in his shirt. While he was still young and foolish, the child would respond to this treatment by bursting into tears. But when he grew cleverer, which happened fairly quickly, he would stay as quiet as a mouse, and would go and hide under the couch, behind the basin that was used to feed the pigs. Apparently he had no desire to get soaked in scalding water, as had happened to him once before.

Sometimes Walek would even stay under the couch for hours on end, until everyone began to gather for dinner or supper. Occasionally, seeing the child's head sticking out from under the couch, his eyes shining with tears from his recent hurt and also with curiosity about the dumplings being served, the farmhands would ask his mother, "Aren't you going to feed the kid you found in the potato patch?"

"You and him can both eat dirt!" answered his mother irritably, and though she had previously intended to give Walek something to eat, now she changed her mind.

"You can't let the lad starve to death, even if he is a foundling," the other women argued.

"Well, starve he will, just to spite you all for poking your noses in!"

And since she was sitting facing away from the couch, Walek got a heel in the mouth.

Then, out of spite for his mother, the farmhands pulled the boy out and fed him.

"Right, Walek," said one, "you can have some dumplings if you kiss the dog on the backside."

The boy executed this command promptly, and then swallowed the big dumplings without even chewing them.

"Now smack your mother in the head and you can have some milk."

"I hope your arms wither up and drop off!" cried the scullery maid, and Walek was off behind the basin.

Sometimes, breathless and trembling, he would fly out into the courtyard and hide in the thick bushes across from the manor. And when his tears had dried, he would look over and see on the veranda a beautiful little table with two chairs, on which sat Lonia and my sister, while the chambermaid tied napkins under their chins, Salusia poured them some soup, and the countess said, "Blow on it, children, so you don't burn your tongues. Is it sweet enough?"

Since the farmhands had gone back to work and there was no one else in the kitchen, the scullery maid came outside and shouted, "Walek! Get yourself in here."

From the way she called, Walek knew it was safe to come out, and he ran off toward the kitchen. There his mother gave him a hunk of bread, a wooden spoon, and some borscht in a huge bowl that could have served six people. He sat on the ground; his mother propped the bowl between his feet and, straightening the shirt on his back, said, "If you kiss the dog on the backside again, I'll beat you black and blue. You mark my words!"

Then she went off to wash the pots.

Suddenly, out of the blue, the farmyard dog appeared and sat opposite the boy. To begin with he snapped his teeth at flies, yawned, and licked himself. Then he sniffed the borscht once, sniffed it again, and carefully poked his tongue into it. Walek bashed him over the head with the spoon. The dog retreated, yawned again, and lapped up some more soup, this time more boldly. After that, the boy could knock him on the head with the spoon as much as he liked, because once the dog's appetite had been whetted he wouldn't have taken his muzzle out of the bowl to save his life. But Walek had also come to the conclusion that the winner would be the one who ate the most, so he ate from one side of the bowl till he was gasping for breath, and the dog lapped away from the other.

When his mother was in a good mood, and Walek was around, he would get tidbits from the gentlefolk's table.

"There you go, you'll like this," the scullery maid would say, giving him some cake crumbs, a plate covered with sauce, a fish head, a wing that hadn't been touched, or a beaker at the bottom of which were a few drops of coffee and undissolved sugar. When he'd sucked everything out of the beaker or licked the plate clean, his mother would ask, "Well, was it good?"

Walek would put his hands on his sides, like the farmhands used to do after lunch, give a profound sigh, and, tipping his old hat back, would reply, "I'm fit to burst, thank the Lord! Well, back to work."

He would leave the kitchen and go off somewhere for half the day.

His games were based on what the grown-ups were doing. At ploughing time he would take a little horsewhip from behind the trough, grab any old picket from the fence or the root of a fallen tree, and would plough for hours on end, of course swaying all the while and calling, "Whoa! Gee up! Gee up!"

When they went fishing, Walek would look for a broken strainer in the rubbish, and would keep dipping it into the water with unflagging patience. Another time he would mount a stick and go and water his horses at the well. Once, by the sheepfold, he found an old pair of bast slippers; he threw them upon the water and went rowing, in his mind's eye of course.

In a word, he played some wonderful games, but he never laughed. His face had assumed a permanently serious expression, which was replaced only occasionally by fear. In his eyes there resided eternal astonishment, as with people who over many years have witnessed extraordinary things.

Walek was clever when it came to disappearing from the house for days on end. The farmhands were never surprised if one morning they found him in a haystack or beneath a tree in the woods. He was also able to stand in the middle of a field for a long time without moving, like a gray post, staring at some unknown thing with his eyes wide open. I once came upon him in this position, and as I was quite close I heard him sigh. I don't know why, but a sigh from such a slight figure terrified me. I felt angry, I don't know who at, and at that moment I began to like Walek. But when I took a few steps toward him more openly, he came to and scuttled off into the bushes with an amazing nimbleness.

At this moment I had the curious idea that God, who looks down always on this child, must have a heavy heart. And I understood why in religious paintings He is always serious, and why in church you have to talk quietly and walk on tiptoe.

This unprepossessing little person caused me to stop skulking around behind the fence and to set off for the park, having first announced to Zosia that from now on I would play with her and Lonia.

Naturally my sister was delighted with this plan.

"Be in the park," she said, "when the two of us go out for a walk. And say hello to the governess, too. She reads books in the summerhouse. But don't talk to her for too long, because she doesn't like to be disturbed. And then you'll see what fun we'll have!"

The same day, at lunch, she said to me with a mysterious expression, "Come at three o'clock. I've already told Lonia you'll be there. When we come out of the manor I'll give a cough."

My sister took up some needlework, while I, of course, went outside, because I never liked to take up space indoors. When I had reached the courtyard, Zosia ran out after me.

"Kazio! Kazio!"

"What is it?"

"When I cough, you'll know what it means?" she said solemnly.

"Sure."

She went back inside, but she called to me again from the window: "I'll give a cough. Don't forget!"

And where was I to go but to the park, though there was still an hour and a half before the time we were supposed to meet. I was so deep in thought that I have no idea whether on that day there were any birds singing in the park, which was usually so full of life. I circled it a couple of times, then I sat in a rowboat that was moored at the bank, and, unable to go rowing, I rocked the boat out of boredom instead.

I was working on my plan to renew my acquaintance with Lonia.

It was to happen as follows. When Zosia coughed, I would emerge from a side path with my eyes down and join the main avenue. Then Zosia would say, "Look, Lonia, it's my brother, Master Kazimierz Leśniewski, a second-form pupil, friend of that poor Józio whom I have told you so much about."

Then Lonia would curtsy, and I would doff my cap and say, "I've been meaning for some time . . . " No, that won't do! "For some time now I've wanted to renew my . . . " No! This is better: "For some time now I've been wanting to pay you my respects, ma'am."

Lonia would then ask, "Have you been here long, sir?" No, no, she wouldn't say that, but: "Pleased to meet you, sir. I've heard so much about you from Zosia." And then what? Then this: "Are you not bored here? You've grown accustomed to the city." And I would reply: "I was bored before I had your company."

At this point, beneath the surface of the water, there appeared a pike that must have been two feet long. In the face of this reality, my daydreams disappeared. There were fish like that in the pond, and I didn't even have a rod!

I leaped out of the boat, meaning to see if I could find a hook at home, and I almost bumped into Lonia, who was just about to start skipping with a red skipping rope.

The fish, the hook, the plan to initiate a formal acquaintance – everything became muddled up in my head. There was a pike! I even forgot to bow to Lonia, and, worse, I forgot to say anything. But that was some pike!

Lonia, who was a pretty girl with auburn hair and an expressive mouth that kept changing its shape, looked down at me and, tossing back her luxurious curls, asked without any introduction, "Is it true that you put a hole in our boat, young man?"

"Me?"

"That's what the gardener told me, and now Mama won't let us go out in it, and she's ordered that the boat be tied up at the side of the pond and the oars put away."

"I swear on my father's name that I didn't put a hole in your boat!"

I was making excuses as if I were talking to the deputy head.

"Are you quite sure?" asked Lonia, staring keenly into my eyes. "It's quite your style, young man."

I didn't like her tone. Damn it! The strongest of my classmates would never have spoken to me like that.

"When I say I *didn't*, then it means I'm *absolutely sure*," I replied, placing heavy emphasis on the important words.

"In that case the gardener told a lie," said Lonia, frowning.

"He did the right thing," I retorted, "because young ladies don't know how to row."

"And you do, young man?"

"I can row and I can swim, including backstroke and doggy paddle."

"Will you row us?"

"If your Mama allows it, I will."

"Then go and see whether there's a hole in the boat."

"There isn't."

"So how did the water get in?"

"From the rain."

"From the rain?"

The conversation broke off. Yet I had succeeded in looking boldly at Lonia, while she, as far as I remember today, did nothing to me. Indeed, without moving from where she was, she began to skip, talking to me in the pauses.

"Why didn't you play with us, young man?"

"I was busy."

"What on earth do you have to do?"

"I have to study."

"No one studies during the holidays."

"In our class you have to study even through the holidays."

Lonia skipped over the rope twice and said, "Adaś is in the fourth form, and he didn't study at Christmas. Oh, I forgot, you don't know Adaś."

"Who told you that I don't know him?" I asked proudly.

"Well, you were in the first form, and he was in the third."

Two more skips over the rope . . . I thought something extraordinary was about to happen to me.

"I had friends from the fourth form," I said, irritated.

"It makes no difference, because Adaś goes to school in Warsaw, while you . . . Where is it you go to school?"

"In Siedlce," I barely got out, my voice hollow.

"I'm going to be going to Warsaw, too," declared Lonia, and added, "Perhaps you could tell Zosia that I'm here already, young man."

And, without waiting for me to agree or refuse, she ran off toward the summerhouse, skipping all the while.

I was stupefied. I couldn't get over the way she had treated me.

To hell with your games, I thought, genuinely angry. Lonia is a rude, inconsiderate . . . she's a brat!

These remarks, however, didn't prevent me from carrying out her command at once. I went back to the house quickly, maybe even too quickly, no doubt because I was so upset.

Zosia was just taking her parasol to go down to the garden.

"Guess what," I said, flinging my cap in the corner, "I've just met Lonia."

"And?" my sister asked curiously.

"Nothing . . . Just that!" I answered, avoiding her gaze.

"Isn't it true that she's so nice, so pretty?"

"Oh, I couldn't give a hoot about that. Oh yes, she asked you to go down there."

"Are you coming too?"

"No."

"Why not?" asked Zosia, looking into my eyes.

"Leave me alone!" I snapped. "I'm not going because I don't feel like it."

There must have been something very categorical in my voice, because my sister left without asking any further questions. Seeing that she was virtually running, I called to her from the window, "Zosia, please, just don't say anything. Say that I . . . say I have a bit of a headache."

"It's all right, don't worry. I won't say anything against you."

"Remember, Zosia, if you love me even a little."

Naturally, we hugged and kissed warmly.

Today it's hard for me to recapture the feelings that gripped me after Zosia left. How could that Lonia dare talk to me in such a way? True, the teachers, especially the deputy head, treated me somewhat unceremoniously, but they were grown-ups. Among my classmates in the first form (now the second), I enjoyed respect. And here in the country – look how my father talked to me, how the farmhands bowed to me, how often the bookkeeper said to me, "My dear Kazimierz, sir, would you care to drop in and smoke a pipe with me?" And I would answer, "Thank you, but I'd rather not grow accustomed to it." And he, "You're a lucky man to have such self-control, my good sir. You wouldn't let yourself be swept away by a governess . . . "

In response to the way the older people treated me, I acted seriously too. The parish priest himself said to my father, "You see, Mr. Leśniewski, my good fellow, what school can do for a lad. A year ago this Kazio was a rogue and a scapegrace. Now, my good sir, he's a regular statesman, a Metternich . . . "

This was what people thought of me. And it took an accident for some slip of a girl who'd never even set foot in a school to have the temerity to tell me that "it's quite your style, young man." Young man? And she's quite the mature lady! Just because she knows some Adaś, she puts on airs. Who's Adaś? He's finished third form, and I'm starting second form. Big difference! If he's stupid, I'll catch up to him and even pass him. And to top it all, she sends me off to fetch Zosia as if I were her flunky. Let's see if I do what you tell me to next time! I swear to God that if she ever tries anything like that again, I'll simply put my hands in my pockets and say: "I don't think you should be taking that tone with me!" Or even better: "My dear Lonia, I see you could use some lessons in politeness." Or even: "My dear Lonia, if you want me to spend time with you . . ."

I could feel the right reply wasn't coming to me, and that irritated me more and more. Even my expression must have changed, because our housekeeper, old Mrs. Wojciechowa, twice came into the room looking at me out of the corner of her eye, until in the end she said, "My goodness, what's got into you, Master Kazio? Have you been up to some mischief, or is it something to do with your father?"

"There's nothing wrong with me."

"I can see that. You won't keep any secrets from me. If you've got yourself into trouble, go to your father and get it off your chest right away."

"I haven't done anything. I'm just a bit tired, that's all."

"If you're tired, then take a rest and have something to eat. I'll get you a slice of bread and honey."

She left, and a moment later came back with a huge slice of bread dripping with honey.

"I'm not going to eat anything. Let me be!"

"Why shouldn't you eat? Here, take this quickly, the honey's dripping onto my fingers. You'll feel better once you've had a bite. People always fret when they're hungry, but as soon as they have something to eat, they're able to think straight. Here, take it!"

I had to take the bread, worried that she'd drip honey on my hair or my uniform. I ate automatically, and I did in fact start to feel more cheerful. I decided that I'd be able to handle Lonia and that I ought to give Walek some of this, because he probably doesn't get to eat honey that often, and besides, I'd come to like him.

At my request Mrs. Wojciechowa, seeing the wonderful effects of her medicine, made me an even bigger slice of bread spread liberally with honey. I took it carefully and went out to look for the kid.

I found him not far from the kitchen. Two farmhands who had just brought some timber from the woods were talking to him and laughing.

"If your mother beats you again," one of them was saying, "you should just up and leave. Will you do that?"

"I dunno how," answered Walek.

"Tie your shoes to a stick, and off you go to the woods and beyond. There's a whole world out there."

"But I ain't got no shoes."

"Then just take a stick. You'll get by with a stick and no shoes."

Seeing me, Walek ran away toward the burdock bushes.

"What were you talking to him like that for?" I asked the farmhands.

"Nothing, we're just having a bit of a laugh with him. He's such an idiot."

Seeing that the honey was starting to run over my fingers, I abandoned my conversation with them and went after Walek. He was standing among the weeds and looking at me.

"Walek!" I called. "Here's some bread and honey for you."

He didn't budge.

"Come here now." I took a few steps forward.

He began to run away.

"You're so daft. Here's your bread, I'm putting it down right here."

I put the bread down on a stone and walked away. But it was only when I disappeared around the corner of the kitchen that Walek approached the stone, looked the bread over cautiously, and finally ate it, with great relish as far as I could tell.

An hour later, as I was on my way to the woods, I noticed that the lad was pattering along behind me at a certain distance. I stopped, and he also came to a halt. When I turned back to go home, he jumped to the side and hid in the bushes. But a short while later he was trailing after me again.

That day I gave him some more bread. He took it from my hand, though he was still timid, and ran off at once. Nevertheless, from that day on he began to follow me, always at a certain distance.

From early morning he would be hanging around outside our windows like a bird to whom a friendly hand throws grain. In the evening he would sit by the kitchen and gaze up at our house. Only when the lights went out would he go to sleep on a sheet behind the stove, with the crickets chirping over his head.

A few days after my first meeting with Lonia, I yielded to Zosia's entreaties and went to the park with her.

"You know," my sister assured me, "Lonia was quite taken with you. She keeps talking about you. She was vexed that you didn't come back that time, and she's been asking when you'll join us."

It was hardly surprising, then, that I gave in, the more so because I myself was somehow drawn to Lonia. It seemed to me that I would get over the melancholy I had felt after the death of Józio only when Lonia and I would walk out arm in arm and have serious conversations. What about? That I do not know to this day. I sensed only that I wanted to speak long and eloquently, and to have Lonia as my only listener.

At the thought of the two of us walking out together something sounded in my heart like a harp and glittered like sunlight on drops of dew. But reality doesn't always match up to one's dreams. When, brought by my sister, I met Lonia again, I spoke to her with the intention of initiating those ideal conversations.

"Do you like to fish?"

At this point the girls grasped each other by the hand, whispered, and ran along the avenue laughing hysterically. I was stunned, and turned in my fingers the fishing rod, the making of which had almost cost me a kick from the gray horse when I pulled a hairworm from her tail.

Just as I was about to leave, offended, the girls came back, and Zosia said, "Lonia asks if she can be on first-name terms with you."

I bowed and out of a sense of confusion said nothing, and they burst out laughing again and ran off toward the pond.

"You know, young man . . . ," began Lonia, but corrected herself at once. "You know, Zosia, Mama definitely won't let us go out in the boat. I told her your brother would take us out, but Mama . . . "

She whispered at length in Zosia's ear, but I guessed right away what it was about. Her Mama was probably worried that I would drown the girls, me, the strong swimmer and second-former!

I was embarrassed. Lonia noticed and suddenly said, "Young man, why don't you . . . "

Once again she corrected herself.

"Zosia, ask your brother to pick us some water lilies. They're so pretty, and I've never had one in my hand."

I was inspired. Now, finally I could show what I was capable of.

There were a lot of lilies growing on the pond, only not by the bank but farther out. I broke off a stick and stepped into the rocking boat.

Lilies have springy stalks. When I hooked them with the stick, they came closer, but then floated away again. I broke off a longer pole with a sort of hook at the end. This time I had better luck. I got a good grip on a lily and pulled it close . . . I stretched out my left hand, but it was still too far away. I knelt in the prow of the boat,

leaned out, and was just about to break off the flower when suddenly I fell full length in the water, the pole slipped out of my hand,
and the lily floated away again.

The girls began to scream. I called, "It's nothing! nothing! The
pond's shallow here." I poured the water out of my cap, put it on
my head, and, wading up to my waist in the pond and up to my
knees in mud, I broke off one lily, a second, a third, a fourth.

"Kazio! For the love of God, come out of there!" my sister called
tearfully.

"That's enough, that's enough now!" Lonia chimed in.

I paid no heed to them. I picked a fifth, a six, a tenth lily, then
some leaves.

I came out of the pond soaked from head to foot, my legs and
sleeves covered in mud. On the bank Zosia was crying, Lonia would-
n't accept the flowers, and behind them, yellow with fright, Walek
was hiding.

I could see that Lonia also had tears in her eyes, but suddenly she
started to laugh.

"See how he looks, Zosia!"

"Lord! What will Papa say?" exclaimed Zosia. "Kazio, wash your
face at least, you're all dirty."

Without thinking I touched my nose with a muddy hand. Lonia
laughed so hard she fell on the grass. Zosia laughed too, wiping her
eyes, and even Walek opened his mouth and emitted a bleating noise.

Now the girls noticed him.

"What's that?" asked Zosia. "Where did he come from?"

"He followed your brother," answered Lonia. "I saw him creep-
ing through the bushes."

"Lord! Look at his hat! What does he want from you, Kazio?"
asked my sister.

"He's been following me around for the last few days."

"Aha! Kazio was probably playing with him when he wouldn't go with us," Lonia put in derisively. "Look at the two of them, Zosia. One sopping with water, the other unwashed. How funny!"

I didn't like being compared to Walek one bit.

"Come on, Kazio, get washed and go home to change, and in the meantime we'll go to the summerhouse," said Zosia, picking up Lonia, who was almost having spasms from an excess of merriment.

They went off. I was left with Walek and, on the grass, a handful of lilies that no one had picked up.

"That's the reward for my sacrifice?" I thought bitterly, tasting mud in my mouth. I took my cap off. It was in a terrible state. It looked like a rag, and the peak was coming away in one place. Streams of water were pouring off my uniform, my waistcoat, and my shirt. My shoes were so full that they squelched when I moved. On me I could feel the cloth turning to wool, the wool to leather, and the leather to wood. And from the summerhouse I could hear Lonia's laughter as she told the governess about my accident.

They would be back in a minute. I tried to wash, but I ran off without finishing. They were coming! I could see their dresses on the avenue, I could hear the governess's fussing. They cut off my way back home, so I turned in another direction, toward the fence.

"Where is he, then?" asked the governess shrilly.

"There he is, there! The two of them are running away," replied Lonia.

Now I saw that Walek was at my heels. I reached the fence, and he was right behind me. I climbed up, so did he. And just when the two of us were sitting facing each other astride the fence as if we were on horseback, Lonia, Zosia, and the governess appeared in the bushes.

"Oh, and with that friend of his!" laughed Lonia.

I jumped down from the fence and rushed across the field toward my house. Walek kept up with me. He was plainly enjoying the chase, because his mouth was open and he was making the bleating noise that was meant to indicate pleasure.

I pulled up short, furious.

"Look, kid, what do you want from me? Why do you keep trailing around after me?" I said to the boy.

Walek was stunned.

"Get away from me, get away!" I said, clenching my fists. "You've embarrassed me, they're all laughing at me. If you cross my path again I'll do you in!"

After I said this I walked away, and the boy was left behind. When I had taken a dozen steps or so I turned around and saw him in the same position. He was looking at me and crying loudly.

I rushed into our kitchen like a phantom, and wherever I walked I left a stream of water. When they saw me the chickens took fright and made for the windows with a squawking and a flapping of wings. The maids started to laugh, and Mrs. Wojciechowa clapped her hands in astonishment.

"The word become flesh! What happened to you?" the old woman exclaimed.

"Can't you see? I fell in the pond, that's all! Just get me some clothes, some shoes and a shirt, Mrs. Wojciechowa. But hurry."

"That Kazio won't give me a moment's peace!" replied Mrs. Wojciechowa. "I don't think your other coat has the buttons sewn on yet. Kaśka, off you go and look for some shoes!"

She started to undo my uniform and take it off, helped by the other maid. It came off in the end, but the shoes were more of a problem. Neither of them would budge an inch. In the end they got the stableboy to help. I had to lie down on the couch, Mrs. Wojciechowa and the maids held me under my arms, and the stableboy began tugging at my shoes. I thought he'd pull my feet off. But in half an hour I was like a doll, all wiped clean, changed, my hair combed. Zosia ran in and sewed the buttons onto my linen suit. Mrs. Wojciechowa wrung out my wet clothing and hung it up to dry in the attic, and that was the end of it.

Nevertheless, my father, when he came home, already knew the whole story. He looked at me mockingly, shook his head, and said, "You silly ass! Now go and ask Lonia for some new trousers."

Before long the distillery owner appeared. He also looked me over and had a laugh, but I overheard him saying to my father in his office, "He's a lively lad! He'd do anything for the girls. Like us in our younger days, Mr. Leśniewski."

I realized that the whole farm must know about what I had done for Lonia, and I was terribly embarrassed.

In the evening the countess, Lonia, and her governess came to visit, and each of them, unbelievably, wore a water lily on her dress. I wished the earth would swallow me up. I wanted to run away, but I was called upon, and I stood before the ladies.

I noticed that the governess was looking at me with a benevolent expression, while the countess stroked my red face and gave me some sweets.

"Little boy," she said, "it's wonderful that you're so gallant, but please, don't ever take the girls out in the boat. All right?"

I kissed her hand and murmured something.

"And don't go out in it yourself either. Do you promise me?"

"I promise."

Then she turned to the governess and said something in French. I heard the word *herro* repeated several times. Unfortunately, my father heard it, too, and put in, "Oh, you're right there, your ladyship. He's a Herod, a real Herod!"

The ladies smiled, and after they left Zosia tried to explain to father that *herro* was spelled *héros,* and in French it didn't mean Herod but hero.

"Hero?" repeated my father. "He's such a hero that he got his school uniform wet and tore his trousers and it'll cost me two hundred zlotys to get Szulim to do the repairs. To hell with the kind of heroism that other people have to pay for!"

I was truly hurt by my father's prosaic attitude. But I thanked God that nothing went any further.

From then on I spent time with Lonia not only in the park but also in the manor. I had lunch there a few times, a source of great discomfort to me, and almost every day I had tea, at which they served coffee, or wild strawberries, or raspberries with sugar and cream.

I often talked with the grown-up ladies. The countess was surprised at how well-read I was, something for which I was indebted to Józio's library, while the governess, Miss Klementyna, thought the world of me. This last-mentioned admiration I owed not so much to my own erudition as to conversations about the bookkeeper: I knew where he worked and what he thought about Miss Klementyna. Eventually that wise person confessed to me that she had no intention of marrying the bookkeeper but only sought to improve him in a moral sense. She declared to me that in her view the role of women in the world was to improve men and that I myself, when I grew up, would have to find a woman who would improve me.

I liked these lectures a lot. And I was ever more eager in bringing Miss Klementyna news of the bookkeeper, and the bookkeeper news of Miss Klementyna, for which I gained the goodwill of both.

From what I remember today, life in the manor had its own character. The countess's fiancé called to see her every few days, several times a day Miss Klementyna visited those parts of the park from which she could see the bookkeeper, or at least, as she put it, hear the tones of his voice, probably as he was swearing at the farmhands. For her own part, one of the ladies' maids wept at a series of windows for the same bookkeeper, while the other maids, following their superiors, divided their affections between the butler, the downstairs kitchen boy, the cook, the cook's boy, and the coachman. Even old Salusia's heart was not free. It belonged to the turkeys, geese, ducks, cockerels, and other feathered companions of various shapes and hues among whom the housekeeper spent her days.

It went without saying that in such a busy environment time was unconstrained for us children. We played from dawn till dusk, and only saw the grown-ups when we were called in to dinner, to supper, or for bedtime.

Thanks to this freedom, my relationship with Lonia developed in a rather unusual fashion. She called me Master Kazio for a few days, then plain Kazio, and she ordered me around and even shouted at me, while I continued to call her miss, spoke less and less, and obeyed her more and more. Sometimes within me there stirred the pride of a person who in a year's time may enter the third form. At such times I cursed the moment when I first followed her orders and went to fetch my sister when she told me to. I said to myself, "What does she think, that I work for her like my father works for her mother?"

In this way I incited myself to rebellion and declared that things had to change. But at the sight of Lonia my courage would abandon me, and even if some were left, Lonia would issue her commands so impatiently, would stamp her foot so, that I had to obey every time. And when I caught a sparrow one time and wouldn't give her it at once, she cried, "Not if you don't want to, then! I don't need your sparrow."

She was so deeply offended and so curious that I began to beg her to accept the sparrow. She would not have it! I scarcely managed to persuade her to take it, of course with Zosia's help, and even so for several days I had to listen to her grumblings.

"I would never in the world have insulted you like that. I can see now just how constant you are! The first day you jump into the water to pick lilies for me, and yesterday you wouldn't even let me play with a little bird for a while. Now I see it all . . . No other boy would have treated me that way."

And when, after endless explanations, I finally asked her not to be angry with me at least, she retorted, "Me, angry? You of all people should know that I'm not angry at you. I was just hurt. But just how hurt I was no one else can even imagine. Ask Zosia how hurt I was."

Then Zosia put on a solemn expression and explained to me that Lonia was deeply, deeply hurt.

"Besides, Lonia herself will tell you how hurt she was," my beloved sister concluded.

Driven from pillar to post in search of a more accurate description of how hurt Lonia had been, I felt my head starting to spin.

I became a machine with which the young ladies did absolutely anything they fancied, because the slightest sign of assertiveness on my part was hurtful either to Lonia or to Zosia, both of whom felt the other's hurt like it was their own.

If poor Józio had risen from the grave, he would not have recognized me in that meek, obedient, browbeaten young man who was constantly fetching something, carrying something, looking for something, who knew nothing about something, or couldn't handle something, and was rebuked every few minutes. And if my classmates had seen me!

One day Miss Klementyna was busier than usual. The bookkeeper had some work to oversee at the stables, a few dozen yards from her beloved summerhouse. Taking advantage of the situation, the three of us slipped away to the park, to the bushes where the blackberries grew.

There were untold numbers of them there. There was a bush at every step, and on each bush a mass of berries black and big as plums. To begin with we picked them together, exchanging exclamations of wonder and delight. After a short while, however, we fell silent and each of us went our own way. I don't know about the girls, but for myself, submerged in the thickest patches, I forgot about the world altogether. What wonderful blackberries they were! These days you won't find even pineapples like that.

Tired of standing, I sat down; tired of sitting, I lay on the bushes as on a padded armchair. It was so warm there, so soft and comfortable, that from somewhere the thought came to me that it must have been like this for Adam in paradise. Lord! Lord! Why was I not Adam? The fruit on the accursed tree would still be growing there to this day, because I couldn't even have been bothered to raise my hand above my head . . .

Stretching out like a snake in the warm sunlight, on the yielding bushes, I felt an indescribable happiness, mostly because I was able not to think at all. From time to time I turned over onto my back, my head hanging below the level of my body. Fanned by the wind, leaves were stroking my face; I looked at the immense sky and, with a sense of unfathomable contentment, I imagined to myself that I was not even there. Lonia, Zosia, the park, dinner, and finally school and the deputy head seemed to me a dream I had had that had passed, maybe a hundred years ago, maybe a thousand. Poor Józio probably experienced such feelings constantly in heaven. How lucky he was!

Eventually I'd even had enough of the blackberries. I could feel the bushes bearing me up gently, I could see each and every little cloud drifting slowly across the azure sky, I could hear the rustle of every single leaf – but for myself, I was thinking about nothing.

Suddenly, something woke me. I leaped to my feet without knowing what was going on. For a split second it was quiet as before, then all at once I heard Lonia crying and calling, "Zosia! Miss Klementyna! Help!"

There is something terrible in a child's cry for help. The word "viper" flashed into my mind. The blackthorn dragged at my clothing, wrapped around my legs, tugged at me, pulled me away; no, it was wrestling with me, fighting me like a living monster, and all the while Lonia was shouting, "Help! Oh my Lord!" and I knew only one thing, as clear as daylight: that I must come to her aid or perish myself.

Exhausted, covered in scratches, and most of all scared to death, I finally fought my way through to where I could hear Lonia's crying.

She was sitting by a bush, trembling and wringing her hands.

"Lonia! What is it?" I cried, using her name for the first time.

"A wasp! A wasp!"

"A wasp?" I repeated, running up to her. "Did it sting you?"

"Not yet, but . . . "

"So what's the . . . "

"It's crawling on me . . . "

"Where?"

The tears fell profusely. She was terribly embarrassed, but fear got the better of her.

"It's crawled into my stocking. Oh Lord. Oh Lord, Zosia!"

I knelt before her, but I didn't yet have the courage to look for the wasp.

"Take it out," I said.

"I'm scared to. Oh Lord!"

She was trembling as if she had a fever. I took a firm grip on myself.

"Where is it?"

"It's on my knee."

"It's not on this one or on that one."

"It's higher up now. Oh, Zosia, Zosia!"

"It's not here either."

Lonia covered her face with her hands.

"It must have gone inside my dress," she said, crying ever more bitterly.

"Here it is!" I exclaimed. "It's a fly."

"Where? A fly?" asked Lonia. "So it is! What a big one. I was sure it was a wasp. I thought I'd die. Goodness! How silly I am."

She wiped her eyes and at once began to laugh.

"Shall I kill it or let it go?" I asked Lonia, showing her the wretched insect.

"Whatever you wish," she said, by now entirely calm.

I was going to kill the fly, but I didn't have the heart. And since both it and its wings had gotten a little crumpled, I put it down carefully on a leaf.

In the meantime, Lonia was staring at me most intently.

"What's wrong?" she asked suddenly.

"Nothing," I answered, attempting to laugh.

I could feel my strength ebbing away rapidly. My heart was clanging like a bell, my eyes clouded over, I broke out in a cold sweat over my whole body, and I swayed on my knees.

"What's wrong, Kazio?"

"Nothing . . . I just thought something awful had happened to you."

If Lonia hadn't grabbed hold of me and laid my head on her knees, I would have broken my nose falling to the ground.

A wave of heat rose to my head. I heard a buzzing in my ears, and Lonia's voice again: "Kazio! Kazio, my dear Kazio . . . What's wrong? Zosia! Oh Lord, he's passed out. What shall I do? Now I'm in a jam!"

She put both her arms around my head and started to kiss me. I could feel her tears on my face. I felt so sorry for her that I summoned all the strength I had left and with great difficulty pulled myself up.

"I'm all right! Don't worry!" my voice came from deep within me.

And in fact, my momentary weakness passed as quickly as it had come. The buzzing in my ears stopped, my eyesight cleared, and I sat up from Lonia's lap, looked into her eyes, and laughed.

Now she began to laugh, too.

"Oh, you bad, naughty boy!" she said. "You caused me such a

fright. How could you have fainted for such a silly reason? I mean, even if it had been a wasp, it wouldn't have eaten me. And what would I have done with you here? There's no water, no one around, Zosia's disappeared somewhere, and I'd have to rescue a big lad like you. You should be ashamed of yourself!"

Of course I was ashamed. What was I thinking of, frightening her like that?

"How are you feeling?" asked Lonia. "Oh, I'm sure you're all right now, you're no longer so pale. You were as white as a sheet before.

"Well," she added a moment later, "I'm certainly going to get into trouble when Mama finds out about this! Oh Lord! I'm afraid even to go home."

"When your Mama finds out about what?" I asked.

"About everything, worst of all the wasp."

"Then don't tell anyone."

"What good would that do?" she asked, turning away.

"Do you think I'd tell?" I replied. "I swear on my father's name that I won't breathe a word to anyone."

"What about Zosia? She can keep a secret."

"I won't tell Zosia. I won't tell anyone."

"Even so, everyone will find out. You're all scratched, your clothes are torn. Wait a minute!" she added after a moment, and wiped my face with her handkerchief. "Lord, you know I even kissed you out of fright, I just didn't know what to do. If anyone found out I'd die of embarrassment, though that wasp really was a problem. Goodness, what troubles I have because of you . . . "

"You've no cause to be worried," I assured her.

"Sure I haven't! It'll all come out, because your hair is full of leaves. Wait a minute, I'll comb it for you. I just hope Zosia's not watching from behind some bush. She can keep a secret, but there's always . . . "

Lonia took a semicircular comb from her own hair and started to comb mine.

"Your hair is always so messy," she said. "You should keep it combed like gentlemen always do. Like that! Part it on the right, not on the left. If your hair was black you'd be as handsome as my Mama's fiancé. But since it's blond, I'll comb it differently. Now you'll look like one of the angels beneath the Madonna. You know the one I mean. Pity I don't have a mirror."

"Kazio! Lonia!" called Zosia at this moment, from the direction of the park.

We both started, and Lonia genuinely took fright.

"It'll all come out!" she said. "Oh, that wasp! And the worst of it was that you fainted . . . "

"Nothing'll come out!" I retorted vigorously. "I won't say a thing."

"Neither will I. You won't even say that you fainted?"

"Of course not."

"Well!" said Lonia admiringly. "Because if it had been me that fainted, I wouldn't be able to help myself . . . "

"Kazio! Lonia!" called my sister, who was now only a few yards away.

"Kazio!" whispered Lonia, placing a finger on my mouth.

"Don't you worry!"

The bushes rustled, and Zosia emerged, wearing an apron.

"Where've you been, Zosia?" we both asked her.

"I went to get an apron for myself and for you, Lonia. Here, these blackberries stain."

"Are we going home straight away?"

"There's no point," answered Zosia. "The gentleman's visiting your Mama, and Miss Klementyna wouldn't dream of leaving the summerhouse. We can sit here till evening if we want. But I'm going to pick some blackberries, because you two have had more of them to eat than I have."

They both began picking berries, and I had also somehow regained my appetite.

Seeing that I was moving away, Lonia called after me, "Kazio, I haven't forgotten!"

And she wagged her finger at me.

At this point, for the umpteenth time I swore to myself that I wouldn't tell a soul either about my fainting fit or about the fly. But I'd scarcely gotten more than a few yards away when I heard Lonia's voice.

"Zosia, you'll never guess what happened here! But no, I can't say a word about it to you. Though if you swear to me that you can keep a secret . . . "

I slipped off as far away as I could into the bushes, feeling ashamed. Even Zosia . . .

We spent another hour among those fateful blackberries. As we headed home, I noticed a significant change in the situation. Zosia was looking at me with horror and curiosity, Lonia wasn't looking at me at all, and I felt as guilty as if I'd committed a murder.

When Lonia bid us good-night, she kissed Zosia affectionately and nodded to me. I took my cap off to her, thinking that I was a fearful good-for-nothing.

After Lonia had left, Zosia turned on me.

"I've heard some things today!" she said solemnly.

"What have I done?" I asked, seriously worried.

"What do you mean, what! First of all you fainted (Lord, and I wasn't there to see it), then that wasp or fly . . . Awful . . . Poor Lonia! I would have died of embarrassment."

"But how was it my fault?" I made so bold as to ask.

"Kazio," she replied, "you don't need to make excuses to me, I'm not accusing you of anything, but all the same . . . "

"All the same" – that was my answer! From that "all the same" it transpired that I was the only one to blame in the whole incident. Not the fly, not Lonia, who had been shouting her head off, but me, because I had come running to the rescue.

Well, yes, but what had I fainted for?

I was inconsolable. The next day I didn't even go to the park, wishing above all not to meet Lonia. The day after that she ordered me to come. When I went, she nodded at me from a distance and talked only with Zosia, from time to time giving me a proud, sad glance, as if I were a criminal.

There were moments when I really thought I had suffered an injustice. But I suppressed these suspicions, telling myself that I had indeed done a terrible thing. At that time I was still unaware that this method constitutes a characteristic feature of feminine logic.

Meanwhile, the girls were walking around the garden at a measured pace, not even thinking about playing skipping games, but just whispering to each other. Suddenly Lonia came to a stop and said in a mournful voice, "You know, Zosia, I could just fancy some blueberries. I can almost smell them . . . "

"I'll bring you some," I put in promptly. "I know a place in the woods where there are lots of them."

"Could you be bothered?" replied Lonia, throwing me a melancholy look.

"What does it matter? Let him go if he wants to," put in Zosia.

I set off, all the more quickly because I'd begun to feel stifled by all those wry faces in the garden. As I passed the kitchen I heard the young ladies laughing, and when I glanced casually over the fence, I noticed they were blithely skipping away. It was clearly only in my presence that they had been behaving so solemnly.

There was an infernal racket in the kitchen. Walek's mother was crying and cursing, and Salusia was shouting at her because Walek had broken a plate.

"I gave the bugger a plate to lick," the maid was lamenting, "and the so-and-so dropped it on the ground, then took off. If I don't kill him today, I think my arms and legs'll drop off . . . "

Then she exclaimed, "Walek! Get yourself in here right now, you little sod. I'll flay you alive if you don't come this second."

I felt sorry for the boy and wanted to smooth things over. It occurred to me, however, that I'd be able to do so just as easily when I came back from the woods, because Walek would probably only reappear in the kitchen at night, and so I went on my way.

The wood was about half an hour's walk from the farm, perhaps a little more. Oaks, pine trees, and hazels grew there, and there were more wild strawberries and blueberries than you could pick. At the edge of the wood the shepherds had thinned out the blueberries somewhat; further in there were more, in patches the size of a courtyard.

When I reached the place, I filled my cap and my handkerchief with berries, eating few myself because I was in a hurry. All the same, an hour or more went by before I set off back home, laden with my spoils. I didn't go straight back but went the long way around, as I felt like a walk through the woods.

When you walk toward the thick of the forest, the trees visibly move aside as if they were making room for you. But as you move forward, just try to turn around. They touch branches as if they were shaking hands, trunk draws closer to trunk until they even start to touch one another, and you won't even notice when there appears behind you a multicolored wall, dense and impenetrable . . .

At such times, it's the easiest thing in the world to get lost. Wherever you walk it looks the same; everywhere the trees part before you, then close up behind you. If you start to hurry, they hurry right behind you, anything just to cut off your return. If you stand still, they stand still too, and, tired, fan themselves with their branches. If you look to the left and right, searching for a path, you notice that some of the trees are hiding behind others, as if trying to make you believe there are fewer of them than you first thought.

The woods are a dangerous place! There, every bird watches where you're going, and every plant tries to trip you up, and when it can't, at the very least it rustles to let the others know where you are. It seems that the woods long for a human face so much that when they see one they use any stratagem to keep it there forever.

The sun was already dropping toward the horizon when I walked out into the open fields. A few hundred yards farther on I met Walek. He was walking quickly toward the woods, leaning on a tall stick.

"Where are you going?" I asked him.

He didn't run away from me. He stood and, indicating the woods with his yellowish little hand, he answered softly, "A long way away!"

"Night's coming, you should get back home."

"But my Mum's going to thrash me."

"Come with me, she won't thrash you."

"Yes she will!"

"Come on, you'll see that she won't do anything to you," I said, going up to him.

The boy took a step back, but didn't run away; he seemed to be wavering.

"Come along."

"I'm scared . . . "

Again I moved toward him, again he retreated. I grew impatient with this ragged kid wavering and retreating. Back there Lonia was waiting for the berries, and he was negotiating his return? I didn't have time for this.

I walked on quickly toward the farm. I had gone about halfway to the house when I turned and saw Walek on a knoll by the woods. He was standing with his stick in his hand staring at me. His dirty old shirt flapped in the wind, and in the rays of the setting sun his battered hat shone about his head like a fiery halo.

I felt somehow moved. I remembered how the farmhands had urged him to take his walking stick and see the world. Could it be . . . ? No, surely he wasn't that foolish. Besides, I didn't have time to go back to him, because the berries were getting squashed, and Lonia was waiting.

I ran into the house, meaning to empty the berries into a basket. I was met on the doorstep by Zosia in a flood of tears.

"What is it?"

"It's terrible," my sister whispered. "Everything's out. Daddy's lost his job with the countess . . . "

The berries spilled out from my cap and my handkerchief. I seized Zosia's hand.

"Zosia, what are you talking about? What's wrong with you?"

"It's true. Daddy no longer has a job. Lonia confided in the governess about the wasp, and the governess told the countess . . . When Daddy went to the manor, the countess told him to take you to Siedlce at once. But Daddy said we'd all leave together . . . "

She burst out crying again.

At this moment I saw my father in the courtyard. I ran to him and threw myself breathlessly on the ground before him.

"Father, I'm so sorry for what I did!" I whispered, hugging his knees.

My father picked me up, shook his head, and replied curtly, "Don't be silly, go home."

Then he said as if to himself, "There's another master here who's getting rid of us because he thinks that an old plenipotentiary won't let him gamble away the fortune of an orphan. And he's right!"

I guessed he was talking about the countess's fiancé. I began to feel better. I kissed my father's rough hand and said more boldly,

"You see, Father, we were picking blackberries. Lonia was stung by a wasp . . . "

"You're as daft as a wasp. If you didn't go hobnobbing with young ladies, you wouldn't have to be searching for wasps and ruining your trousers in the pond. Go home and don't cross the threshold again until they've all left."

"They're leaving?" I whispered barely audibly.

"They're going to Warsaw in a couple of days, and by the time they get back we'll be gone."

That evening was a sad one. There were delicious dumplings in milk for supper, but none of us ate. Zosia kept wiping her red eyes while I was laying desperate plans.

Before bedtime I crept into my sister's room.

"Zosia," I said to her decisively, "I . . . I have to marry Lonia!"

She looked at me, horrified.

"When?" she asked.

"It makes no difference."

"But right now the priest won't marry you, and then afterward she'll be in Warsaw and you'll be in Siedlce. Besides, what would Father say, or the countess?"

"I can see you're not prepared to help me," I replied, and left without kissing her good-night.

From that moment on I don't remember anything. Days and nights passed, and I stayed in my bed, by which sat either my sister or Mrs. Wojciechowa, or occasionally the doctor's assistant. I don't know if I overheard it or if I imagined that Lonia had already left and that Walek had disappeared. Once I even thought that I could see above me the tear-stained face of the scullery maid, who was sobbing and asking, "Master Leśniewski, you haven't seen Walek anywhere, have you?"

Me? Walek? I didn't understand a word of it. But later I imagined that I was picking blueberries in the wood and that Walek was peeping at me from behind every tree. I called him, but he ran away; I chased after him, but I couldn't catch him. The blackthorn was tugging at me and pulling me back, the blackberry bushes were tripping me up, the trees were dancing, and between the moss-covered trunks there flashed the boy's dirty old shirt.

Sometimes I dreamed that I myself was Walek, and other times that Walek, Lonia, and I were one person. At these times I could always see woods or dense bushes, someone was always calling for help, but I couldn't move.

It was terrible what I had to endure.

》 《

When I got up from my bed, the holidays were almost over and it was time to go to school. I spent a few more days at home, and it was not until the evening before I was to leave that I dragged myself out into the courtyard.

The blinds were down in the windows of the manor. So they really had left? I walked round to the kitchen, looking for Walek. He wasn't there. I asked some girl about him.

"Oh!" she replied. "Walek's gone, Master Leśniewski."

I was afraid to ask more. I went to the park.

Lord, how sad it was there. I wandered aimlessly along paths that were damp from the recent rain. The grass had yellowed, the pond was even more overgrown, and the boat was full of water. On the main avenue there were great big puddles in which the dusk was reflected. The earth was black, the trunks of the trees were black, their branches drooping and their leaves withered. Sorrow rent my soul and summoned forth one shade after another from its depths. Now Józio's, now Lonia's, now Walek's . . .

Then there came a gust of wind; the tops of the trees soughed and from the swinging branches there fell large drops like tears. Even

God could see that the trees were weeping. I don't know if they were crying because of me, or because of my friends, but for certain I wept with them.

It was dark when I left the park. In the kitchen the farmhands were eating their evening meal. By the obscure light that fell upon the earth from a bright band of clouds, I recognized the scullery maid. She was staring toward the woods and murmuring, "Walek! Walek! Come on home now. I've been sick with worry because of you, you naughty child . . . "

I ran off home as fast as I could, because I thought my heart would break.

## »»»» ««««
# The Fungi of This World

I once found myself in Puławy with a certain botanist. We sat on a bench by the Sybilla Museum, next to a huge boulder covered with mosses or fungi, which my learned companion had been studying for several years.

I asked him what he found so interesting in the irregular dark gray, silvery, green, yellow, or red patches.

He looked at me suspiciously, but then, realizing that he was dealing with a layman, he began to explain:

"The patches you see are not inanimate marks but groups of living beings. Invisible to the naked eye, they are born, they move in ways we cannot see, they marry, produce offspring, and finally they die.

"Even more noteworthy, they form, as it were, communities, which you can see here as these patches of various colors. They prepare the ground for future generations; they spread, colonize unoccupied territory, they even fight among themselves.

"That silvery patch the size of your hand: Two years ago it was no bigger than a four-grosz piece. That little off-white mark didn't even exist a year ago; it comes from the big patch that occupies the top of the boulder.

"As for these two, the yellow and the red, they are in conflict with each other. At one time the yellow covered a huge area, but its neighbor gradually ousted it and took its place. And look at the green one: Can you see how its gray neighbor is making inroads into it, how many dark gray strips, specks, and clusters can be seen against the green background?"

"It's rather like relations among human beings," I put in.

"Not so," replied the botanist. "These societies have no language, no arts, no consciousness, no emotions. In a word, they lack the souls and hearts that we humans possess. Here everything goes on blindly, mechanically, without sympathies or antipathies."

A few years later I found myself by the same boulder one night, and by the light of the moon I examined the changes that had taken place in the shapes and sizes of the various fungi.

Someone tapped me on the shoulder. It was my botanist friend. I offered him a seat, but he stood before me, blocking out the moonlight, and whispered something inaudible.

The museum, the bench, and the boulder disappeared. I sensed about me an indistinct brightness and a boundless void. When I turned to the side, I saw something like a globe from a geography class glistening with a faint light, as big as the boulder by which we had been standing a moment before.

The globe was turning slowly, revealing ever new places. Here was the continent of Asia with the little peninsula of Europe; here was Africa, the two Americas . . .

As I peered closer, on the inhabited continents I noticed the same patches, dark gray, off-white, yellow, and red, just like on the boulder. They were composed of a multitude of barely perceptible points, which seemed immobile but were in fact moving very slowly: In the course of an hour an individual point covered no more than a two-minute arc, and that not in a straight line but oscillating upon the axis of its own line of movement.

The points joined, separated, perished, made their appearance on the surface of the globe; yet all these events were unworthy of special attention. It was only the movement of whole patches that was significant, as they grew smaller or larger, appeared in new locations, penetrated each other, or drove each other out of positions occupied.

All the while the globe went on turning. I had the impression that it performed hundreds of thousands of rotations.

"Is this supposed to be the history of humankind?" I asked the botanist, who was standing beside me.

He nodded.

"Very well. But where are the arts, learning?"

He smiled ruefully.

"Where are consciousness, love, hatred, desire?"

"Ha, ha, ha!" he laughed softly.

"In a word, where are human souls and hearts?"

"Ha, ha, ha!"

His behavior filled me with indignation.

"Just who are you?" I asked.

At this moment I found myself back in the park next to the boulder, whose shapeless patches were bathed in moonlight.

My companion had vanished, but I had already recognized him by his mocking tone and his melancholy.

# Shadows

As the sun's brightness fades from the sky, twilight emerges from the earth. Twilight, the great army of the night with its thousands of columns and millions of soldiers. A mighty force, which since time immemorial has been doing battle with the light, fleeing each morning, victorious every evening; it holds sway from sunset to sunrise, and in the day, broken up, it conceals itself in hiding places, and waits.

It waits in the ravines of the mountains and the cellars of the city, in the depths of the forest and the bottom of dark lakes. It waits in hiding in the ancient caves of the earth, in mines, in ditches, in the corners of houses, and in cracks in the wall. Scattered and seemingly absent, it yet fills every crevice. It is there in every crease in the bark of a tree, and in folds of clothing. It lies under every least grain of sand, attaches itself to the finest piece of spider's silk, and waits. Flushed from one location, in an instant it moves somewhere new, exploiting every opportunity to return to the place from which it was expelled, to squeeze into unoccupied spots, and to flood the whole earth.

When the sun disappears, the army of night emerges from its refuges, silent and wary. It fills the corridors of houses, doorways, and poorly lit stairs; it crawls from beneath cupboards and tables into the middle of the room, gathering around the curtains; it passes through the skylights of basements and through windowpanes into the street, storming the walls and roofs in silence, and patiently lying in wait on the rooftops till the pink clouds in the west lose their color.

A moment later, there is a sudden explosion of darkness stretching from the earth to the sky. Animals take cover in their lairs, humans run for home; like a plant without water, life shrivels and begins to dry up. Colors and shapes melt into nothingness; and fear, deception, and vice take over the world.

At this moment, on the emptying streets of Warsaw, a strange human figure appears, bearing a small flame over his head. He scurries along the sidewalk as if he were being chased by the darkness. At each lamppost he pauses for a moment and, lighting a cheerful light, he disappears like a shadow.

This happens every day of the year. Whether spring is breathing across the land with the scent of flowers or whether a midsummer storm is gathering, whether the boisterous winds of autumn are blowing up clouds of dust in the streets or whether wintry snows are swirling in the air, as soon as evening comes, he runs about the streets with his flame, bringing light; then he vanishes like a shadow.

Where do you come from, and where do you hide, so that we do not know your face or hear your voice? Do you have a wife or a mother who awaits your return? Or children, who lean your lamp in the corner then clamber onto your lap and hug you? Do you have friends to share your joys and your troubles, or at least acquaintances with whom you can exchange commonplaces?

Do you even have a house where you can be found? Or a name you can be called by? Feelings and desires, which would make you a person like the rest of us? Or are you indeed a being without form, silent and intangible, appearing only at dusk, bringing light then vanishing like a shadow?

I was told that he was a real person, and I was even given his address. I went there, and asked the caretaker, "Does the man who lights the lamps in the streets live here?"

"He does."

"Whereabouts?"

"In that room over there."

The room was locked. I looked through the window, but all I could see was a couch against the wall and next to it a lantern on a long pole. The lamplighter was not in.

"Can you at least tell me what he looks like?"

"Hard to say," answered the caretaker with a shrug. "I don't know him all that well myself; he's never at home during the day."

Six months later I went back.

"I don't suppose the lamplighter is in today?"

"Oh," said the caretaker, "he's not in and he won't be. They buried him yesterday. He died."

The caretaker became pensive.

I asked about certain details and rode over to the cemetery.

"Gravedigger, show me where they buried the lamplighter yesterday."

"The lamplighter?" he repeated. "Who knows? We had thirty new arrivals yesterday."

"He was buried in the poorest part of the cemetery."

"Twenty-five of them were sent there."

"He was in an unpainted coffin."

"There were sixteen of them like that."

In this way I never got to know his face or his name, and I never even saw his grave. And after his death he became what he had been during his life: a being seen only at dusk, as mute and elusive as a shadow.

In the darkness of life, where humankind blunders about, unseeing and unhappy; where some crash into obstacles, others fall into the abyss, and no one is sure of the way; where people, hampered by superstition, are prey to accident, destitution, and hatred – in the unlit wilderness of life there are also lamplighters. Each of them carries a tiny flame over his head; each of them brings light along the way; each lives unknown, works unrecognized, and then vanishes like a shadow . . .

# In the Mountains

"My dear fellow," said a friend of mine, a real character, "my dear fellow, the homeopaths have a remarkable principle: 'Cure like with like.' Even allopaths cure smallpox with smallpox, and Pasteur has proposed treating rabies with rabies. But why bother with such examples? I'll tell you of a case I saw where a man was cured of imaginary fears by real-life peril."

After this introduction my friend lit a cigar and went on:

"I caught my first glimpse of the Alps twenty years ago, when I arrived in Thusis. A few days after my arrival I went off on a short walk with a group of companions. On that day, however, I had such a fright that I immediately left Thusis, and for many years afterward I couldn't even bear the sight of mountains.

"There were six of us on that trip: myself and one other Pole, a German, an Englishman, and two French ladies. We were all staying at the same hotel. We didn't take a guide with us as the Englishman knew the area well, and the peak we were to climb looked as visible and as accessible as that armchair there in the middle of the room. True, through the telescope I could see some furrows running vertically and horizontally across the mountainside, but as they looked no bigger than ditches, I thought nothing of it. I was even surprised that on such a short walk we were setting off from the hotel at nine in the morning; but, since I didn't want to let on that I knew nothing about mountain-climbing, I didn't say anything, and on the way I acted like a true mountaineer who has trod the Himalayas. This won the respect of the whole company, and the particular regard of the German.

"Of course, the feeling was mutual, for he was a most agreeable chap. However, he had one fault: He suffered from vertigo.

"We had great fun on the way. Everyone played about, even the Englishman; I was the only serious one, while at places where the path was steep the German would look behind him and quote passages from Virgil. He claimed it was the best method for distracting attention from something one doesn't want to look at.

"'So you feel dizzy even here?' I asked.

"'Yes,' he replied abruptly, 'but let's not talk about it, or I won't be able to take another step.'

"I fell silent, and my German companion began reciting Virgil louder and louder, glancing back ever more frequently. At one point he went so far as to grab my arm and whisper in my ear, 'Your calm is a source of courage for me. If you weren't here, I'd not budge another inch – or I'd break my neck.'

"I broke into a cold sweat, for my inner state was in complete contrast to my poor companion's image of me.

"Above all, I was concerned that although we had been walking for two hours, the mountain we were supposed to be climbing was no closer; the whole time it looked to be about a kilometer away. But my worries reached a new extreme when suddenly the mountain toward which we were headed vanished, and in its place I saw huge masses of earth and rocks, which began somewhere far down in the valley and seemed to stretch all the way up to the heavens.

"The slope we were ascending took the form of a gigantic flight of stairs, with each step a hundred feet or so in height. At the foot of one of these steps I thought that it would lead straight to the summit, but after we had been walking up it for a quarter of an hour I found that instead of being at the summit we were on another step, or in a small clearing beyond which was another step. And so on endlessly.

"In the meantime, the path grew wilder. The woods, grass, undergrowth, even the soil, all disappeared. We were crossing a layer of rocks that grew bigger and slippier under our feet. We were encircled by an ever thicker multitude of mountain peaks adorned with fluffy clouds, or by ravines breathing forth a bluish fog.

"At times the wrinkles in the mountain grew smooth; its great steps and terraces vanished, and in their place I could see a sloping wall which dropped off steeply all the way to a sapphire-colored forest that lay silently a kilometer below us. Once, when I forgot for a moment that I was in the mountains, I had the impression that I was standing on a plain that suddenly tilted under my feet; at one end it rose right into the sky, while the other end sloped away into the bowels of the earth. My head began to spin, and to prevent myself from stumbling I seized the arm of the German, who was walking in front of me. He quickened his step and we reached a place that was less steep.

"'Thank you,' he whispered, shaking my hand in gratitude. 'I feel better now. You saved my life.'

"I was flabbergasted. Meanwhile, ahead of us the ladies were smoothing their shawls and dresses, concerned about their appearance.

"'It's terribly hot!' said one.

"'This path is rather difficult!' complained the other.

"After a quarter of an hour along an easier stretch of path the slope we had been ascending came to an end. I saw that we were surrounded on all sides by mountaintops that were either bare or covered with snow, and that between them and us there was nothing, that is, nothing but air. For some unknown reason, at that moment I felt a sense of pride and delight at nothing in particular.

"'We have reached the summit,' said the Englishman. He bowed to the ladies and lit a cigar.

"'What a beautiful view!' they both exclaimed.

"They took mirrors from their handbags and began straightening their somewhat disheveled hair.

"'Two o'clock!' remarked my compatriot in Polish. 'No damned lunch today. We might even end up missing dinner.'

"The German, meanwhile, had sat himself on the ground, and, his head lowered, was declaiming Virgil.

"'Can you see Thusis?' I asked him. 'It looks no bigger than a little bean.'

"'I can't see anything and I don't wish to,' he replied. 'And above all, I don't know whether I'll be able to get back down!'

"The Englishman noticed how pale he was, shook his head, and passed him a flask of cognac. The poor fellow took a drink, rested a while, and calmed down.

"We had been sitting there for fifteen minutes or so when a rather chilly wind blew up. I happened to be looking down toward Thusis, and I witnessed an extraordinary sight. In the deep ravine that lay beneath us, the blue mist took on a lighter color; it turned to light blue, then grew lighter still, until it was completely white. And then all the valley began rapidly to fill up, so that it looked as if we were surrounded by a milky sea on which the tops of the mountains were sailing. And not just sailing, for they were gradually starting to sink and drown. I could clearly see the mist and the mountains moving in relation to each other, but I was terrified when I noticed that the summit on which we were sitting was beginning to drop downward. I would have sworn that we were falling onto the cloud that was spread below us, and toward which we were moving at great speed.

"'What does this mean?' one of the ladies asked the Englishman.

"'The mist is rising,' he answered somewhat darkly. 'We have to go down,' he added.

"So it's not that we are falling but that the mist is rising up toward us! I thought to myself, much calmer now.

"But clouds have swift wings. We had not even all risen to our feet when the mist had surrounded us on all sides, and despite the fact that it was the middle of the day it grew so dark that we could barely see a few paces ahead of us. We felt moisture on our hands and faces; then rain started to fall, then sleet, and finally it began snowing as thickly as in a Polish blizzard.

"Nevertheless, we held hands and pushed on, for the path was safe and the Englishman knew it like the back of his hand. At times the slippery rocks would slide out from under our feet, and we would slither a few feet downhill, laughing all the while. The German laughed loudest of all. He had been in a capital mood from the moment the mist had concealed the side of the mountain and the abyss that lay below it.

"During one such slide we dropped not four or five but fifty feet. The ladies had already begun to cry 'Oh! oh!' when we slowed down and felt hard rock underfoot.

"The German was the first to his feet. He happily lifted his walking stick and was about to set off again, but the Englishman stopped him.

"'You will excuse me,' he said, 'but first I must take a look to see where we are.'

"He felt his way forward for a few paces and disappeared abruptly into the mist.

"'Hello there! Hello!'

"He came back, but we could see concern in his face.

"'Would a compass be of any use?' asked my compatriot.

"'But of course, please give it to me!' answered the Englishman, impatiently grabbing the little compass with which the Pole had decorated his watch chain.

"The Englishman looked, turned the compass, shook his head, and finally clicked his tongue.

"'We shall have to stay here until the mist lifts,' he said with a smile to the ladies.

"And to us he whispered, 'We strayed from the path; we're way over on the other side of the mountain.'

"'How high up are we?' asked the German.

"'Perhaps halfway up the mountain, though I can't be at all sure.'

"'Are there any cliffs here?' inquired the German again.

"'I don't know that either,' replied the Englishman. 'In any case, the mountainside here is extremely steep.'

"The ladies sat glumly.

"'What a pity we don't have a little stove to make hot chocolate,' one of them remarked.

"It was after four when a strong wind from the side blew up and uncovered the horizon for a short time.

"I shuddered. I saw that we were sitting on a sort of ledge that was about twenty feet wide. Behind us was the steep side of the mountain, covered in slippery rocks, which we had no chance at that time of climbing; in front of us, a kilometer away, was the valley.

"There was no hope at all of climbing down from the ledge toward the valley, because at this point the rocky mountainside dropped away almost vertically.

"'When will we be setting off again?' one of the ladies asked.

"'When the mist clears,' replied the Englishman.

"'And if it doesn't clear by nightfall?'

"'Then we shall spend the night here.'

"'Surely you're joking?'

"'Not in the slightest,' he replied gravely. 'We have fallen into a trap, and we must be patient.'

"'Then call for help, gentlemen,' put in the other lady. 'There are people about after all, perhaps someone will hear.'

"'That's just what we intend to do.'

"The other Pole had a revolver, and began to fire in the direction of the village. But the reports were so faint that I doubted whether anyone could have heard it.

"In the meantime, the mist had grown even thicker. The ladies wrapped themselves in their shawls and sat cheerlessly; the German paced to and fro, looking greatly perturbed.

"Suddenly he took me by the arm and led me to one side. He had a crazed expression on his face.

"'My friend,' he said in a changed voice, 'I know we're sitting on the edge of a cliff; and although I can't see it, at the very thought of it my head spins so terribly that I can't bear it any longer.'

"'So what do you intend to do?' I asked, taken aback.

"'I shall throw myself off! I'd rather perish than suffer like this. You're the only one I'm telling of my intention; the others mustn't know anything.'

"'Have you gone mad?'

"'Yes, I feel that I have gone mad . . . '

"At this moment the Englishman came up, and before I knew what was happening, he had seized hold of the German. He tried to tie his hands, and to me he muttered, 'Throw a kerchief over his head.'

"But the poor fellow broke away, pushed us both back, and ran along the ledge to the left.

"A moment later we heard a heavy thud and the muffled clatter of falling rocks.

"'What's going on over there?' asked one of the ladies, hearing the noise.

"'Nothing,' answered the Englishman in a hollow voice. 'Our companion is looking for a way up.'

"And he whispered to me, 'Don't mention a word of this or the others will follow in his footsteps. In a situation like this, panic is infectious. We're in a tight spot.'

"He took a sizable shot of cognac, gave me a drink, and then began singing an aria from an operetta in a tuneful tenor. The French ladies brightened up and started to sing along with him. Even my compatriot forgot about his dinner and accompanied them in a discordant bass, repeatedly getting the melody wrong.

"Only I was silent, shocked, and frightened. That singing on top of the precipice, after such a terrifying incident, revealed to me the superhuman courage of the Englishman, but also the extremely perilous nature of our position.

"'Sing along with us!' one of the ladies called to me. 'It's just the ticket when you're bored and cold.'

"'And it may draw the attention of the locals,' added the other.

"The three of them began a new aria, even more cheerful than the last. This time the Pole unceremoniously shouted out in Polish, 'To hell with you and your mountain, Mr. Englishman! If I weren't afraid of the Swiss, I'd eat you instead of veal for my supper!'

"The Englishman politely turned his pallid countenance to him and marked time with his hand.

"Then I heard a voice from down below. The Englishman leaped to his feet and ran to the part of the ledge where the German had thrown himself off.

"'Hello there!' came a voice from below.

"'Hello!' we responded in unison.

"The two ladies kissed each other from joy.

"'I didn't kill myself!' cried the voice. 'Come down this way! There's an excellent little path!'

"We were astonished to recognize the voice of our German companion.

"'You can jump off the ledge, gentlemen – it's only a few feet high. But the ladies will have to be carried down,' shouted the German.

"'Thank God!' exclaimed my compatriot. 'At least I'll get to eat supper today!'

"And he jumped right into the mist.

"Once again we heard a clatter of stones, and the voice of the Pole protesting.

"'Dash this path of his! I think I've twisted my ankle.'

"After this, we heard a conversation down below. He had obviously already met up with the German.

"One by one we all got down, despite the protests of the ladies, who categorically refused to stand on the Englishman's shoulders. In the end, however, they relented; for at this point the cliff formed a kind of threshold five or six feet high, from which one either had to jump or climb down with the help of someone standing below.

"Once we had left the fateful ledge we found ourselves on a steep hillside littered with rocks. Thus, we did not walk so much as slither down noisily and at great speed, four of us holding hands – the two ladies in the middle and the Englishman and I at either end. Beneath us and a little to the side we could make out two shadows moving through the mist: This was my fellow Pole and the German would-be suicide. Although we were moving fast, for several minutes we continued to slide down the steep slope. However, as we dropped lower, the mist thinned out, and we could see the valley and some of the shepherds' chalets.

"When, a quarter of an hour later, we all came out onto a meadow, the Englishman, taking the German by the arm, turned to the ladies and said, 'Would you believe, ladies, that an hour ago this man tried to kill himself?'

"The suicide, embarrassed, moved to one side, and the French ladies, seeing how seriously the Englishman spoke, began to laugh. Even the Pole thought it a splendid joke. But when we told them about the whole incident, one lady burst into tears and the other had an attack of nerves.

"It was true that we owed our lives to the temporary madness of our companion. For the ledge overlooked a precipice, and it was only at the point where the German had jumped that it was possible to descend into the valley without risking one's life.

"The remainder of his adventure was fairly straightforward.

"When he threw himself off the cliff, he landed on a layer of small stones, and seeking to put an end to his vertigo as quickly as possible, he ran blindly forward. After a few minutes he reached the edge of the mist, and found a safe path. At this point, once he had grown calmer, with considerable effort he climbed back in order to lead us down.

"And what do think?" asked my friend. "As a result of this incident the German was completely cured of his fear of heights. He even joined a mountain-climbing club, and recently I've seen his name on the list of those climbers who have conquered the highest peaks.

"Like is cured with like."

# From the Legends of
# Ancient Egypt

See how paltry are human hopes in the face of the order of the world! See how paltry they are in the face of the judgments written in fiery signs in the heavens by the Eternal One!

One hundred-year-old Ramses, the mighty ruler of Egypt, was dying. This powerful man, whose voice had for half a century caused millions to tremble, had been overcome with a stifling affliction that drew the blood from his heart, the strength from his arm, and at times even the consciousness from his mind. The great pharaoh lay like a felled cedar upon the skin of an Indian tiger, his legs covered with the victory cloak of the Ethiop king. Hard even on himself, he summoned the wisest physician from the temple at Karnak and said, "I know that you have strong medicines which either kill or cure outright. Prepare one for me for my sickness, so all this might finish once and for all, one way or the other."

The doctor hesitated.

"Think, Ramses," he whispered, "since the time you descended from the heavens the Nile has flooded a hundred times. Can I give you medicine that would be dangerous even for the youngest of your warriors?"

Ramses sat up in his bed.

"I must be truly sick," he cried, "when you, priest, dare to advise me! Be silent and do as I order. My thirty-year-old grandson and successor, Horus, is alive, after all, and Egypt should not have a ruler who cannot even climb into a chariot or wield a spear."

When the priest handed him the medicine with a trembling hand, Ramses drank it all as a thirsty man drinks a cup of water. Then he summoned the most renowned astrologer of Thebes and ordered him to recount truthfully what was written in the stars.

"Saturn is in conjunction with the moon," said the wise man, "which foretells the death of a member of your dynasty, Ramses. You were wrong to drink that medicine today, for the plans of humans are futile in the face of the judgments that the Eternal One writes in the heavens."

"Of course the stars have foretold my death," replied Ramses. "When will it happen?" he asked, turning to the physician.

"Before the sun rises, Ramses, either you will have the health and strength of the rhinoceros, or your sacred ring will sit upon Horus's finger."

"Summon Horus to the Chamber of the Pharaohs," whispered Ramses in a voice that was already growing weaker. "Have him wait there for my last words and for the ring, so that there shall be no break in the rule of the pharaohs."

Horus, who had a compassionate heart, wept at the imminent death of his grandfather. But since there could be no break in the pharaohs' reign, he went to the Chamber of the Pharaohs, accompanied by a large train of attendants.

He sat on the terrace, the marble steps of which ran down all the way to the river, and gazed about, filled with an indistinct sense of sadness.

The moon, next to which burned the ominous star of Saturn, was at this time gilding the brown waters of the Nile, painting shadows of the huge pyramids on the meadows and orchards, and lighting up the whole valley for miles around. Although it was the middle of the night, lamps shone in the cottages and houses, and the people had come out of their homes. On the Nile there were as many boats as on a holiday; unnumbered multitudes thronged the palm groves, the riverbanks, the marketplaces, the streets, and the area surrounding Ramses' palace. And yet despite all this, there was such a silence that Horus could hear the rustle of the rushes in the water and the plaintive howling of the hyenas as they searched for food.

"Why are they all gathering like this?" Horus asked one of the courtiers, pointing to the countless expanse of human heads.

"My lord, they wish to greet you as the new pharaoh and hear from your own lips of the good works you have planned for them."

At this moment, for the first time the prince's heart was struck by the pride of greatness, as the sea strikes against a steep shoreline.

"And what is the meaning of those lights over there?" Horus continued.

"The priests have gone to the grave of your mother, Zephora, to transfer her remains to the catacombs of the pharaohs."

Horus's heart was once again moved at the thought of his mother. As a punishment for the charity she had shown toward the slaves, stern Ramses had ordered her body to be buried among those same slaves.

"I can hear the neighing of horses," said Horus, listening intently. "Who is leaving at this hour?"

"The chancellor, my lord, gave the order for messengers to be sent to your old tutor, Yetron."

Horus sighed at the thought of his dear friend, whom Ramses had sent into exile because he had instilled in the soul of Ramses' grandson and successor a horror of war and pity for the oppressed masses.

"And that little light across the Nile?"

"With that light, Horus," replied the courtier, "the faithful Berenice greets you from her imprisonment in the convent. The archpriest has already sent the pharaoh's boat for her, and as soon as the sacred ring shines on your finger, the heavy doors of the convent will open and she will return to you, longing and loving."

When he heard these words, Horus asked no more questions; he fell silent and covered his eyes with his hand.

Suddenly he winced with pain.

"What is it, Horus?"

"A bee just stung me on the foot," answered Horus, who had turned pale.

The courtier examined his foot by the greenish light of the moon.

"Praise be to Osiris," he said, "that it was not a spider. Their poison can be fatal at this time of the year."

Oh how paltry are human hopes in the face of the immutable judgments!

At this moment the commander in chief of the army entered and, bowing to Horus, said, "The great Ramses, sensing that his body is growing cold, sent me to you with an order: 'Go to Horus, for I am not long for this world, and obey him as you have obeyed me. Even if he should order Upper Egypt to be ceded to the Ethiopians and a fraternal union established with those enemies of ours, do it when you see my ring on his finger, for the immortal Osiris speaks through the mouth of the pharaohs.'"

"I shall not give Egypt over to Ethiopia," said the prince, "but I shall arrange a peace treaty, for I do not wish to spill the blood of my people. Write an edict at once, and have a group of mounted messengers in readiness, so that when the first fires are lit in my honor they should hasten in the direction of the southern sun and bring mercy to the Ethiopians. And write a second edict that from this day to the end of time no prisoner of war is to have his tongue torn out on the field of battle. This is my will."

The commander in chief prostrated himself and then retired to write what had been ordered. The prince asked the courtier to examine his foot again, as it was very painful.

"It is a little swollen, Horus," said the courtier. "What would have happened if you had been bitten by a spider rather than stung by a bee!"

Now the chancellor of all the nation entered and, bowing to the prince, said, "Mighty Ramses, realizing that his sight is beginning to fail, has sent me to you with this order: 'Go to Horus and obey him blindly. Even if he should order you to release all the slaves from their chains and to return all the land to the common people, you will do it when you see my sacred ring on his finger, for the immortal Osiris speaks through the mouths of the pharaohs.'"

"My wishes do not extend so far," said Horus. "But write an edict declaring the land lease and taxes for the common people are to be reduced by half, that slaves are to have three days each week free of work, and that they may not be beaten without an order from the court. And write one more edict recalling from exile my teacher, Yetron, who is the wisest and noblest of Egyptians. This is my will."

The chancellor prostrated himself. Before he had left to write the edicts, the archpriest entered.

"Horus," he said, "at any moment now great Ramses will depart for the kingdom of the spirits, and his heart will be weighed by Osiris on his infallible scales. And when the sacred ring of the pharaohs gleams on your finger, command and I shall obey, even if you were to demolish the magnificent temple of Amon, for immortal Osiris speaks through the mouths of the pharaohs."

"I shall not demolish anything, but I shall build new temples and enrich the priesthood's treasury. I demand only that you write an edict to order the ceremonial transfer of the remains of my mother, Zephora, to the catacombs, and a second edict to have my beloved Berenice released from her imprisonment in the convent. This is my will."

"You act wisely," replied the archpriest. "Everything is prepared for your orders to be carried out, and I will write the edicts at once.

When you touch them with the ring of the pharaohs, I will light this lamp to signal the bounty you have shown to the common people, the love you have bestowed upon Berenice, and the freedom you have granted her."

The wise physician of Karnak entered.

"Horus," he said, "I am not surprised at your pallor, for Ramses, your grandfather, is dying. He could not withstand the powerful medicine, which I was reluctant to administer to him, that most mighty of rulers. Only the archpriest's deputy has remained with him, so that when he passes away the sacred ring will be taken from his finger and given to you as a sign of your absolute power. But you seem to be turning even paler, Horus."

"Take a look at my foot," moaned Horus, and collapsed into a golden chair, the arms of which were sculpted in the form of hawks' heads.

The physician knelt, looked at Horus's foot, and drew back in horror.

"Horus," he whispered, "you have been bitten by a poisonous spider!"

"Am I to die? At such a moment?" asked Horus in a barely audible voice.

Then he added, "Will it happen soon? Tell me the truth."

"Before the moon drops behind that palm tree."

"I see . . . and will Ramses live much longer?"

"I do not know. Perhaps they are already bringing his ring."

At this moment the ministers came in with the completed edicts.

"Chancellor!" called Horus, seizing him by the hand. "If I were to die at this moment, would you carry out my orders?"

"May you live to be as old as your grandfather, Horus!" answered the chancellor. "But even if you were to follow right after him to stand before the judgment of Osiris, every one of your edicts will be obeyed, if only you touch them with the sacred ring of the pharaohs."

"The ring!" repeated Horus. "But where is it?"

"One of the courtiers told me that Ramses is taking his last breaths," whispered the commander in chief.

"I have sent word to my deputy," added the archpriest, "to tell him to take the ring off the moment that Ramses' heart stops beating."

"Thank you," said Horus. "I am sad, so sad. And yet I shall not die entirely . . . Blessings will remain after I am gone, peace, the happiness of the people, and my Berenice shall regain her freedom. How long now?" he asked the physician.

"At the speed of a soldierly march, death is a thousand paces from you," replied the physician gravely.

"Do you not hear anyone coming?" said Horus.

There was silence.

The moon was drawing close to the palm tree and had already touched its first leaves. The fine sand sounded quietly in the hourglasses.

"How long?" whispered Horus.

"Eight hundred paces," answered the physician. "Horus, I am not sure that you will have time to touch all of the edicts with the sacred ring, even if they should bring it to you at once."

"Give me the edicts," said the prince, straining to hear if someone was running in from Ramses' chambers. "And you, doctor," he said, turning to the physician, "tell me how long I still have, so that I may lay the ring at least upon those edicts that are dearest to me."

"Six hundred paces," whispered the physician.

The edict ordering the reduction of the land lease for the people and of work for the slaves fell from Horus's hand to the ground.

"Five hundred . . . "

The edict concerning a peace treaty with the Ethiopians slipped off the prince's lap.

"Is no one coming?"

"Four hundred," responded the physician.

Horus thought for a moment. The order to transfer Zephora's remains dropped to the ground.

"Three hundred . . . "

The same fate befell the edict recalling Yetron from exile.

"Two hundred."

Horus's lips turned livid. With a stiff hand he threw down the edict forbidding the pulling out of the tongues of prisoners of war. There remained only the order to free Berenice.

"One hundred . . . "

In the deathly silence there came the sound of sandaled feet. The archpriest's deputy ran into the room. Horus stretched out his hand.

"A miracle has occurred!" cried the newcomer. "The mighty Ramses has regained his health. He rose vigorously from his bed, and at sunrise he wishes to go lion-hunting. As a sign of his grace, you, Horus, are invited to join him!"

Horus cast his dying gaze across the Nile, where the light shone in Berenice's prison. Two bloody tears rolled down his cheeks.

"Have you no answer, Horus?" said the deputy in surprise.

"Can you not see that he is dead?" whispered the wise physician of Karnak.

See, then, how paltry are human hopes in the face of the judgments which the Eternal One writes in fiery signs across the heavens.

## »»» «««
# A Dream

There was once a poor student in the fourth year of medical school.

He gave private lessons for six rubles a month to an engine driver on the Terespol Railway who lived in the Praga district, and for three rubles to a shopkeeper on Podwale Street. He himself lived on Piwna Street in a fourth-floor room for which the rent was four rubles, a sum he systematically failed to pay, not because he sought to bring about the ruin of the landlord, but because he never had a penny to his name.

He wore a student's uniform faded at the seams, with buttons that were so worn you could see the copper underneath. His trousers were so threadbare that they could barely pass as the logarithms of real trousers, while he himself referred to his pockets as Toricelli's vacuum. They were so very empty that in the end they grew ashamed and quit the garment, and their place was taken by holes so deep they went right to the center of the earth.

As a result of this singular financial situation, the poor student had a sunken chest and a hollow stomach. He hung his head not out of unhappiness but because that poor head contained far more learning than could be carried on such a scrawny neck.

"If I were God, I'd organize the world differently," he would sometimes say. "I'd invent for myself private lessons at thirty rubles a month, I'd eat dinner every day, I'd buy myself a winter coat, I'd pay my rent. But as things stand . . . "

Sometimes he would imagine the future and think: I'd give a hundred ducats to the person who told me whether or not I'd graduate from medical school. Because with this stupid cough, with these fevers, this expectoration . . . But then again, what do I care? It won't be my fault if Europe loses an outstanding doctor. I'd be such a wonderful healer! I'd write every patient the same prescription: a dry flat, heated every day. They can skip breakfast and supper, but dinner is a must; their clothes should be in good condition and should be appropriate to each of the four seasons. In addition, they should possess at least two shirts of their own, and stay away from doctors and medicines.

One day, before Christmas, our friend picked up five rubles for the private lessons in Praga, but then found himself in a quandary. He had meant to pay the landlord the rent for July, but you see . . . He had paid back a loan of three rubles to a fellow student who was leaving town, he had given eighty-five kopecks to the grocer for foodstuffs, he owed the caretaker a ruble . . . Where was he supposed to find the July rent?

He was so concerned about his unbalanced budget that it was afternoon before he returned home to Piwna Street. When he gave the caretaker his ruble and asked for the key to his room, the caretaker scratched his head and replied, "You know, sir, they've already moved in on the fourth floor."

"Who? How? What banditry is this?" exclaimed the student, reaching instinctively into his pocket, where bandits usually keep their revolvers and ordinary mortals their money.

"The landlord said," explained the caretaker, "that you haven't paid your rent for six months, sir, so he ordered your things to be brought down to my place, and he let the room to a roofer. They're poor folk, sir; he has a wife and three kids, and they've already borrowed some potatoes and some coal from me. The roofer said that if your room hadn't come along, they probably would all have frozen to death on the street."

The penniless student fell deep in thought.

"Well, if that's the case," he said, "I can let them have it. But if Bloch or Kronenberg had moved in there, I'd have shown the landlord what it means to neglect your obligations."

He nodded and went out onto the street, without even asking about his belongings, an act worthy of a truly wise man whose earthly possessions consist of a toothbrush, half a towel, and a magnificent anatomical atlas.

He had stopped thinking about either the roofer or the landlord. He could feel that he had a slight fever, and that after a whole day without food he ought to get a bite to eat, though he didn't feel hungry: a fever, and also perhaps experience, can mean a lot in such circumstances. So he entered a little shop. The gourmet in him selected two dry sausages, and the practical man a hunk of wholegrain bread; he then magisterially ordered the entire purchase to be wrapped in some thick sugar paper. He had the impression that the shop assistant suspected he might be setting off on an arctic expedition and that she was staring at him in admiration; in reality she suspected that he might be chronically destitute and was carefully looking to check that the coin he had given her wasn't counterfeit.

Taking his ten groszes' change, our friend found himself on the street once and for all; past him, through the snow that was melting into mud, drove carts with meat and bread, and sleighs bearing lovers of poetic experiences. Suddenly, on the corner of the sidewalk, an old woman all in rags seized him by the hand and started shouting at the top of her voice, "Sir! Sir! We're so poor!"

"I bet she caught a whiff of the dried sausage – these starvelings have an excellent sense of smell!" thought the medical student, and, to avoid a scene, he gave the woman his last ten-grosz piece.

"May the good Lord bring you happiness!" cried the beggar woman, who must at one time have been a fine lady. At any rate, this was indicated by her exclamations, which were filled with turns of phrase that betrayed refined sentiments.

The poor student fled from her touch like a naked man from boiling water.

What an embarrassing woman! he thought. Her kerchief and my student's uniform look so much alike that people might think we're related.

At the same time, against the background of the tinkling of sleigh bells, the clatter of sleighs on the cobblestones, and the rattle of carriages, he seemed to hear her blessing, spoken in her noble if stuffed-up voice: "May the good Lord bring you happiness!"

Happiness? he thought, walking along the pavement, jostled by passersby. What is happiness? I've often heard the word, but although I don't lack for anything in life and I'm entitled to call myself entirely content, I wouldn't dare to claim that I have ever been happy.

I mean, that party at Bajer's house was something. I'll be damned if I didn't eat five smoked sausages and half a pound of cheese all on my own, not to mention the rolls. And how about that punch? Genuine Goa arrack from Fuks's, burgundy from Maliniak's, lemons . . . I believe the lemons were real . . . I ate and drank like an archduke. If I'm not mistaken, there were even young ladies from a first-class restaurant where they only serve things in portions. Yet I can't say that that was happiness; though after that punch I felt flushed by the time I'd reached the third floor . . .

Excitement induced by punch, even ladies from a first-class restaurant, were not true happiness. So what was missing at that party? They had wine, women, and song, and yet it all ended in an upset stomach. So: What is happiness?

Twelve years ago, he had traveled home for Christmas in a light coat, and he had been so cold that he thought he would freeze to death on the journey. His fingers and ears were stinging, he could no longer feel his nose, his legs had gone numb, and shivers ran through his entire body. But when he reached home, and he was given a mug of hot tea with milk and went to bed, when the warmth began to return to his frozen legs, he experienced a bliss he had never known before.

He recalled fondly how his ears had burned, how his shivers had been left outside; and he had been highly amused by the shadow of his father's head, with its unnaturally large nose, moving across the wall. How gaily the candle had burned, and how calmly he himself had fallen asleep, glad that the frost had tormented him so thoroughly.

Afterward there had been many more frosts in his life, rains, hungers, and every kind of misfortune. But, strangely, he wouldn't have exchanged any of these privations for an evening of punch and young ladies, or even for a private lesson for thirty rubles. Because each instance of suffering left in his soul a sort of radiance, a sweetness and warmth nothing else could replace.

"Is that happiness then?" he thought. "How funny!"

At this moment he noticed that he was in the Saski Gardens, where dusk was beginning to fall. Beyond the dark branches of the trees and the iron railings of the gardens, lights were starting to appear in windows.

There was only a handful of people, who were hurrying toward the gates as if the night and the cold were driving them along. A few dogs were frolicking in the snow; one of them, with a characteristically slight figure, its tail between its legs, was staring at him from a distance, moving its rear as if it were about to sit down on its hind legs and rub its front paws together.

This sight reminded the poor student that he, too, was fearfully cold, so he put down the package with the sausage and bread on the bench and began to run up and down the path, beating his arms against his sides and rubbing his ears.

It has to be admitted, he thought to himself, seeing the blissful effects of his exercises, that humans are far superior creatures to dogs, who can't even warm their own ears.

All of a sudden he heard an ominous snapping noise from under the bench. He looked down. His package lay ripped open on the snow; the sausages had disappeared, and the remains of the bread were being mauled by the same dog which a moment earlier had been watching its friends' games with such melancholy. Now, too, it sat on its hindquarters with its tail tucked right under it; but its figure seemed a little fuller . . .

"You little . . . !" shouted the poor student. In a single bound he leaped up to the dog and gave it a hefty kick in its white teeth.

The dog yelped, staggered, and scuttled off toward the nearest gate, howling plaintively, "Ow, ow! Ow, ow! Ow, ow! Ow, ow!"

It was only now, looking at the torn paper and what was left of the unfinished bread, that our friend became fully aware that he was cold, that he was very thirsty, that he didn't have a roof over his head, and that say what you will, a fourth-year medical student ought not to be in such a compromising situation.

I'm not going to wait here on the street till I'm frozen stiff and they take me to the police station, he thought. There's a perfectly respectable place I can go: one of my classmates is on duty in the Christ Child Clinic, so I'll go there and relieve him. And in that way I'll get a good night's sleep, and something to eat and drink . . .

Ten minutes later he was already at the clinic, where he did indeed find a colleague on duty, and offered to take his place for the night with the patients. His colleague looked at him closely, assured him that he wouldn't leave his patients for all the tea in China, but told him that he would give him a bed in another room that happened to be vacant. His friend was even so kind as to help him undress, order some tea to be brought, put him to bed, tuck him in, and even slip a thermometer under his arm.

"Surely you don't think I'm ill, do you?" our friend asked, laughing. "All it is is that my landlord threw me out today and I don't have anywhere to sleep. If it wasn't for that I wouldn't have dreamed of coming to the clinic."

The colleague on duty nodded to his guest, adding mentally that if it weren't for his unnaturally empty stomach, slight inflammation of the lungs, forty-degree Celsius temperature, and pulse of a hundred and twenty, our friend could consider himself to be in excellent health.

Meanwhile, the poor medical student was feeling better with every hour that passed. He was delighted with the hospital bed; he kept calling his colleague in for philosophical debates on the nature of true happiness and the purpose of human life. Around ten in the evening he was so well that not only was he continuously laughing and singing, but he also absolutely had to go back out to the city, where, according to his observations, it was already summer and the sun was out. He virtually had to be forced to stay in bed, until after a struggle he fell into a state of complete torpor in which he could neither hear voices nor see the people moving around him.

Before his eyes, which were closed to earthly things, there opened up another world.

He seemed to have found himself in the country, staring at the sky as the sun set. The sky looked like an emerald-green ocean covered with gold and silver islands occupied by people, animals, and plants in strange forms.

I have a fever, of course, the sick man thought, but what's the harm in looking, since it's so interesting?

And so he observed this new land, smiling skeptically like a person who is shown pictures in a magic lantern and is told fairy tales.

Above all else, he was struck by the appearance of objects. The leaves of the trees were green, like in the real world; their bark was brown, sand was yellow, the earth dull brown, and the flowers pink, white, and blue; but all these hues were marked by an unimaginable delicacy and radiance. Colors like these can only ever be seen in clouds or in droplets of dew. Furthermore, the student had the impression that each object not only reflected some powerful external light but was also translucent and shone with its own mysterious inner glow. This effect created a wonderous play of subtle, vital colors.

Thanks to this light, if you looked carefully you could see the pulsating movement of stones, which contracted and expanded, rippled on the surface and inside at every change in the temperature or air pressure, even at every movement or noise that was heard in their vicinity. You could see the sometimes rapid, sometimes slower circulation of sap in plants, the breath of their leaves, and the formation of new buds. And it seemed, too, upon closer scrutiny, that you could see ideas drifting like clouds through people's minds and the fluctuating colors of feelings in their hearts.

In addition, every tremor of a stone, rustle of a leaf, breath of wind, and even change in human physiognomy was accompanied by a delicate whisper halfway between melody and speech, which either explained and recounted something to the listener on its own or joined with other voices into a fuller melody or a longer story. In this way, without disturbing each other, individual flowers conversed with a whole forest, drops of water with the ocean, grains of sand with vast mountain chains. There was no need for any special methods for studying the secrets of nature, since each being revealed and recounted its own mysteries in a language that was vivid and harmonious yet also simple and clear.

In this curious land, where humans, animals and even pieces of brick were alive, had feelings, and talked with each other, where the sand glittered like gold and a cobblestone refracted the light as well as any diamond, the poor student, peering closer, noticed an extra-ordinary sight.

Everything there was beautiful: the men, the women, the plants, and the stones; but the most beautiful things were those which in our earthly life we deem to be poor and in suffering. Silks, velvets, pearls, and gold seemed dull and commonplace amid the general splendor; whereas coarse linen, rough homespun coats, the bast clogs of the peasants, and beggars' rags were somehow unusual and drew one's attention. Regular features and statuesque faces were tedious in their sameness, while thin, broken, scarred bodies aroused one's interest. At the sight of a beautiful person the poor student waved his hand and thought, They're just like millions of others; it's clear they've not encountered any obstacles in life.

But every infirmity and wound made him curious, and he said to himself, "That chap must have been through the mill!"

The same interest was stirred by splintered trees, the ruins of buildings, and whole regions destroyed by earthquake. The student didn't ask where well-formed and decorative things were from, because in this world everything was well-formed, decorative, and brightly colored. But he was fascinated by anything misshapen, every damaged entity. These entities were like ledgers in which important events were recorded.

"It's odd," he said, "how all this reminds me of the saying: 'Blessed are the little ones and those who suffer.' I must admit that these little ones are very picturesque, and those who suffer have a dramatic look about them."

Not far from a rocky mountain of sapphire and topaz, from which a stream of water flowed like a rainbow and beneath which a wretched Caesar was hiding from the specters of hundreds of thousands of dead soldiers, the student saw a group of women. They included bankers' wives in pearl necklaces, viscountesses in diamond bracelets, countesses in lace and ostrich feathers; and they were jealously and ruefully crowding around an old Jewish woman who was sitting by a barrel of herring.

The gowns of these ladies, against the background of a meadow of emeralds speckled with rubies, sapphires, and amethysts, and crossed by a stream of diamonds, looked like old dishrags, while the Jewish woman's quilted fustian jacket, with the padding poking out in places, had the color and luster of pure bronze adorned with wisps of silver. And the beautiful faces of the women were somehow sorrowful, and even, terrible to tell, soulless. They seemed like corpses in which there was barely a faint glimmer of consciousness constantly fading and fearful of being extinguished.

As he looked closer, the student could tell that these ladies had never done anything and had never experienced anything bad in life. Their spiritual resources were virtually nonexistent, constantly growing dim and threatening to turn into nothingness. To revive their atrophying minds somewhat, the wretched creatures gathered around the old herring seller, who took pity on them and allowed them to gaze into the window of her life and to draw from it, as it were, breath for their own eternally dying hearts.

The herring seller's story was a very simple one: Every week for thirty years she had given a herring and a piece of bread to whichever poor person first passed by her barrel on Friday morning.

The student looked into the window of her life and saw what looked like a line of people of various ages, sitting, standing, or lying on the pavement, in the snow, by a fence, on some stairs, on scaffolding; and each of them was eating a herring and a piece of bread, and on each could be seen images from their life. One of them had been so hungry he had been about to kill himself, but when he received the gift from the old woman he had found a new desire to live. Another was going to have to steal, but was given something to eat in time and was saved from prison. A third was about to abandon his tiny children, yet another to kill a person for money, but each had been led away from the wrong path by a little herring and a slice of bread.

The student felt the hunger and the rage of these poor folk, and then their joy and the better thoughts that began to appear. He saw their families saved from destitution, and the people who almost became victims of their desperation. In the midst of this great throng there passed a portly banker, who, once he had seen the compassionate old woman giving a poor man a herring, introduced free lunches for the needy and, like that old woman, saved many a person from their undoing.

In a word, through the window of the old Jewish woman's life there could be seen a vast world of people who had been suffering and were brought relief, who had been angry and were calmed, who had been desperate and had found hope. All of them multiplied and brought about new sufferings and new joys. And there was such lively movement among them that the poor society ladies, whose souls were dying, looked at this vibrant picture, became more animated, and regained a faint consciousness of existence, only, alas, to feel its emptiness even more painfully.

All the while the old Jewish woman in the torn jacket, her arms folded on her lap, screwed up her eyes and nodded her head, smiling compassionately. She had no need to look into the window of her own life, because her merciful soul was strewn with memories like a tree with blossom in springtime.

"That old woman I gave ten groszes to really did bring me happiness," said the student. "From what I can see I'm beginning to realize that the greatest honor is suffering, and the greatest happiness is in good deeds. The damn things multiply like rabbits: Each one produces a hundred new deeds, and each of that hundred another hundred. While poor Caesar looks like a fellow who's been sued for centuries by the invalids of Rome for their lost legs and heads (a

Draconian fate!), and the grand society ladies are permanently fading away with some sort of spiritual anemia.

"In this way," he added, "I myself can lead a very pleasant life here. My uniform is full of holes, my stomach is empty enough to compete with those people from the old herring seller's story, and as a result I haven't done anything so bad that it could spoil things for me here . . . "

At this moment he heard a frightful voice crying, "Ow, ow! Ow, ow! Ow, ow!"

He shuddered and felt as if daggers were being stabbed into his ears. He experienced such intense pain that it caused all of the delights of his dream to fade away.

The yelping moved away and gradually grew quieter, and the frightened student thought: What the hell was that (if I can use such a word in a place like this)! It must have been that dog I booted in the Saski Gardens. Pardon me! If he puts on another concert like that, I'd better clear out of here!

Well, if that kind of wrong produces such a show, I wonder what happens to those noblemen who believed it was fashionable to flog their coachmen?

"It would be a good idea, though," he said upon reflection, "to see what my own balance of good deeds is like. Am I like that fortunate herring seller, who through her window can see legions of those she has helped, or am I more like those beautiful women who are dying like fish out of water?"

He had barely finished talking when he noticed that from his heart there extended thousands of rays like golden threads, which reached out toward the earth and fastened on to various places: one to the grave of his parents, another to the house where he had spent his childhood, another to the trees beneath which he had played, the stones he had sat upon when he was tired, the spring he had drunk from. Other rays from his heart were attached to his friends, his favorite books, to young ladies he knew, even to newspapers and the gods in the theater.

These were all objects and people he loved. And thanks to the rays or threads that linked him with them, his own life at this moment grew a thousand times stronger. He felt the joy of one of his friends, who was presently traveling home for the holidays; that of another, who was getting ready to visit a certain charming young lady; he followed the train of thought of a third, who was playing chess, and a fourth who was studying for an exam. A sweet melancholy flowed into his soul from the snow-covered trees and from the old house, whose rotten shutters banged in the wind.

But among the thousand golden rays that brought him another's joy or a sweet sorrow, there were a few black threads that linked him to people and things he did not like. These black threads spoiled his happiness, because whether the person he didn't like was joyful or sad, the black thread tugged at his heart in the same way, causing a sharp, stinging pain.

"So it's true that love brings happiness and hatred suffering?" he said pensively, sensing that it was not possible to snap off any of the threads, either golden or black. "So perhaps the admonition to 'love thine enemy' has some real value? Can it really be true that through love and hatred we coexist with those close to us, and they become, as it were, an inseparable part of our souls?

"Oh, those are just old wives' tales," he exclaimed. "I must have quite a fever if such nonsense comes into my head in the fourth year of medical school. Are those black threads really going to torment me for all time?" he wondered further. And his reason told him that it was for all time, because what has once become fact can never die either in nature or in the spirit. If every high tide leaves its mark on the shore, if every geological era is recorded in the very rocks, why shouldn't the waves of human thoughts and feelings also be recorded somewhere? In time they may become covered with new layers, but they will never be wiped away . . .

"What a stupid story," muttered the poor student, and to drive away the sad thoughts that had crept into his heart like vermin along the threads of hatred, he decided to explore a new question: In human life, what is the purpose of suffering, and what is the purpose of joy?

As he thought this, a great change took place in his dream: Instead of the colorful, bright region, he saw a dark smithy in which two gigantic, shapeless figures were at work.

One giant had a bellows and was blowing at a fire from which sparks smaller than poppy seeds shot out, while the other seized the sparks and encased them in spheres of granite as big as the dome on the Carmelite church.

"Good day!" said the student. "What are you doing there, masters?"

"I'm driving out the seeds of souls," said the one with the bellows.

"And I'm encasing them in human bodies," added the other.

"Wow!" whistled the student. "I'd make so bold as to doubt whether such a frail little seed could break through such a massive earthly shell. That granite sphere must be six feet in diameter. How can the tiny seed of the soul sprout from it?"

"If you were given a thinner earthly covering," muttered the other giant, "you'd ruin it in no time, you rogues!"

"The third master'll tell you how it's done, sir," answered the one with the bellows, who was clearly more easygoing.

Now the poor student saw on the threshold of the smithy a third, even more lugubrious creature, who was performing a bizarre task. He took the granite sphere with the spark trapped inside, and with a fearful steel spike and a thousand-pound hammer he drove a hole into the granite right down to its center. At each blow, the granite moaned and shed bloody tears. But all at once, from inside, a slender stalk of light emerged. Then the giant put the sphere in the open air outside the smithy, and there the stalk grew and branched out (or withered), while the giant took another sphere, again drove the spike into its center, again brought out a new stalk of light, which grew once it was put in the open air.

And this went on and on.

"Excuse me," the poor student said to the monster, tipping his cap, "what are you doing, master?"

"I'm helping souls to grow," said the creature.

"The granite is actually screaming," said the student.

"But just look what happens with the soul, sir . . . "

The student walked outside the smithy and looked at the heaps of granite forms. Each of them had two, three, sometimes even twenty radiant little stalks, upon which winds blew from various directions. When there blew a mild, gentle wind, like the pure joy of a human heart, the stalks grew a multitude of small branches, and what seemed like a forest of light appeared around the mass of granite. But when there came a wind that was violent and burning, like passion, some of the branches, even the whole forest of the soul, shriveled up.

And the monster went on driving holes into the granite, which wept and released ever new shoots from its stone bosom.

"Who are you, master?" asked the student, amazed and horrified by the bloody work.

"I am Suffering," replied the specter with the terrible spike. "If it were not for me, your souls would remain forever poppy seeds slumbering in a solid mass of matter."

"Goodness, I must have a hell of a fever," thought the student, rushing out of the smithy.

He was concerned about his condition, so he said, "Let's try and think logically, according to the principles of anatomy, physiology, pharmacology, and obstetrics. My brain isn't functioning properly, and so I imagine that even suffering has a purpose, that it causes the growth of the human soul. Whereas if I considered matters scientifically, I would understand clearly that there is no purpose either in suffering or in nature as a whole. After all, this is irrefutably proven by the existence of nipples in men, and of the human external ear, which is a useless organ, since we can't even wave flies away with it, as cows do, for example. To continue: Because I'm sick, I dream that our earthly life prepares the human soul for a higher life, like grammar school preparing you for the university. While if I were healthy in body and mind, I would believe with the philosopher Hartmann that the whole living world endeavors to destroy the unconscious absolute, just as vermin in Swiss cheese endeavor to destroy the cheese. This absolute of Hartmann's, that is, the unconscious Swiss cheese, created itself and also created its vermin, but unconsciously, so that they would eat it and so that they would eat each other, also unconsciously."

When he had finished his chain of argument the poor student cried out joyfully, "Thank the Lord, I can see my fever isn't so great that it prevents me from thinking precisely and in accordance with the latest developments in philosophy."

Suddenly he noticed that he was standing on a boundless expanse of white, fluffy clouds, in the middle of which there stood a magnificent statue of some person, taller than the tallest mountains on earth. This figure wore a white robe that cascaded down in folds to its feet; its arms were crossed on its chest and its face was plunged in thought. The folds of its robe looked like mountain ranges separated by deep chasms, while across these heights and depths there scuttled creatures the size of ants who bore an uncanny resemblance to humans in the caps and gowns of university professors.

The poor student realized at once that this immense figure was the image of Reality, and that the ants crawling about upon it were attempting, with telescopes, compasses, protractors and chemical reagents, to study the true shape of that statue.

It was obvious that the ants were working intensively and possessed great knowledge. Unfortunately, the statue was a million billion times larger than they were. As a result, none of the scientists was able to take the whole in visually or even to see any larger part of it. And so they explored it gropingly, laboriously, and extremely slowly, so that it took them over a dozen generations to explore one fold, making mistakes and quarreling among themselves. To grasp the form of Reality it was necessary to examine several hundred horizontal and vertical sections, the circumferences of which extended several hundred miles. Yet up till now only a dozen or so sections had been studied, and those only in the lower parts of the statue, while a similar number of measurements had been taken.

In spite of this, discussions were held concerning the whole, which some considered a regular and functional figure, others a lifeless and unordered heap of accidents. The latter were the most audacious ones.

"I have a telescope," one was exclaiming, "so powerful that through it I can even see the end of my nose, but I have not perceived any design in nature."

"A telescope is nothing!" retorted another. "I've studied a number of corns from the feet of eminent people, and I have found no soul."

"And I can't even see any life in nature," added a third, "despite the fact that I've created an artificial urine that is exactly the same in weight, color, odor, and taste . . . "

"Any jackass could do that better and cheaper," interrupted the owner of the telescope.

"But in my universal distillator I'm now going to create a whole artificial person . . . "

Mathematicians had been studying the foot of Reality, and since they had been working longest and in the most orderly fashion, they soon finished their map and discovered in it a striking regularity. This allowed them to conclude that the whole must also be exceptionally regular, and they claimed that their formulae could be applied even to those parts of the statue that no inquiry had yet considered.

But the researchers of corns and the creators of artificial urine shouted them down, and so the work proceeded slowly and amid general confusion.

Seeing this, the poor student thought: Obviously I am the most perfect of people, because I understand clearly what the wisest cannot grasp. Reality is not chaos, but it is a whole, and it is not only regular but also beautiful; whereas I myself . . .

At this moment there rang out the yelping of the dog – "Ow, ow!" – which shocked the sick student so much he opened his eyes.

This time he was no longer in the land of happiness, nor in the dark smithy where human lives are forged, nor on an expanse of clouds above which rose Reality, but in a hospital bed. He was surrounded by his fellow students, whose faces expressed concern and wonder.

"What are you all staring at me for?" he asked.

"You can speak?" cried one of them. "So you're going to live . . . "

"You already had one foot in the grave," added another.

"Or in the next world," replied the patient, recalling his strange dream.

"In the next world already? How are things over there? What's new?" joked his colleagues.

The poor student waved a hand dismissively and thought: You can joke as much as you want; I know what I know . . .

And when he regained his health, not only did he not complain about the fact that he was poor, but he was even glad of it. And whenever he was in a tight corner, he remembered the rays of light springing out of the granite sphere from the blows of Suffering, and said to himself that at this moment his soul was growing stronger.

# European Classics